"I want to cancel the announcement of my engagement in the paper."

Josie started to nod. Her first day at the *Sunshine Coast News* was not going well, but when she heard Rowena Dale sniffling on the other end of the phone, she couldn't help but ask, "Are you all right?"

"No, I'm a fool. I'm damned near eighty, and I should know better by now. Do you?"

"Do I what?" Josie asked.

"Do you know enough about men to figure out when they're up to no good?"

Josie thought back to her immediate and intense attraction to Gray MacInnis. "I'm not sure if I do. How can I learn?"

Josie leaned back in the chair and pulled a pad and pen toward her.

"One—Always pretend you're poor, even if you're not. Two—Don't trust extremely good-looking men. Three—Time is important. Time to get past the immediate attraction, time to get to know the man."

Josie interrupted. "How much time?"

"Years would be best. Four—This one's not easy. Self-respect. Five—Sex isn't love, although it often feels like it. Six—Learn from your mistakes. Seven—If a man much younger or smarter or better-looking than you is falling all over you, don't forget to ask why. Eight—Never, ever, put up with rudeness in a partner. Nine—Women aren't perfect, either."

Rowena paused to get her breath. "Ten—Remember, you don't get smarter just because you get older."

Kate Austin

Kate Austin has worked as a legal assistant, a commercial fisher, a brewery manager, a teacher, a technical writer and a herring popper, while managing to read an average of a book a day. Go ahead—ask her anything. If she doesn't know the answer, she'll make it up because she's been reading and writing fiction for as long as she can remember.

She blames her mother and her two grandmothers for her reading and writing obsession—all of them were avid readers and they passed the books and the obsession on to her. She lives in Vancouver, Canada, where she can walk on the beach whenever necessary, even in the rain.

She'd be delighted to hear from readers through her Web site: www.kateaustin.ca.

KATE AUSTIN

THE
SUNSHINE
COAST
NEWS

THE SUNSHINE COAST NEWS

copyright © 2006 Kate Austin

isbn 0373880820

TheNextNovel.com

 HARLEQUIN®

PRINTED IN U.S.A.

From the Author

The Sunshine Coast is a real place. Gibsons Landing, Sechelt and Pender Harbor exist. A peninsula accessible only by ferry, it is set in the midst of the rainy Pacific Northwest.

By some fluke of the weather gods, the Sunshine Coast is just that: sunny. Of course it rains—it is the Pacific Northwest, after all—but the spring, summer and fall boast plenty of sunshine, much more than the mainland only a few miles and a forty-minute ferry ride away.

To all the wonderful, brilliant, caring women
I have had the privilege of knowing over the years.
Without you, life wouldn't be worth living.

CHAPTER 1

Each afternoon, crows circled the building like the rings of Saturn or moons of Jupiter. The birds represented another thing which made no sense to Josie, but at least they were consistent and she remained grateful for this minor favor. The world had mostly stopped making sense almost two years ago.

It wasn't a single event that had knocked Josie's life askew, but a series of small, seemingly unconnected and random incidents of misfortune. Josie had grown up in a family blessed with good luck. She'd always taken it for granted.

Her father, no matter what downturn the economy took and how many of his fellow employees lost theirs, always ended up with a better job than the one he'd started with. Her mother, an avid player of games of chance, never lost money, and when they needed a little extra cash for a vacation, for piano lessons or a new car, she won the jackpot bingo at Our Lady of Perpetual Grace on Friday nights.

Fred and Marlene became best friends and lovers the very day they met at the student union during their final year at the University of Toronto. Marlene quit three months short of a degree in Roman history and culture to have Josie and work part-time in telephone sales while Fred finished his accounting course.

Even now, Marlene could, and did at Christmas, Thanksgiving and Easter, recite the spiel for: waterless cookware, encyclopedias, half a dozen different magazines, the sharpest knives ever made, a device to peel and core apples with a single touch. Marlene sold them all effortlessly and without regard to their usefulness.

She sold them because she knew how a woman felt at three o'clock on a Friday afternoon after a week of cranky kids, dirty laundry and a tired, indifferent husband. She understood the loneliness of an older woman with a voice full of sadness. Not, of course, that any of these things were part of Marlene's life, but they had all been part of her mother's, so her sympathy and patience were boundless.

Marlene knew to hang up if a man answered, or a brisk nononsense woman, otherwise she listened, spoke words of encouragement and hope, and mostly sold whatever she was selling that month. She thought of these sales as trades—her support and the woman's subsequent sense of at least temporary well-being in exchange for a few dollars for Marlene and her family.

The product was irrelevant. In fact, she sold different products to the same women over and over again. To Marlene, and to her customers, it wasn't about the fat-free grill with attached rotisserie large enough for two whole chickens; it was about the conversation.

Marlene believed in the value of talk therapy long before it became universally popular. It didn't matter where they lived—and they moved fifteen times before Josie finished high school—Marlene was at the center of a circle of bright, interesting women. Women who talked. Josie learned everything she knew from those women.

She knew, without ever having her heart broken, to avoid the boys in tight jeans and T-shirts who hung around in the parking lot after school. She knew to find a good hairdresser and stick with her, no matter how much it cost for a haircut. She knew how to handle difficult bosses, the ones who yelled, the ones who schemed, the ones whose hands landed places they shouldn't.

She knew how to make and keep friends, to write letters instead of just e-mails, to phone the minute she thought of it instead of waiting for the right time. She knew to put away a little money for a rainy day, to think before she spoke, to wait for the right man.

She learned how to cook and sew, to build bookshelves, to give her car a tune-up. She learned to fix a leaky toilet and knew to clean out the furnace for the winter. Even though she'd never done it, she could tell you how to grow asparagus and transplant lilac bushes.

She learned how to deflect a jealous woman's anger, how to recognize a broken heart, how to prevent a child from drowning. She learned how to love a man, and how to be loved in return. She learned to count the stars in the sky, the grains of sand on a beach, the ants in an anthill. She learned about lucky numbers and how to pick a winning horse. Josie grew into adulthood already knowing things some women never learned.

The oddest thing about all this knowledge was that once she knew it, and despite the fact that she never used most of it, Josie never forgot it. Those women, their voices, had somehow managed to hardwire her brain with a lifetime's worth of information.

Josie saved thousands of dollars because she knew these things. She didn't need to take courses, she could fix her own car and toilet and bicycle, and she never fell in love with a man who would steal her savings.

She knew everything except how to handle bad luck. She'd never thought of her life as lucky, after all, she was almost forty and still unmarried. If that didn't constitute bad luck, she had no idea what did. She had friends who'd had two or even three husbands. Josie hadn't found even one. She'd never been engaged, or truly in love. Where was the luck in that?

But once her luck changed, she could look back on her life, on her parents' life, and see what had always been perfectly obvious to everyone else. The Harrises were a charmed family.

Josie didn't remember being in a single fight, not with Fred, not even with Marlene. She never heard an argument between her parents. Her friends told stories of their vicious teenage knockdown, drag-out battles with their mothers. Josie remembered shopping trips and baking cookies with Marlene, playing Scrabble and Monopoly with Fred and walks in the park with both of them.

The only angry words she heard as a child were on television and she knew they had nothing to do with her life. So when bad luck came knocking, Josie was totally unprepared.

The first incident might have been a fluke. Josie arrived at Gabrielle's for her regular appointment to find her hairdresser had eloped with a waiter. Not only that, but he was ten years younger than she was, and handsome and desperately in love. They were moving to Mexico, opening a restaurant and having a baby.

Josie learned all this from the man who bought Gabe's shop while he butchered her hair and bitched about Gabe's clients. Josie still hadn't found anyone to replace Gabe, and she'd tried every good and even indifferent salon in the city, so now she settled for ten-dollar haircuts at discount clip joints.

She'd forgiven Gabe, even sent a wedding present, quickly followed by a baby gift, but her luck had been swept into the garbage with her hair that day. Josie simply hadn't recognized it at the time.

Because it got worse. She got fired from her job, the best job she'd ever had. Not for being incompetent—Josie was smart and punctual and she loved her job (which usually counted for more than intelligence)—or even for an understandable mistake, but for being in the wrong place at the wrong time.

Josie's intuition failed her that morning. She knew Don Mollard, knew he wasn't at his best in the mornings, and on the mornings after his five teenage daughters went home to their mother he was impossible. He loved those rowdy girls without a single reservation and couldn't bear to see them go even for a week at a time. So Josie learned to stay out of his way on Friday mornings, to give him time to get used to their absence.

Afterwards, she wondered what had gotten into her. She walked into his office without knocking and sat down in the chair across from the desk. She looked at her list and began.

"We're meeting with Palleson on Monday. Are the specs ready?"

She hadn't even looked at Don before she started talking. If she had, she would have seen the way his cheeks had fallen in on themselves. She would have noticed his red-rimmed eyes and most importantly, for she'd seen and recognized it a hundred times, she would have seen the mark of heartbreak on his face.

Josie first saw the mark on Phyllis, her best friend in high school. Josie watched her fall passionately in love with the president of the photography club. Phyllis was tall and slim with beautiful high breasts and the boy took exquisite photographs of the shadows those breasts cast on that perfect body. Art, he'd called it, so Phyllis couldn't object. In those days, at that high school, art was incontrovertible, the highest value.

Then he sent the photographs to *Playboy* and there was Phyllis, naked, in a magazine her father and most of his friends bought every month. For the articles, they said, but Phyllis and everyone else knew that even in the unlikely event they read the articles, they'd still spend most of their time with the pictures. And her face, as well as everything else, was clear for all to see and recognize.

She left town to spend the rest of the school year with an aunt but not before Josie saw what had happened to her. Her face changed overnight.

It wasn't just sadness, though that was part of it, it was as if the bones had somehow shifted in her skull. They flattened out, leaving great planes of unsupported skin, while at the same time becoming more prominent, so Josie could clearly see the shape of them. No one else noticed anything except the sadness. Only Josie saw the heartbreak and knew Phyllis would never be the same.

And she'd learned that the two things—heartbreak and sadness—weren't always equal. Mostly sadness was simply that. A parent dying, a lover lost, sometimes only a tragic book or movie. These engendered sadness. People got over sadness. Only occasionally was the sorrow so overwhelming that it broke a heart.

And that's what Josie should have seen on Don's face that Friday morning, what she would have seen if she'd been paying attention.

But she'd only learned a couple of months later, long after he'd fired her, why Don's sorrow had turned to heartbreak overnight. She ran into him in her neighborhood coffee shop on a snowy Sunday morning.

"Josie," he mumbled. "How are you?"

"Fine," she said, grabbing his arm and leading him to a table in the back. "But you're not. What's up?"

He raised his face to hers and she gasped. "Don?"

His face, once ruddy and unlined, now bore all the signs of disaster. Deep crevices radiated out from his eyes, his nostrils, his mouth, scoring shadows into his sallow skin. He looked as if he hadn't slept since Josie had walked out of his office.

"I haven't," he said, reading her mind as if she'd spoken out loud.

"Tracy took the girls away. Their cell phones are disconnected, there's no forwarding address and I'm losing my mind worrying about them. I've sold the business, hired detectives, but they've vanished."

Josie knew right then that even if Don did find his daughters, he would never be the same man she had known.

He'd spend the rest of his life trying to keep those girls safe, never again leaving them to go to work, or allowing them to go to school, instead he'd do whatever it took to keep them in his sight. He had lost them once and he would never let it happen again.

So getting fired was her own fault. Don needed to punish someone for the loss of his daughters and Josie was there. Wrong place, wrong time. Sheer stupidity on Josie's part... jinxed by the hair thing.

She quickly found another job, even without a reference.

The boss was the kind of guy she'd learned about from Marlene's friends. He lied, even about taking the last five dollars out of petty cash, cheated on everything from his wife to his income tax, missed meetings, left jobs unfinished, never told anyone where he was going or when he'd be back.

He refused to answer his pager or cell phone. He flirted, outrageously, with any woman who walked through the door, including the staff. Josie spent half her time calming angry clerks, receptionists and bookkeepers, and the other half hiring new ones. In every way, he was the worst man in the world to work for.

But Josie hung in there. Six weeks after she'd taken the job, she knew what a horror it was, but by then she was also beginning to recognize that her luck had changed.

In quick succession, her furnace and half a dozen smaller appliances gave out. Then her transmission and front porch required replacing, putting a huge dent in her savings.

Fred and Marlene, conveniently residing across town, decided right before Christmas to move to the Sunshine Coast, a five-hour and six-hundred-dollar plane ride away. Her favorite sushi bar closed and her yoga teacher left on a pilgrimage to India. Three of her friends found the men of their dreams and settled into nesting phase, complete with intimations of motherhood. Another admitted she was a lesbian and ran away to San Francisco to celebrate.

So Josie went in to work every day, dealt as best she could with the cloud of bad luck hovering over her, with the daily onslaught of screwups, messes, asses and idiots who passed through her office, and then went home. Her social life had been reduced to conversations with the check-out guys in the grocery store, all of whom were sixteen and had severe acne, and the occasional hello from the next-door neighbors as she parked her car.

This isolation was Josie's fault. She knew that but she didn't know how to fix it. She'd never had to look for things to do or people to do them with; her problem had been the opposite. She'd had to learn to say no or she would have been out every night of the week. The skills she needed now were skills she'd never learned.

So she stood at the window and watched the crows circle

the office and tried not to think about anything else. She concentrated on the pattern, the way they flew clockwise at the twentieth floor, then did an about-face and flew counter-clockwise around the tenth, then flew straight up her side of the building and disappeared above her. Once in a while a few other birds got caught up in the flyby.

The seagulls screamed and tried to go against the flow but they were outnumbered and outsmarted. Josie watched as they slunk off to hover and observe from a safe distance. The starlings were more successful in insinuating themselves into the pack, their dark feathers and smaller mass allowing them to fit in more easily than the huge white seagulls. Josie only recognized the starlings by the flash of oily color from their wings on sunny days and there weren't many of those.

Even the weather changed. Maybe that was why Fred and Marlene moved to the West Coast. Maybe that's why her friends were nesting and Jill ran away to San Francisco. Maybe it wasn't all Josie's fault. It wasn't the rain that bothered her, or sleet, or snow. It was the almost permanent cloud cover. Josie couldn't remember the last time she'd seen the sun.

She started spending Saturday and Sunday afternoons at the office. There was plenty of work—Jonco was a chaotic environment expressly designed to be run by an office manager (her) who had no life.

There were half a dozen disasters every week. Lost plans, last-minute deliveries, employees quitting without notice. Josie had been there almost two years without a day off. There was no time for it, not even to visit Fred and Marlene, though they talked on the phone two or three times a week.

But the real reason she was at the office on the weekends was to watch the crows. Or at least that's what she told herself. Research. Ornithological research. And that was a very sick thing. Josie knew it even as she got into her car to drive to the office.

She looked forward to the hours in the deserted building, walking through the lobby to the elevators and seeing no one. The building looked like a sleeping child, clean and fresh and completely relaxed. Josie knew this building and she knew it enjoyed the silence of the weekends. It wasn't a building filled with successful lawyers, architects and software companies who disregarded the concept of official working hours and weekends off. It was a slightly dingy building in the western suburbs.

Josie's building was occupied by businesses who couldn't afford first- or even second- or third-class space, people who didn't work overtime or on the weekends. They ran the kind of businesses that were always on the edge: of bankruptcy, of police intervention, of collapsing in on themselves under the weight of simply existing.

Jonco was definitely in the right place. Josie sometimes played a little lottery in her head, betting on what would get Jonco and when. Angry suppliers, even angrier clients? The tax people or the police? Maybe even John Johnson's wife, Muriel.

Any of these endings were possible, although once Josie met Muriel a few times, she put her money on the wife. She liked Muriel as much as she disliked her husband. They occasionally chatted on the phone if Josie, as happened regularly, was sitting in for a misplaced receptionist.

The elevator hummed and grumbled in the silence. Josie had recently acquired a slight anxiety about being in the elevator in the empty building. It came along with her newfound aversion to flying and freeway driving and crossing the road at busy intersections. She also acquired a tendency to read the obituaries before the comics and to avoid big dogs and dark corners.

These anxieties were all new to Josie and she sometimes felt as if she were piling a whole lifetime's worth of fear into a single year. She added new anxieties every week.

And they never made any sense, at least any that Josie could understand. The flying and elevators, well, people did die in plane crashes and elevator accidents, you heard about it all the time. But grocery stores in busy malls? As soon as the sun went down, Josie avoided them. And what about the color orange? Now that was plain crazy.

She didn't tell Fred and Marlene about this change in her life. They wouldn't understand. They still led the same charmed life as always, finding the perfect condo right on the beach and a couple who wanted to trade straight across for their little house off the Danforth.

Marlene loved the women she met, played bingo and continued to win enough to pay for what she called her "little treats"—manicures, new hats, trips to the city for concerts and plays. She even won enough to buy the baby grand she'd always wanted and still couldn't play. Fred played golf, badly, but with great joy and enthusiasm, and puttered around the condo. They were as happy as ever, and as lucky.

Josie wasn't sure who was wrong—her or her parents. And

she didn't know if it mattered. All she knew was that the crows had somehow become the center of her life, their daily circling her anchor. She felt as if her soul circumnavigated the building with them in a seemingly aimless circuit.

On quiet days, when the sun hung just behind the clouds, casting a faint yellow glow on the glass, Josie thought she could see into the window as she flew by, and catch a glimpse of herself. Watching. Waiting. Confused and frightened and wondering what might happen next.

CHAPTER 2

She didn't have to wonder for long. Marlene phoned on Monday.

"Josie?"

Marlene's faltering voice, so different from her usual brisk tones, set Josie's panic cells quivering.

"Marlene? Are you okay? Is Fred okay? What's wrong?"

The only response was a tired little whimper, as if Marlene was too exhausted, too overwhelmed by circumstances, to answer even the simplest questions.

"Mom?"

The one word guaranteed to snap Marlene out of her incoherence. Josie had never, even as a child, called her parents by anything except their given names. It wasn't a sixties thing, the decade had barely begun when Josie was born. It was a friendship thing. Marlene had determined that she and Fred and Josie were to be best friends, and so they had been since the first time they saw each other in the lime-green birthing room at the White Oaks Hospital.

Friendship was another thing Josie had learned from those bright, interesting women. They honestly cared about each other. But she also learned it at home, watching Marlene and

Fred and when she grew old enough to participate, by being part of it herself.

If you're very lucky—and Josie used to be—you have friendships that last a lifetime. Usually, like Fred and Marlene, you meet those special friends later in life, when you have learned enough to admire and appreciate them. Josie, born into a charmed family, had that kind of friendship since she was a baby.

When you're older, falling into this kind of friendship can be like falling in love. It can happen with the first conversation when you discover you have a million things in common, when you can't stop talking and you feel as if you've known each other forever, and as if you never want to leave their presence. You tell secrets you've never told anyone else, you laugh until you're hysterical, you know what they're going to say before they say it. And you're so happy you feel as if the sun shone just for you.

So the word Mom felt awkward on Josie's tongue. The feeling it left in her mouth when she spoke it made her think of the last receptionist, the one who came in for her interview wearing a tongue ring. Josie couldn't keep her eyes off it, wondering, watching the way it altered the shape of her mouth, and imagining how it felt when she ate or drank or kissed.

"Mom?"

The first use didn't have the immediate effect Josie had been counting on.

"It's Fred."

The vague sense of dread Josie had felt since the beginning of the conversation focused in on Fred.

"Is he okay?"

Josie's two years' worth of bad luck gave her a million possibilities to worry about. But she settled on a stroke. Of course that's what it was. Fred had always eaten red meat, was an avaricious drinker of coffee, and ate fried eggs and bacon almost every morning. Vegetables, with the exception of potatoes (if you could call them a vegetable), weren't on his menu. With a diet like that, of course he'd had a stroke. Or maybe it was cancer. Malignant melanoma from all the sun he got playing golf without a hat.

"He's left me. For Florence."

And Marlene began to wail. After careful and deliberate consideration, Josie joined her. Josie knew the two phones weren't connected by anything as prosaic as lines but she pictured them anyway, three thousand miles of telephone poles marching through the scrub of Northern Ontario, across the flat prairies, up and over the Rockies, and down to the Sunshine Coast. And every single one of them thrumming with the combined force of Josie and Marlene's pain.

As it passed through Thunder Bay, Swift Current, Moose Jaw, Princeton and Hope, the lights would dim and the sleeping women in those quiet towns would wake and roll over to touch their husbands. But that wouldn't be enough.

They'd lie back down, drape their arms and legs over their men to make sure they'd still be in the right bed when they woke. And they'd lie awake all night trying desperately to get inside their husband's dreams because they needed to know. *Who was he dreaming of?*

Those few women fortunate or unfortunate enough to slip into a husband's dream, spent the rest of their lives wondering what it meant. Because being in someone else's dream wasn't like hearing someone tell you about it, not even like eavesdropping where things overheard make sense. It was more like being on a Tilt-a-Whirl, seeing flashes of color from the carnival midway in one-second bursts. Unless you knew what to expect it was impossible to put the bursts together in any logical or sensible way without the dreamer's unifying logic. They remained short bursts of color; they didn't connect.

But anyone who slips into another's dream never forgets feeling as if that dream was the only one that could make sense of their life, their relationships, their world.

Someone else's dreams are addicting. So those women also spent the rest of their lives trying to get back into their husband's dreams—often staying in a terrible relationship for that reason—with exactly the same success they'd have if they tried to get back the feeling of their very first kiss.

All the things Josie and Marlene learned from the talk sessions flew out the window and joined the crows, circling just out of reach.

Nothing is forever, they'd said, make the best of what you have and when the time comes, let it go without losing your temper and making a fool of yourself. Without having heard more than those five words—*He's left me. For Florence.*—Josie knew that Marlene had lost her temper, maybe for the first time in her life, and had made a fool of herself.

Josie imagined her sweet, generous, loving mother screaming on the front porch of Florence's house, saw her smashing the red clay pots full of impatiens and geraniums on the patio steps. She saw her calling a great swarm of insects with the strength of her fury, a huge, hovering cloud of tiny stinging gnats and flies.

Josie saw, as clearly as if she'd been there, the insects surrounding Marlene, fanning her with their wings, the mass of them expanding as Marlene's rage beckoned more and more of them, until her screams of rage vanished beneath the hum of their wings.

She saw Marlene walk home in the warmth of the late afternoon, invisible, the weight of the sun pressing her into the earth. The bugs deserted her at the front door. Marlene walked down the hall to the bedroom and slept for twenty-four hours. She phoned Josie the minute she woke up, her eyes so swollen from crying in her sleep that she was blind.

Marlene never told this story, but Josie knew it was true. The pictures were as clear as if she'd been there, watching from the curb as Marlene roared across the street. She saw Florence, and Fred, cowering behind the drapes in Florence's front room, debating about calling the police. But how would they explain the insects? They waited until dark before venturing outside to sweep up the dirt and dead plants and smashed pots.

What they wanted, Josie thought, was to wake up the next morning and find Marlene gone, vanished without a trace, so they could begin their new life together without any inconvenient reminders of the pain they'd caused in finding it.

"Do you want me to come and get you?"

"No. I'm staying right here. I won't give them the satisfaction of leaving. That would make it too easy. I want them to see me every day across the street, to check for me before they walk out their door. I know she can't afford to move and I won't, so they're stuck with me. And don't you come out here either. Or phone Fred. He doesn't deserve to hear from you. Let *him* lose someone he loves."

Josie thought of all the advice, the simple, perfect, accurate advice she'd listened to over the years in her mother's living room. And she realized that none of it was going to help her now. Because Marlene had heard it, too. She'd been the main proponent of cutting your losses and moving on, and now she was doing everything wrong. And there was nothing Josie could do about it.

"You stay right there, young lady."

Marlene had changed overnight into an old woman who called her daughter *young lady*. Josie didn't answer. She didn't want to lie to Marlene, but she was leaving for the Sunshine Coast the minute she hung up.

Josie pictured Marlene in the condo she'd never seen. This mess was her fault, her bad luck spilling over. *Phone when you think of it, don't wait for the right time.* The same applied to visiting. Two years without her and her parents' marriage, the happiest marriage in the universe, fell apart. She'd caused this mess; she'd have to fix it.

"She was *my* best friend, that witch. She hypnotized him, I know she did. Fred isn't even interested in sex anymore, he can't be bothered. The doctor told him about Viagra—not that he could have missed knowing about it with all those damned commercials on TV—but he said he didn't need it. I think those commercials gave him ideas. All those men with huge grins on their stupid faces and those women looking well-fucked. No, all he needed was a younger woman."

Josie's face flushed even though there was no one to see her embarrassment. She wasn't one of those kids that had experienced a primal moment that forever defined her sexuality. If it wasn't for her own birth as evidence, she would have had a hard time believing her mother—or her father!—had ever even been in the same bed together.

She couldn't believe her mother knew about Viagra and certainly couldn't imagine her using the f-word. Especially to Josie. And now she had a totally gruesome image in her head and it wouldn't go away. Still in shock, Josie couldn't think of a thing to say that wouldn't make things worse.

"And don't you phone me. I'm going to be busy. I'll phone you."

Josie sat at the kitchen table and worried about what Marlene was going to be busy at. Heartbreak could make a woman do anything, absolutely anything. If Florence hypnotized Fred, then he was only living a life he'd wanted anyway. Hypnotism couldn't change a person, not deep down inside. But heartbreak could. It could reshape your bones and it could make you do things you'd never, even in your most deeply buried dreams, imagine possible.

Heartbreak could turn a young woman old overnight. It could turn her deaf or dumb or blind. It could steal all the connections she'd made in her life, leaving her standing there with a thousand dangling threads in her hands, which used to lead to family, to friends and faith and hope and love. It could turn a spendthrift into a miser. It could send her running away, searching for a place she'd never find. Or it could root her in one spot for the rest of her life, poisoning the earth around her with her pain.

Josie wasn't sure what heartbreak had done to Marlene, but it had done something, something serious. She had to get out there, and soon. If Marlene wasn't expecting her to phone, Josie had plenty of time. That solved the money problem. She'd drive—she was too scared to fly anyway. A gas credit card and a little cash for food would get her there.

She bought a cheap cooler and filled it with road food, the unhealthy carbo-laden kind she only ate when she traveled. Cheetos, tuna and egg-salad sandwiches, high-octane soda and red licorice. She threw in a handful of CDs without checking the titles and the box from the second bedroom that she hoped contained at least part of her summer wardrobe.

She got out of the city and onto the highway just as the sun set right in her eyes. She stopped at the first drugstore to buy cheap sunglasses. Josie had forgotten she'd spend the next week driving straight into the sun, leaving the gray clouds behind and heading into blue skies.

"Sure," she said, raising her voice to hear it over the thunder of the trucks passing, "blue skies and sunshine. That'll be great. A winter holiday. I need one. Just not this one."

Josie tried not to anticipate the scene at her parents' condo but she couldn't help it. She had always thought her parents would die together, peacefully, in their sleep. Probably just before they turned one hundred. She knew she'd be the one to find them, hands clasped, smiles on their faces. She'd bury

them together and visit their graves every Sunday afternoon
until she joined them. The headstone would say:

Beloved:
Fred 1936 – 2036
Marlene 1937 – 2036
Josie 1961 –

And they'd be together forever, all three of them. Josie had
it all worked out. And now this.

Marlene would come to the door in a ratty old bathrobe
(did she even own a ratty old bathrobe? Josie couldn't imagine it). Her hair would hang in strings around her face and
she'd smell. Josie wrinkled her nose at the thought. The
condo would smell, too.

Of cat pee. And that was as weird as the ratty old bathrobe because Josie had spent years begging Marlene to let her
have a cat and she'd said no. *They smell*, she'd said. *Not in my
house*, she'd said. But Josie knew when she got to the Sunshine Coast, there'd be dozens of cats milling around Marlene's feet, mewling for food. The curtains would be drawn,
the furniture scratched and stained, the carpets a huge kitty
litter box. Newspapers would be piled everywhere and open
tins of cat food would line the floors.

Marlene's nails, once her pride and joy, would be tattered
and yellow. A cigarette—she'd never smoked in her life—
would dangle from her lips, spilling ashes as she moved. Josie
dared not think about the fire hazards. Marlene's face was
lined and old, the wrinkles cut so deeply they seemed to

reach right to the bones underneath. When she opened her mouth, Josie stepped back. She'd thought the cats smelled.

Josie checked her voice mail at every pit stop. She could return calls from the road and no one—Marlene, she meant—would know she'd left home. She'd find a phone booth somewhere off the highway to return the call. That would work.

But no one phoned. Not Marlene. Not Fred. Not even work. No one knew, or cared, that Josie was on the road, first hundreds and then thousands of miles away from home, racing to get to her parents before they ruined her life forever.

"Snap out of it." This time she raised her voice so she could hear it over the Dixie Chicks. She'd ended up with the Chicks, an old Tom Jones CD of Marlene's, a homemade CD of Jill's amateur choral group signing show tunes, badly, and three classical CDs—Purcell, whom she hated, Mozart's Requiem and Chopin. Not the best of collections for this trip.

Josie felt the self-pity creeping up on her as the clouds and rain changed to blue skies and sunshine. She hated it, but couldn't seem to stop herself. Fred and Marlene, their perfect relationship, their good humor and joy in each other, in Josie, in life, were the things that sustained her.

Take those away and Josie's conversion was complete. She spent the first half of her life living a charmed life, and now she'd spend the rest of it walking around with a black cloud over her head like that cartoon character whose name she could never remember, or spell. Joe something, she thought.

And though she knew she should be grateful for the first half, she wasn't at all sure she could cope with the second.

She'd have to learn a whole new set of skills, including how to deflect bad luck. She had already stopped playing bingo and going to the racetrack. She couldn't afford to lose any more money.

She'd tried the races once since her luck changed, and put a hundred dollars on a sure thing passed on by a friend who wrote for the racing papers. The horse trailed around behind the pack looking as if he was running in the following race.

Same thing at bingo. Josie hadn't thought it possible to play a whole night's worth of bingo and never get within ten numbers of a jackpot. She was sure it was statistically impossible. So she gave up all games of chance, wouldn't even go into lottery pools at the office because she didn't want to influence the draw. Obviously her bad luck was spilling over onto her family and Josie could see that it was only a matter of time before it would affect her coworkers, too.

When she thought about it, and five days on the road gave her plenty of time to think, it wasn't affecting her friends. Their lives were great—new men, new babies, new everything. They glowed with good luck. The contrast made Josie's situation even more obvious.

She'd always been the one to cheer up her friends, to suggest a movie or a bottle of wine. Now they sent her flowers—just because—and phoned her to see how she was doing.

"Come to dinner," they'd say, "you have to see the new couch."

But Josie knew they were calling because they felt sorry for her and for the first time in her life, resorted to white lies.

"Sorry, I've made plans. A movie with a guy I met at work."

Or in the grocery store or a line somewhere. And they chose to believe her, because they wanted to spend their time with their new men, and not with Josie. They owed her, that was all.

But the isolation she'd experienced over the past two years stood her in good stead on the trip. She knew how to go days without conversation. She knew how to turn off her mind, and think of nothing except the passing scenery. She knew how to sleep so deeply she couldn't remember her dreams and to sleep anywhere. So the days and the miles passed.

She'd traveled across the prairies, racing on those long straight highways as if monsters chased her car, stopping to sleep at the side of the road, the seat pushed back as far as it would go, closing her eyes, aching from concentrating on the horizon for so many hours.

She'd been dizzy driving through the mountains, the car turning and turning, first up, then down, then up again, until Josie no longer knew which was east or west. Popping out of the mountains early on a Saturday afternoon she was now almost at her destination.

She stopped at a gas station and washed her face and hair in the sink. She used the scratchy paper towels to wipe away the smell of the road from the rest of her body and the tiny mirror to apply makeup and comb the knots from her hair. She was as ready as she could be.

She bought a map, worked out the route and then put her mind on autopilot. Thinking wasn't going to help, not now.

CHAPTER 3

Josie wanted to see Marlene, Fred and Florence, before any of them saw her. She drove down their street wearing her dark glasses and a scarf over her hair, looking for a place to watch for them. She needed to see how they looked, how they moved. She especially needed to see Fred and Florence together.

She maintained a faint hope that Fred had returned home, but it wasn't really sustainable in the light of day. She checked her voice mail every few hours and the only message she'd received over the past five days was from John Johnson, firing her in absentia. Marlene would have called to tell her of Fred's return, if only to crow over her victory. And she knew how worried Josie was. Surely Marlene wouldn't leave her in suspense?

Josie knew her wish to be a fantasy, impossible to maintain. But without it, Josie thought she might collapse. Or run screaming all the way back across the country to huddle in her bed, frightened and unable to cope. She needed to believe in Fred and Marlene. The thought of them, happy in the sunshine on the Sunshine Coast, had kept Josie going as the rest of her world fell apart around her.

They were her proof that the world wasn't totally screwed up. She pictured Fred and Marlene sitting on a bench overlooking the ocean and she felt better. This despite the fact that Marlene couldn't sit still long enough to contemplate anything; she was a mover, not a sitter. But it was the idea of them Josie cherished, the belief that the two of them continued to live the perfect life. That's all Josie wanted, just to know it was possible.

A tiny parking lot led to the beach beside Marlene's condo. Benches perched on a thin patch of grass, their front legs almost in the sand. But they faced the wrong way, away from the building. Josie parked the car in the lot, backing in so she faced the street, and settled down to wait.

It seemed odd to be still. Josie felt like a sailor trying to get his balance back after being at sea for months. The vertigo affected everything: her eyes, her hearing, her stomach, even her body temperature.

The street shimmered. Josie blinked her eyes and tried again. It still moved. The heat could do that; Josie had seen it in Toronto. In August, on those still, airless days, the pavement squirmed in the afternoon heat. The sun beat anyone foolish enough to venture out into it with the strength of a prize fighter until you wanted to lay down, and be counted out so you could be carried off to an air-conditioned room somewhere.

But it was only the beginning of April, and even on the Sunshine Coast it was cool enough for a sweater and only just warm enough to be driving with the windows open. The street moved and Josie's stomach protested until she pushed back the seat and closed her eyes.

The salt-tinged air felt good on her face as she wiggled deeper into her seat. Josie felt safe and comfortable in the car, the sun warming the cool air off the ocean. She couldn't open her eyes even if she wanted to.

The past week caught up to her and she fell into sleep. Not the deep dreamless sleep she willed for herself each night, but a shallow, chaotic sleep filled with impossible images. She traveled her childhood, stopping for a time in each of the houses she lived in as she grew up, walking down a hundred streets, all of them only vaguely familiar.

The dream had no coherence; rather it shifted color and shape like a kaleidoscope. But Josie, even in her sleep, knew where the images came from. They were a reflection of her happy childhood, when nothing could go wrong. When Fred and Marlene ruled her world. And it reflected her profound unhappiness with the state of her world today.

She wanted to wake up. She could cope better, pretend better, when she was in control. Josie fought against sleep like a swimmer in dangerous waters. She got her head above the salty waves for a quick breath of air then slowly submerged again. The world was tinged with green light, the sun filtered through layers of water and seaweed.

Everything was perfectly clear and quite beautiful and Josie was tempted to surrender to it. She might have done so but for a voice calling her name.

"Josie. Josie. Wake up." Someone shook her shoulder through the open window.

She reluctantly opened her eyes and focused them on Fred, wearing the usual goofy grin on his face, and for a minute Josie believed the entire week had been some kind of hallucination. She smiled back.

"Hi, Fred."

His grin grew wider as he pulled a tiny redheaded woman in a bright pink tracksuit out from behind his back where she'd been hiding.

"Josie, meet Florence. Flo, this is my daughter, come three thousand miles to visit. Isn't she a beauty?"

This last was addressed to Josie, his arm resting protectively over Florence's shoulders.

"I've missed you, honey. You should have moved out here a long time ago. Are you staying?"

His eyes wandered over the interior of the car, their light dimming as he realized she didn't have all her worldly goods crammed into the small space, but he brightened up immediately.

"Oh, you got a mover. That was smart. Josie's a bright girl, Flo. You'll see. I've never beaten her at Monopoly, not even once. Maybe we can play tonight?"

His head bounced back and forth between the two women like a Ping-Pong ball, searching their faces for clues. Josie knew exactly what he was thinking. He hadn't changed over the years except to become more himself, more cheerful, more exuberant, more of everything. Fred may have made a living as an accountant, but at heart he was an entertainer. And a good one. Josie found herself nodding.

"Monopoly sounds good," she said, before she could stop herself, and then backtracked. "But I have to see Marlene."

"You're staying with her?" Fred's voice wavered a little although he bravely maintained his grin.

"I hope so. But..."

"She doesn't know you're here, does she?"

Florence's voice was as tiny as she was. Josie had to strain to hear her words over the faint crashing of the waves. She sounded like a chorus of silver bells. A luscious tinkling Josie wanted to hear again and again.

"No. She told me not to come and I haven't heard from her in a week."

"Neither have we, not since…"

The memory of that day passed over Fred's face, a pall of anguish clouding his features. Florence took his hand and brought it to her face, holding it to her cheek while she talked.

"We've seen her, though, so we know she's okay. And no one else will even speak to us, so we know what she's been doing."

Josie squirmed. She could imagine exactly what Marlene had been doing and for the first time she felt sorry for Fred and Florence. Marlene was the most persuasive woman Josie had ever met. She could make life hell for them. And obviously that was exactly what she was doing.

"Could we have dinner tomorrow night? Play Monopoly?"

Josie would have promised almost anything to take that look off Fred's face. He looked as if someone had kicked him in the stomach and he just hadn't fallen over yet. He couldn't muster a grin, but his mouth twitched.

"That would be great. We're right over there," he pointed to a tiny house on the beach. "Come over any time. If we're not in, there's a key under the geraniums. Or try the beach."

Florence still had his hand in hers and the two of them

walked away down the beach swinging their linked hands like teenagers.

This was going to be harder than she thought. Josie hadn't expected to like Florence, or feel sorry for the two of them. But she should have remembered about Marlene. No one—not Fred, not Josie, not anyone—could tell Marlene anything once she'd made up her mind.

Oh, she couched her point of view in such reasonable terms, and spoke in such a reasonable voice, smiling while she did it so that you couldn't help but agree with her. But once she'd decided, she was like a pit bull. She was right and you were wrong and not even the most lucid discussion would sway her.

When Josie was thirteen, she'd got her ears pierced. All her friends had pierced theirs years before, but Marlene was adamant that Josie wait until she was fifteen. Marlene had her ears pierced at fifteen, so that would be good enough for Josie. Foolishly, though, Josie had spoken to Fred first and he, equally foolish, said yes and gave her the money.

Both Fred and Josie knew that Josie's appearance was Marlene's exclusive dominion but Josie was so excited about it, Fred said yes before he even thought. Josie, knowing it was a bad idea but unable to stop herself, had rushed downtown and done it right there and then. She had an idea that presenting Marlene with a fait accompli would forestall any problems. She was wrong.

Of course she was wrong.

Fred tried to shoulder the blame, even going so far as to tell Marlene about the piercing while Josie was still out. Josie

arrived home to find Fred sitting in a kitchen chair while
Marlene stood over him, speaking in her calmest voice, telling him exactly how wrong he'd been. She flicked her eyes
at Josie, taking in the small gold hooks in an instant, and then
she did the thing Marlene did best. She switched tactics and
turned into Joan of Arc, Martyr.

"I meant it to be a special day. Just the two of us. Mother
and daughter together. Josie did one of the most important
things a girl can do. You robbed me."

Her face crumpled as she spoke, her voice becoming softer
so they had to lean forward to hear it. She imbued it with
the faintest hint of tears, nothing over-the-top, but Josie and
Fred were experts, they knew the tears were there, waiting
for the perfect moment to appear.

The ear piercing equated to an entire summer in the dog-
house. Josie couldn't imagine what this transgression would
rate. Somewhere along the lines of a lifetime, was her guess.
And she wasn't just thinking of Fred. Josie herself was already
in trouble. She'd come to the Sunshine Coast against direct
orders, and she'd spoken to Fred and, God forbid, Florence.

Even worse, she'd promised to have dinner with them and
there was no way to hide that from Marlene. All she had to
do was watch out her window while Josie walked down the
street to the cottage on the beach. And even if Marlene
didn't see her, someone else would. She'd know. Josie couldn't
even imagine how angry Marlene would be.

She stood at Marlene's door and hesitated, just for a minute. Someone had let her in the security door so Marlene
didn't know she was here. What if she turned around, right

now, and went back across the country without seeing Marlene? She'd never know Josie had disobeyed her. The only people who knew couldn't betray her secret. Marlene wasn't talking to them.

Josie's cowardly self had already turned away from the door and was walking back to the main entrance before Josie got it under control.

"You can't do that," she whispered. "Fred's heart would be broken. And Marlene needs you, really she does."

It was hard for Josie to believe Marlene needed anyone. Marlene had her life, and her family, under tight control. Time was apportioned out in blocks. So much allotted for cutting the grass, homework, TV, ballet lessons—so much for sleeping, school, playing Monopoly (no matter that the game might not be finished), walking in the park.

Josie still planned her weeks the same way she'd watched Marlene do all her life. She sat down on Sunday night at seven o'clock and wrote out her weekly plan. Josie had notebooks going back twenty years. But recently her plans had begun to take on an odd look.

Marlene would not be impressed.

They were filled with notations like: Sunday afternoon—watch crows, contemplate life; Friday night—avoid bingo. The past week's plan had only one entry: drive to Sunshine Coast—get Fred and Marlene back together.

The older notebooks were filled with neat blocks carefully checked off as the tasks were accomplished. The current notebook had no checkmarks. Even contemplating life wasn't completed.

She'd spent hundreds of hours over the past two years thinking about life, her life, mostly, though once in a while she managed to take a broader view, if only for a few minutes. When Jill ran away to San Francisco to become a lesbian, Josie had taken the time to think about what it would feel like to discover your true identity so late in life.

Maybe Josie, too, had another woman buried deep under her skin, someone who would take over, explode out and live a completely different life than the safe and secure one Josie had managed until now. Maybe this other woman would abandon the notebooks, stop being on time for everything, do things impulsively, find a man and some new friends and a great job. Or maybe she'd sell her house and live off the proceeds until she was broke. She could do anything.

Jill, one of her dearest friends, had been almost sixty when she discovered she was a lesbian. Mother of two, grandmother of five, she'd left all that behind and had been so happy, lit up like a Christmas tree covered with a thousand twinkling lights, when Josie saw her off at the airport. Josie would trade her present life for that joy in an instant.

If that other woman presented herself, Josie would leap at the chance. She wouldn't hesitate for a minute, even if the opportunity wasn't in her schedule. Even if it meant abandoning everything, and giving up her sensible, structured life. She'd do it. And she'd start by knocking on the damned door.

The first knock sounded a bit tentative, like a mouse scratching in the walls. But Josie stepped back and waited. She probably didn't even need to knock; Marlene always seemed to sense her presence. If Josie walked barefoot into the house from the yard, Marlene knew the instant her foot crossed the threshold.

"Don't forget to wash your hands, darling. And take that cake out of the oven," speaking the instant before the timer went off.

Marlene knew about Josie's first and only cigarette despite the entire pack of breath mints gobbled on her way home.

She knew Josie's grades before she opened her report card.

She knew where Josie went and with whom, even when Josie herself thought her travels were completely spontaneous.

She knew about Josie's first kiss even though Josie had scrubbed her face with snow before she came in the front door. Marlene had the lecture planned, right down to Josie's responses and Fred's few interjections, before Josie left the house that night.

Josie knew all about where babies came from, sexually transmitted diseases and the risk of promiscuity before she began to menstruate. Marlene was thorough. And ruthless. She made sure Josie knew all there was to know, even things Josie could do without, like leprosy.

For years, Josie thought she'd get it from kissing.

She checked her fingers and toes every single morning to make sure they were still firmly attached. She woke in the night, convinced they were tingling and expecting them to turn black. Marlene used leprosy the same way she'd used dirty old men when Josie was younger. And it worked. She spent all her teenage years scared of kissing.

She still kissed, but always in the back of her mind lurked the fear of leprosy. She didn't enjoy it. Marlene's plan, exactly.

But Marlene and Fred were Josie's best friends and it didn't serve any purpose for her to be standing in front of the door thinking about the past, wishing for it back. The world had changed for the worse. Josie might be responsible for that, but she wasn't going to take the blame for not doing anything about the future. She knocked again, hard enough to hurt her knuckles.

"Is that you, Heather? Wait a minute, I'll just turn the kettle off."

Tea? Marlene was making tea? What in the hell did that mean? And who was Heather? Marlene collected so many friends Josie had never been able to keep track of them. She collected them and Josie couldn't keep up. But Heather wouldn't be far behind if Marlene had the kettle on. That was good. Marlene would be on her best behavior for her guest.

The door opened.

"Josie. What are doing here? I don't want you…"

Before she could finish the sentence help arrived in the form of a young woman carrying a notebook and a tape recorder. Marlene's voice switched immediately from anger mode to professional.

"Come in, come in. Heather, this is my daughter, Josie. She's just arrived from Toronto."

Only the glare over Marlene's shoulder as she escorted Heather into the living room gave her away.

The next two hours were the oddest Josie had ever spent in Marlene's presence. She didn't mention Fred, not once. It was as if he'd never existed. But Heather seemed to be writing, or at least transcribing, Marlene's life story. So where was Fred in all of it?

For that matter, where was Josie? She was sitting on the same rose-colored couch as Heather. She'd been there for every single event Marlene described, yet not a single mention of her. Marlene seemed to have forgotten her existence.

Or worse. Maybe, Josie thought, this was the way Marlene saw her life. A single woman overcoming the odds. A successful salesperson who'd eventually moved on to Mary Kay and had been selling it for years. She had shipped her third pink Cadillac across the country when they'd moved to the Sunshine Coast.

Josie wanted to give her the benefit of the doubt but listening to that sweet voice going on and on about her accomplishments without any acknowledgment of Josie, without a single word about Fred, gave Josie the heebie-jeebies.

She sat in Marlene's living room and stared at the ocean through the window. Something had shifted inside, and she didn't know how to cope with the sensations. Everything she'd believed about her life—her charmed life—was in question.

If Marlene thought of her at all, obviously, she thought of her as a hindrance. Josie had admired Marlene when she sent Josie away to university at great cost and personal distress. Marlene didn't consider her own feelings but did what was best for Josie.

Suddenly, feelings Josie had buried for years came spewing up at her. She had hated every minute of school, hated being so far away from home. The notebooks, the week ahead carefully laid out to avoid any downtime, helped the days pass faster. Josie got her degree in the shortest time possible and rushed right home where Marlene had found her the sweetest little apartment.

"It's too bad it's across town, but it's cheap. I know you'll love it. Fred moved all your things over last week. He painted the kitchen and the bathroom your favorite colors. I bought you a new bedspread and some pillows for that old couch from the basement. It looks great. We'll take you over right now."

Josie could still picture the look on Fred's face as he dropped her at the curb. (Marlene wouldn't let him go up with Josie.) He didn't say a word, just summoned up a sickly grin while Marlene took over, doing what she always did, arranging Josie's life.

But Josie agreed with what Marlene had done, knowing it was in her best interests. Moving in with her parents after being away for three years was a step backward, wasn't it? She needed to move forward, stay independent, be her own woman.

Marlene handed Josie a set of keys and said, "Here you go, darling. Don't forget we're expecting you for dinner on Sunday. Six sharp. The bus stop is just down the street." She waved her hand at the corner. "It probably takes an hour on Sunday. I'll phone you."

And she did phone, religiously, every two or three days. Still did, for that matter, with the exception of the past week. She chatted for a couple of minutes and then passed the phone to Fred. Josie was certain the phone calls were marked in Marlene's notebooks just as they were in hers. In Josie's case, though, they were marked with stars and flowers. She suspected now that for Marlene they were just another task to be accomplished and checked off.

The soothing tones of Marlene at her sweetest washed over Josie as she stared out the window. The sun struck sparks off the waves, diamonds of light dancing across the water like fairies. Josie drifted, no longer listening to what Marlene said, just hearing the tone of her voice.

No wonder she had so many friends. No wonder she could convince anyone of anything. No wonder she was such a good salesperson. Her voice made its hearers feel as if they were slipping into a hot tub on a cold winter's night. Soothing, warm, intoxicating.

The room faded around her and she followed Marlene's voice back to her childhood. She remembered the nights she lay in her bed, the door slightly open so she'd have a little light—Marlene didn't believe in night-lights. Josie had been scared of the dark all her life and still slept with a light on in her bedroom.

She remembered listening to Marlene talking on the phone. This was Marlene's work, Josie knew that, knew better than to interrupt her, but it didn't sound like work to Josie. It sounded like fun.

A few times, early on, Josie had left her bed and wandered out to the living room where Marlene curled up with the phone, a glass of wine on the table next to her. Josie believed if she were really quiet, she could sneak behind the couch and lie on the floor to listen.

But no matter how quiet she was, how carefully she held her breath, Marlene always knew she was there. She reached over the back of the couch, grabbed Josie's hair to pull her to her feet, gesturing with her free hand to send her back to her room. Marlene's voice didn't even falter.

Back in those days, Josie hadn't wondered where Fred spent his evenings. The living room was Marlene's domain. Fred's favorite saying was *early to bed, early to rise*, so after he kissed Josie good-night, where else could he be but asleep in bed? She wanted, for a single night, to be that little girl again so she could find him, follow his voice instead of Marlene's, watch him instead of her mother.

She pictured him in bed, the covers neatly folded back, his pajamas clean and starched. He had fallen asleep with his glasses on. His book lay across his chest. Josie walked up to his side of the bed, her head level with his chest, and gently took the book from his unresisting hands. She marked his place before putting the book on the dresser. She had to climb up on the bed to reach his face. She pulled his glasses off and kissed his cheek. She stayed, secure in his presence, until Marlene's laughter woke her from her dream. She scrambled off the bed and back to her own room.

Josie knew it hadn't been like that. Fred had likely been banished to a bedroom in the basement or the attic, depending on the house. Marlene didn't like anyone to overhear her while she was on the phone and once Josie went to university, Marlene soundproofed Josie's room and turned it into an office. Josie slept on the hide-a-bed in the living room when she came to visit.

The interview finally over, Marlene saw Heather to the door, promising to see her tomorrow. Josie wondered how long the rewriting of Marlene's history had been going on, how many afternoons Heather had sat on the pink sofa and listened to the story.

Josie wondered, absurdly, who was paying for it.

"I'm exhausted," Marlene said, coming back into the living room.

She didn't look it, she looked exhilarated. But she fell into her favorite chair and looked distastefully at the dishes on the coffee table. Josie got the hint. She could postpone the showdown.

It was Marlene's best china, yellow roses and a gold trim, and it had never been in the dishwasher, nor a single piece chipped. Josie washed it, taking her time while trying not to fret about the ordeal waiting for her in the other room. But she could only spend so long with three teacups and luncheon plates and eventually even the counter was clean and the floor swept, the tea towel hung to dry and the dishes put away.

Marlene hadn't moved an inch so far as Josie could see. She sat in her chair, back straight, legs crossed at the ankle, hands clasped loosely in her lap. She held herself like royalty and no wonder. She'd modeled herself on them. Her public demeanor had always been that of a queen. Marlene's eyes were closed and Josie took the opportunity to study her.

She'd aged; there was no denying that.

Hairline cracks appeared in her face under the glare of the pitiless afternoon sun. Her lipstick, reapplied relentlessly throughout the day, was now lost in the crevices of her lips, stripes of color and not-color calling attention to themselves.

Her hair, still blond and perfectly coifed, had faded and coarsened. Marlene wasn't old yet. She worked hard to avoid that horror, but the signs of it could be seen in her face and her neck, on her arms and in her hair.

Josie was confused. Marlene had spent the past two hours pretending Josie, who was sitting right across from her, had never existed. She had ordered Josie to stay home as if the last thing she wanted was to see her daughter. But… For the first time in her life, Josie looked at Marlene and felt sorry for her. She looked at her aging face and wondered at the strength of will it must have taken to maintain that poise, to reapply that lipstick and dress so perfectly in the face of disaster.

Josie sure hadn't managed that poise and discipline. Her world had fallen apart and she had fallen with it.

She reached out her hand for her mother but quickly retracted it at the look in Marlene's eyes.

Josie didn't speak. Anything she might say would only make matters worse. Marlene had this conversation planned in her mind. She'd had two hours to think about what to say and Josie's best bet was to go along with it. Her only bet, really. So she waited for Marlene to begin.

"You shouldn't be here."

"But you need me."

"You'll just make things worse. I've got everything under control."

"But…"

"No buts, Josie. I have a plan and your presence isn't part of it. The next ferry leaves in two hours. You've got plenty of time."

"But I've just driven three thousand miles to get here."

"You should have listened to me in the first place. I told you not to come."

"I wanted to be with you, help you. I wanted to see you."

"What you wanted doesn't matter. You can't be here. Not now. You'll spoil everything."

Josie hoped her shock didn't show in her face. Up until now, she realized, Marlene had always managed to couch her orders in such reasonable terms that Josie (and presumably Fred as well) hadn't noticed that they were orders. But all pretence of disguise had disappeared along with Fred. Marlene didn't leave Josie much time to think about that change.

Marlene opened her eyes wide and looked directly at Josie, who was surprised by the lack of emotion in them. Marlene wasn't sad or scared or worried, she didn't even look mad. All Josie saw was determination.

"I can't go home. Not now. Not today."

"You can't stay here."

Marlene's determination overwhelmed her. Josie stood up and started for the door, for the ferry, for home. But what did she have to lose?

"I'm not going home. I'm staying here until this gets straightened out."

She stood with her back to Marlene, her hand on the doorknob.

"I'm not leaving."

Josie expected a bolt of lightning to strike her dead for disobedience, for cheekiness, for changing the habits of a lifetime. Her vertigo returned and she began to shake. The only thing keeping her upright was her damp hand on the doorknob. Her stomach twisted in on itself, and sweat pooled under her breasts and at the base of her spine. She struggled for breath.

"I'm. Not. Leaving."

"You can't stay here. I have no room or time for you. Josie, listen to me," Marlene's voice was as persuasive as ever, and Josie listened against her will, her back to the room, to Marlene.

The voice enveloped her and Josie almost found herself captivated by its magic.

"Fred made a mistake. He knows that, but he can't figure out how to get out of it. You know him, he doesn't like to hurt anybody, even that…" The voice hardened for just a second. "He doesn't like to hurt anyone. So I have a plan. But it doesn't involve you. You're a hindrance. Josie, you have to go home. Do it for your old mother."

The voice didn't change, but Josie snapped out of her enthrallment at that phrase. Marlene had lost her edge. She'd never have used a phrase so at odds with her philosophy in the past. She was so angry, she wasn't thinking, or planning. She was reacting, using anything to get her way. And with that, Josie knew that Marlene's plan wasn't to get Fred back, it was to punish him. And Florence.

The knob turned and she fell into the hallway, still alive and strong enough to walk away. She couldn't believe it. She'd disagreed with Marlene and lived to tell the tale. The door closed softly behind her. Josie felt Marlene on the other side, felt her waiting. But Josie wasn't going home. She had a dinner date for tomorrow night, and today she needed to find a job and a place to stay. That would be enough for one day.

CHAPTER 4

The small communities of the Sunshine Coast—Gibsons Landing, Pender Harbour, Sechelt—strung out along the highway like pearls on a necklace. When Josie set out from Marlene's condo, she headed back down to Gibsons to start her job search. She needed to support herself while she solved her parents' problems.

She'd thought it would be easy. She'd show up, Fred would immediately realize what a terrible mistake he'd made and Marlene, after a little fuss, would forgive him. Life as Josie knew it would return and so would she. To Toronto.

Instead, waves of the past threatened to drown her. As for Fred, she was beginning to sympathize. She knew nothing about Florence other than her penchant for clothes just slightly too young for her and her silver bell voice, but what if she made Fred happy?

Josie's nausea returned. It had taken up permanent residence, along with a low-grade headache and a slight fever. She needed to sleep. In a bed and for a very long time.

She'd noticed a small motel on her way up, nestled in one of the hundreds of bays along the highway. The Sand Dollar Motel became her home away from home with the presentation of her not-quite-maxed-out credit card to the woman at the front desk.

"You're the lucky one, aren't you? If you'd come even a couple of weeks from now, honey, you'd be sleeping in your car. But tourist season isn't here yet so I can give you a room and a deal."

The room was cheap and clean and colorful. Especially colorful. Bright green carpet clashed with orange chairs and pink floral curtains. The bathroom looked like it had been transported forward in time from the fifties. It boasted olive-green fixtures, black-and-white tiles and a faded fluorescent tube humming overhead.

But it was off the highway and that was a bonus on the Sunshine Coast where the highway ran parallel to the shore and for most of its journey hugged the coastline like tight jeans hugged a man's butt. Almost every building sat next to the highway, and the best of them filled in the narrow strip of land between the road and the beach.

Josie sat in the window watching the light fade, first from the mountains, finally, much later, from the ocean. The water captured the dying light, holding faint shards of pink and yellow and the palest of blues, refusing to surrender them to the night. Josie couldn't tell the exact moment when the last hint of color vanished, only that it was there and then it was gone in the same way her luck disappeared.

There was no warning, one day it was there, the next it wasn't. At the time, Josie tried desperately to deny the change, choosing initially to blame Gabe or Don Mollard or someone, anyone, for her problems. *It wasn't about her*, she wanted to say, *it was about them*. The trouble with this course was that if she continued along that path, she'd end up blaming every single person she knew. And quite a few she didn't.

She'd have to blame the bank for her bounced checks instead of her own carelessness. The grocery clerk for the broken eggs in the bag she'd dropped on the way out of the store. The fishmonger for the food poisoning from the shrimp she left out on the counter. The list would be endless. And the task of enumerating all the wrongs caused would take Josie more hours than she had.

She hoped, with the hopelessness of a compulsive gambler, that her ability to acknowledge her own complicity would convince the gods to stop punishing her.

"I know it's me," she'd say. "It's about me, not anyone else."

And then she'd wait. And wait. Because of course the gods didn't answer. Josie knew why. She'd had more than her share of luck. It was someone else's turn. She felt a tinge of bitterness, wishing they'd planned things better, been a little less unfair.

It wasn't right to have given her half of a life brimming with good luck and then rip every single bit of it away. They could have left her something. The ability to find a parking space, buy toilet paper on sale, have a few good friends who hadn't just got married or delivered their first child, a good job, a happy family. Even one of those things would make her life better.

Josie dragged her suitcase out of the trunk and into her room. She threw the clothes into drawers and then pulled a velvet bag from the bottom of the suitcase where it had traveled the three thousand miles nestled between her favorite shoes and three pairs of socks. She cleared the dusty shells and sand dollars from the windowsill, then fetched a damp cloth from the bathroom to wipe off the salty residue.

Josie had changed over the past two years.

Things she'd laughed at when her friends or coworkers did them became habit. She routinely threw salt over her left shoulder, avoided ladders and black cats. She never opened cans upside down, never took off a sock she'd mistakenly put on inside out. She didn't step on cracks on sidewalks and lifted her feet when she crossed a bridge or a bump in the road. She favored the numbers seven and eleven, and shunned the number thirteen.

She even decided to go to church for the first time in her life.

She tried the Second Avenue United down the street, but its practical approach to faith didn't feel right. She tried half a dozen churches of various sects before wandering into St. Mary's one rainy Sunday morning. The ceremony and solemnity of it held some kind of promise for her.

She believed if she knelt and crossed herself at the right time, the gods (she never did understand the Holy Trinity concept and continued to think of them as three quite separate and distinct beings) would reward her. Maybe even return to her at least a small portion of her luck.

She loved the sound of the priest's voice echoing through the almost empty space.

She loved the smell of the incense and the ringing of the bells.

She loved the black-clad women dotted throughout the pews, their heads bowed, gnarled hands grasping rosaries.

Josie understood almost nothing of what was said, and sneaked out of her back pew before the priest could capture her on the steps, but she continued to turn up Sunday after Sunday. She bought a rosary and carried it in her purse.

When she waited for a bus, or in line for coffee, she held the rosary in her hands and ran the beads through her fingers. She took to wearing a scarf over her hair. She studied the women until she could cross herself just like them and then did so before she stepped out into a busy road, got into an elevator or saw a bike courier racing down the sidewalk toward her.

She gathered to herself the cloak of Catholicism until the day she realized her luck hadn't changed and people were staring at her on the street. She gave up on churches after that.

Josie took the rosary from the velvet bag. She laid it carefully on the windowsill, the beads cool and smooth against her fingers. She still thought about the church sometimes, although it wasn't the church, not really. It was the women.

Or maybe just one particular woman. She was tall, much taller than Josie although not much older, and heavy through the middle. She wore thick black shoes, a dark wool coat reaching down to her ankles even in the middle of summer. She had mittens on her hands and a white rosary dangling from them. A black scarf hid her hair but her eyes shone from beneath it. Her face was as white as the rosary.

Josie knew this woman in a way she didn't know the others because she left the church each Sunday before Josie did, not even waiting for the final Amen before she sprung up from her seat and hurried down the center aisle to the doors.

When she walked past Josie, she dropped her eyes, but not before Josie had seen the joy in them.

That woman, obviously as poor and downtrodden as it was possible to be, had found the meaning of life.

Josie wanted that for herself. And she tried, really she did. She assumed the woman humbled herself before the gods and begged for the strength to accept her lot, so Josie tried the same.

It just made her angry.

She assumed the woman left the church and spent the day doing good deeds, so Josie did that, too. Except it didn't work for her. She cut her finger so badly at the soup kitchen she had to be rushed to the emergency room. She yelled at the old people she was supposed to trundle around in their wheelchairs. She was allergic to the dogs and cats at the pound.

So she gave it all up, but she still thought about that woman. Her face reminded Josie of Jill's face when she left for San Francisco, the same unreasoning joy lit both of them. Josie used to look like that. She had the photographs to prove it.

Taking the small, framed picture from the velvet bag she placed it next to the rosary. It was taken three years ago at an office picnic. Josie sat on a child's swing set, her knees bent almost to her chest to keep her feet off the ground. She wore a smile so broad the sun sparkled off her teeth.

Josie carried that photograph to remind her of who she used to be and who she hoped to be again. But when she looked at it, she barely recognized the woman in the picture. Her sun-streaked hair had flown out behind her as she pumped and laughed and pumped some more.

The woman in the picture had freckles across her nose and on the skin in the deep vee of her T-shirt. Her lips were pink, her green eyes bright against the rosy cheeks. Her legs were tanned as she pumped the swing as high as it could go. The woman in the picture could do that because she was short enough—five-foot-nothing—so her legs didn't hit the ground when she arrived at the bottom of the swinging arc.

More than anything else, the woman in that picture looked happy.

She knew, intellectually, that it portrayed a slightly younger self, but she felt no connection to her. It was as if a knife had come down from the sky to cut Josie's life in two, leaving only the most nebulous remembrances of the first half.

In quick succession, she pulled out a rabbit's foot, a four-leaf clover encased in plastic, a piece of Chinese jade, a sprig of holly. She pulled out a charm bag of purple leather a friend had sent from New Orleans.

She laid each of them on the windowsill, then added a plaster Virgin Mary, a carved Buddha, a bronze Ganesh and a fake ivory elephant which she aligned with its trunk facing west.

She added tarot cards wrapped in silk and a Navajo corn doll. A kitchen witch, a tiny green leprechaun, her grandmother's blue-stoned brooch. A well-read book about lucky places with Stonehenge on the cover. A stone from Graceland and a blade of grass from Westminster Abbey.

And that wasn't all. Next was the tiny beaded bracelet saying Baby Girl Harris she'd worn in the hospital. A pale green agate and a perfect shell from a holiday on the ocean when she was twelve, an old garnet ring she'd found in a thrift shop and a single pearl earring she'd picked up on the street.

Her luck, the only luck she still possessed, lay spread out before her on the windowsill. Josie touched each item, lightly, as she would touch the cheek of a sleeping child. The placement had become ritual and she shifted one or two objects, just slightly, then rested her forehead on the cool glass and stared out at the black night.

Every hint of day was gone and the only light remaining was a faint bulb at the end of the dock. It cast a weak circle of light on the dock, but it didn't reach the ocean or the sky. Josie wondered what it would feel like to be that light, the uselessness of its presence against the immensity of the darkness.

Her life felt like it was at its lowest point, the darkness threatening to overpower her. Like the light, Josie had two choices. She could continue to shine, faintly, knowing her presence wasn't helping, or she could give up, douse her light and leave the night to the darkness.

As Josie flipped the switch on the bedside lamp and crawled into bed, the decision was in balance. Sleep settled over her like a net.

Josie woke the next morning as stiff and sore as if she'd spent the night climbing a mountain. Even her teeth ached. The shower seemed a mile away and she contemplated staying in bed, but her stomach wouldn't allow it. She hadn't eaten anything since the small slice of lemon pound cake Marlene deemed appropriate for afternoon tea.

The shower washed away a little of the stiffness but none of the despair. Fred and Marlene were separated, Josie was unemployed in a strange town, and with her luck, the only job she'd get would be…well, something awful, anyway. The view outside her window had vanished overnight into low-lying clouds. And she still had a headache.

No cars remained in the parking spaces before the numbered doors. Josie glanced at her watch; it was only eight o'clock and she'd heard no one leave. She was the only resident, and it was dark, and gloomy, and even a little frightening. She pushed the thought of Norman Bates from her mind.

A bell jangled, loud in the silence, when she opened the door to the office. The woman who'd proclaimed Josie lucky yesterday afternoon sat in front of a TV, the faces on it tinted green to match the room's decor.

"Hey," she said. "You're up early. Are you going to stay another day? The fog should burn off by lunchtime. Supposed to be another pretty day. You shouldn't miss it. This is my favorite time of year. Beautiful weather, neither too hot or too cold, and no damn tourists to screw up my life. Present company excepted, of course. Are you here on vacation? Not many people travel before school's out. I wonder why that is? Hardly anyone has kids anymore so why don't they travel off-season and avoid the crowds? Maybe it's just a habit, all those years in school. We're all so used to having holidays in July and August we can't imagine having them any other time. But they'd save so much money…"

Josie thought the woman—the name tag on her ample bosom said Mercedes—would talk forever if she wasn't stopped.

"I need a local paper and a recommendation for a place for breakfast."

"Here's the paper, hon. I've done the crossword, but otherwise it's good as new. 'Course it is only local, but Gray's a pretty good reporter. Best place for breakfast is the Way-Inn. Turn left and go down the hill. If you hit the water, you've gone too far. Make sure you have hash browns, Sam has a way with potatoes you won't believe. If he wasn't married to the sweetest girl in the world—you'll meet Rose, she's the waitress, cashier and busboy at the Way-Inn—I'd grab him myself."

Josie walked out the door with the paper under her arm and names swirling in her head. She'd had more interaction with new people over the last twenty-four hours than she'd had in months. Florence, Heather, Mercedes. And soon Rose and Sam. Josie's headache increased the pressure on her temples.

How was she going to cope with all these people? And a new job? And Fred and Marlene? No way to answer those questions, and handling the people was a thing that just had to be done.

Josie had two years' worth of experience just doing it. Not in the Nike way, not celebrating her body, but in the everyday plodding way that made up most people's lives. These ordinary things weren't easy for Josie, not anymore, but she did them, and mostly they turned into habits she no longer had to think about.

Because when she thought about them, she wondered about their usefulness. What, exactly, was she accomplishing by acting as if everything was normal when it was as far from normal as possible?

But those habits kept her going today, as they had for months, moved her into the car and left and down the hill.

Beyond making a mental note to pick up some Advil and maybe something for her stomach—the nausea was still there, as was the fever—she ignored her headache and concentrated on the scenery. What there was of it.

A few trees loomed out of the mist, black and ghostly. Yellow lights with halos appeared and disappeared behind swirls of white.

Josie heard the ocean but couldn't see it.

The hill steepened and the car responded, moving faster and faster. Josie's heart began to race with the car, and sweat broke out on her forehead.

She panicked, slamming on the brakes and stopping in the middle of the road.

She heard Mercedes in her head, "If you hit the water, you've gone too far."

Josie put the car back in gear and slowly began her descent. She focused on the road, her foot an inch above the brake, hoping for some kind of sign. Any kind. A street sign, a stop sign, a sign proclaiming Way-Inn.

By the time she reached the bottom of the hill, the ocean and the restaurant, half a dozen cars trailed her. Much politer than Toronto drivers, they didn't honk, simply slowed to match her plodding pace.

One by one, led by Josie, they pulled into the Way-Inn parking lot. Already spooked by the hill and the slow cavalcade appearing behind her out of the mist, Josie pried her hands from the steering wheel and locked the doors. She waited until everyone had silently vanished into the restaurant.

Hunger finally forced her out and across the parking lot

toward the red neon sign "GOO FOO." The door swung open and a chorus of voices and an opera of good smells brought tears to her eyes. She ignored them and sat down in the first booth from the door. And stood up again.

"Oh, God, I'm sorry. I didn't see you." The tears spilled over her lids. "I'm such an idiot."

"Hey." A soft voice reached her. "Don't worry about it. The place is packed, always is this time of the morning. You'd have to share, anyways, so it might as well be with me."

The tall, thin man on the other side of the booth put out his hand without acknowledging her tears.

"I'm Gray. That's my paper you're carrying under your arm so really we've already been introduced. I recommend the hash browns. And here comes Rose with another cup and the coffee," he said, forestalling any protest.

"Josie Harris," she said, appreciating his efforts to ignore her tears. It couldn't be easy because she felt them raining down her cheeks. They wouldn't be stopped. Run? Or stay? Either way would be embarrassing.

She imagined the headline: Unknown Woman Has Nervous Breakdown At The Way-Inn, Drowns Reporter's Eggs In Tears.

And the story.

Except there was no story, not really. Josie was just another woman with a messed-up life. And it wasn't even spectacularly messed-up. No childhood abuse, no rich cheating husband, no embezzlement of funds. Not even an excess of plastic surgery or an affair with a prominent politician or a convicted murderer. She had one speeding ticket and some overdue library books. That was the extent of it. No one would be interested; no one would want to write about it. She opted for the coffee and the handful of napkins Rose offered her.

"Thanks." Josie included both of them in her nod, speaking through the persistent tears. "Bacon and eggs and hash browns, please."

She ignored the tears because there was nothing she could do about them. It felt like her body was trying to rectify an imbalance, to restore itself to some preferred state without the weight of all that liquid.

The tears continued to fall, soaking the collar of her shirt despite the napkin she held to her chin to capture them. Rose returned with breakfast and another handful of napkins.

Rose said, "It happened to my mother once. One morning she sat down across from my father with a cup of coffee in her hand and she started crying. Couldn't stop. Scared the hell out of Dad. He asked what was wrong and she insisted it was nothing. Her life was perfect. She cried all that day and part of the next until she stopped as suddenly as she'd started. She never did know what triggered it."

Josie looked at the drenched napkin in her hand, the pile of them on the table, and sighed.

"Are my eyes red?" she asked, looking up at Rose.

"Nope. Not even a hint."

"And my nose isn't stuffed up, either. And obviously I can talk."

"So eat your breakfast. What else can you do? Want some more coffee?"

"Yeah, thanks. If this," gesturing at the tears, "is going on for a day, I need all the liquid I can get."

Josie moved her plate away from the edge of the table. She liked salt on her eggs but she'd rather it wasn't liquid. She felt the man across the table studying her as she figured out a way to eat her breakfast. She wiped her face, then took a quick bite, repeated it until she'd eaten everything on her plate, hunger overcoming whatever faint shred of humiliation remained.

"It's so weird. You don't even look like you're crying. Your face is like one of those Virgins the *National Enquirer* always has on the front page, tears pouring from their eyes and they don't notice, don't even wrinkle their noses or stick out their tongues to taste the tears."

Josie looked at him for the first time since she sat down. What she saw on his face panicked her.

"Don't you dare write about this." She threw a ten-dollar bill on the table and stormed from the restaurant, tears and hair flying. "Damn, damn, damn. The *Enquirer?* Oh God."

Josie knew there was no way to stop a reporter with a story. She'd seen it happen to a coworker whose son tried to commit suicide by jumping off the Bloor Viaduct onto Don Valley Parkway, causing a five-hour traffic jam in the middle of August. Five men had heart attacks in their cars from the combination of rage and heat.

Two of them died, because ambulances couldn't get through the traffic, one never drove again, and the other two blamed Robbie for the fact they had to stop smoking, learn to eat better and get some exercise. One woman delivered twins with the help of a taxi driver.

Two people fell in love and returned six months later to marry by the side of the Parkway. Robbie ended up in Sunnybrook—he could breathe but that was it. He was gone although his heart kept beating.

The reporter harassed Robert's family, phoning them in the middle of the night to catch them off guard, shooting photos of them as they went to work or shopping or to the hospital.

He sneaked into the hospital to sit by Robbie's bed and spew hatred, until the nurses caught him and threw him out. He just wanted a balanced story, he said, a reaction from the boy. Robbie was only fifteen when it happened.

Every August for five years, the reporter tried again, and then ran the story.

Vegetable Boy Ignores News Of His Victim's Families.

After the third year, Robbie's family moved away, taking Robbie with them, but the reporter didn't stop. When he no longer had Robbie and his family, he concentrated on the others.

He humiliated the man who could no longer drive, scared the twins by following them to school, reported the breakup of the marriage as if the two bank employees were Sonny and Cher.

Josie was determined to avoid the reporter even though she'd found him attractive and nice and not too scary. She was going to avoid everyone until the tears stopped. She'd stay in her room and order pizza when she got hungry. She'd phone Fred… She couldn't phone Fred, she didn't know Florence's last name and she definitely couldn't ask Marlene for it, though she was sure to know. She'd drive up, leave a note on the door. "Job hunting," she'd say, "Here's where I'm staying. Phone me and we'll pick another day."

She left the note on Florence's front door, pulling up cautiously to make sure no one was home before leaping out of the car, sticking the note in the doorjamb, then racing away like Mario Andretti.

She stopped at a tiny grocery store on the way back from Fred's, put on her dark glasses, grabbed a napkin to mop up the excess before running inside for five boxes of tissues, some bottled water and chocolate. The clerk looked at her curiously but Josie pretended it was just because she was wearing dark glasses on such a gloomy day.

Josie returned to her room and tried not to think about the tears. If they hadn't stopped by the morning, something would have to be done, otherwise she'd put it down to the flu. Headache, fever, nausea, tendency to weep. All symptoms, and she'd had them yesterday, even this morning before breakfast. Now the tears flourished, crowding out everything else like morning glory taking over a garden.

Josie knew what to do about morning glory. Cutting it back wasn't enough. You had to follow each tendril back to the root and dig it up, to the very last strand. Its roots grew deep, twining around other plants, insinuating itself into other lives until it became almost impossible to distinguish one from the other.

Ridding a garden of morning glory became a war rife with collateral damage. To root out the morning glory meant ripping the hearts from other, more loved plants. Even though

Josie believed in the necessity of it, she hated it, unable to separate the good—killing the morning glory—from the evil—killing the clematis and roses and pussy willows.

So her wish had been granted. The nausea was gone, and the headache and the fever. And she was left with the tears. Josie was going to have to learn to be careful what she wished for.

CHAPTER 5

I come from a long line of drunks and braggarts. My father's favorite saying was, If you never drink, you'll always be sober, *repeated with the certitude of a drunk at the end of a long drinking day.*

I don't drink much, never have. I'm scared I might end up like them, all those lives wasted in bottles full of liquid promise.

Gray couldn't help himself. He thought better, communicated better, while looking into the screen of his computer and so he typed what he'd been unable to say. He'd never give it to her, probably never see her again, but he wrote it anyway.

He'd wanted to impress the crying woman, but instead he'd scared her. He'd meant it as a compliment; the silent weeping made her even more beautiful than she already was. Gray was attracted to tragic women. He craved the role of a savior rescuing damsels in distress.

He'd rescued a single one, his sole experience—the girl he married right out of high school and divorced almost twenty years later when her affairs with younger and younger men became so obvious Gray couldn't ignore them any longer.

He knew it was his fault, knew he couldn't give her what she needed. His letters weren't enough; she wanted a real man. But the letters were what he knew, who he was. He wrote her every day from the first day they met in the coffee shop where she worked.

Sometimes he wrote two or three times a day, especially if things weren't going well. He poured out his heart to her in perfectly constructed sentences. He courted her with letters, and he assumed that she married him because of them.

Every day, he pulled out a piece of his soul and described it for her until she knew everything about him, things even he hadn't known until he'd written them down. He wrote about his love for her, and the passion she inspired in him. He wrote odes, though he was no poet. He wrote of her hair, her eyes, her breasts.

He wrote about his past, the stories he was working on that very minute, the future he planned for them together, the children and grandchildren and great-grandchildren he wanted them to have.

Twenty years worth of letters, more words than the longest novel ever written, more love than in all the romance novels published every year, more pain than a lifetime of soap operas.

When he cleaned out her closet after the divorce he found the letters. For the first few years, she'd read and saved them, tying them up in bundles with ribbon surrounding them, keeping them safe. Then she'd begun throwing them into the boxes without commemorating them in any way. At the top of the final box, the piles of envelopes weren't even opened.

The only things he brought with him to the Sunshine Coast were those boxes. He couldn't open them, or even put them away.

They sat on an old card table in his living room, gathering dust. He'd never reread them, or opened a single envelope. He knew if he did the words of that naive young man would haunt him for the rest of his life. But he couldn't do anything else with them, either.

He'd once carried them to the car for the trip to the dump, then carried them right back inside as soon as he realized that someone might find them. The dump was another thrift shop for the residents of the peninsula. Dump hunting was a favorite weekend pastime, along with twilight visits for a sight of the scavenging bears.

And one gorgeous May evening he collected driftwood and built a bonfire on the beach below his cottage. He carried the boxes down to the beach and sat beside them, a glass of wine in his hand. He contemplated the life of that young man and knew it was time to let him go. He opened the first box and pulled out a handful of yellowing envelopes.

Gray didn't burn the letters for the same reason he didn't throw them away. Someone showed up just as he opened the first box and he couldn't bear the idea of someone else seeing his soul in flames.

A man had strolled across the sand and stopped at the bonfire, holding out his hands to its warmth. He smiled at Gray, nodded as if to say, *Go about your business, I just want to enjoy the fire.* The man's lips hadn't moved except for the smile, but Gray heard those words as clearly as if the man *had* spoken them out loud.

The envelopes grew heavy in his hands. The flicking light of the fire made it difficult to read the faded handwriting but Gray brought the writing closer to his face.

"Holy tar and damnation," he whispered, echoing his father's favorite saying. The print faded away and Gray saw his father.

He stood on the rickety porch of the house they'd shared for eighteen years, Gray's duffel bag at his feet. It was morning, so his father's hands shook. He smiled at Gray and handed him an envelope.

"This is for you, boy. Now get the hell out of here or you'll miss your bus."

Gray didn't open the letter until he reached his dorm room. Two one hundred dollar bills—he still wondered where his father had got them—and a small piece of paper.

"I love you, boy," it said. "And I'm more proud of you than I can say. Never forget that."

A log crashed into the fire and the gaunt man across it began to walk away. He looked back over his shoulder and nodded one more time before disappearing into the darkness.

Words were his life, Gray thought, looking down at the envelopes in his hand. "My father might have written this," he said, running his thumb over the ink. "This could be his handwriting."

He dropped the envelopes back into the box, the box went back into the car, then back into his living room.

"Not yet," he grunted, carrying the boxes up the beach. "It's not time yet."

Those letters contained his soul and Gray couldn't be sure that inside those letters wasn't the only place where it still existed. He sometimes thought he might have transferred too much of himself into the words, leaving too little to be going on with.

So he kept the boxes and mostly ignored them except to make sure they stayed out of the damp. He installed a smoke detector and alarm system linked directly to the fire department. If he was right, he couldn't afford to lose the letters, not until he found a way to get his soul back.

So I divorced her and moved up here from the city, bought the paper and I've been here ever since. Are you my damsel in distress? Can I save you? In the way I was unable to save my wife? Or my father? Or myself?

Gray deleted the letter he'd begun to the weeping woman. He never wrote letters anymore. No, that wasn't quite true. He never *sent* letters anymore, except for business correspondence.

He still wrote letters, to his dead father, to his divorced wife, to women he saw once and whose names he didn't know, to the fairies he imagined he saw on the beach when the spring moon enchanted him. But he destroyed those letters the moment they were written, and felt the slight zing in his abdomen which signaled the return of the piece of his soul he'd put into the writing. He knew he couldn't afford to lose any more of himself.

Gray was forty-nine years old and he lived the life of an old man. He knew he did, enough women had told him so. Rose and Mercedes, the cashiers at the Safeway and the drugstore, the widow who came in to the office to answer the phone and take down classified ads.

Gibsons was filled with tough, insightful women of a certain age and every single one of them had designated herself Gray's substitute mother. They never fought over their role; rather they conspired with each other to introduce him to every single or divorced or separated woman of almost any age within a hundred mile radius of his house.

He met nieces, daughters, visitors from out of town, the new plumber, the manicurist at Gibsons' one hair salon. They tried to set him up with blind dates every weekend, and even though he'd mostly been saying no for almost ten years, they kept trying.

Gray's few dates were almost invariably disasters, because after he said hello, he was lost. Because he imagined himself a knight in shining armor, he wanted a woman to save. All the pre-arranged-date-women wanted to save him.

He knew exactly how Rose or Mrs. Suzuki or Mercedes (or any of the other women who tried to set him up) would describe him.

"Gray is a terrific guy," they'd say. "He's a bit sad, really, and lonely. But he's smart and he's got a good job and he's attractive." He could even picture the sparkle in their eyes when they got to this part of the description. "He just needs someone to look after him." A slight hint of his backstory: wife, father, etc., and it was done.

The trouble of course was that Gray wanted someone who he could look after, someone who needed him, so all those smart, attractive women who brought him food, who offered to manage his house, his finances, his life, just put him off.

He tried, he really did. Four dates with Sophie, the niece of the Safeway manager. Almost five with Janine, the new beautician. But they wanted a man who no longer existed, if he ever had. Gray MacInnis did not need to be looked after, he hadn't needed to be looked after since he was a child.

But the women of Gibsons had taken Gray under their collective wing with the ease of dedicated mothers. It was as if they knew he'd never had one of his own though he never told anyone, except his now-divorced wife, about his past. How his mother died when he was five from acute liver disease. How his father raised him, schooling Gray at home because he couldn't wake up in time to take him to the bus stop.

Gray grew to love those few hours in the early afternoon which his father had designated school time exactly as much as he loathed the nights.

And he'd learned to be self-sufficient. He did the laundry, made his own meals, did the shopping at the strip mall down the road. There was never quite enough money from the welfare to make it through the month. Gray became an avid bargain hunter and coupon clipper.

He made his own dinner and prepared extra food for his father. Nine nights out of ten he ended up throwing the extra food away after his father passed out in the chair in front of the TV.

But his father was a smart man. He made sure Gray got a better education than a country school could have given him. Made sure the house was neat and the empty bottles well hidden for the visit of the school inspector once a year. Most importantly he filled in all the forms for an official diploma so Gray could go to college if he wanted to.

He thought he did until, in his first week of classes, scared to death of all the people and noise and action, he met the woman of his dreams in a coffee shop. He got a job as a copyboy on the night shift of a small newspaper, gave her a miniscule diamond, and expected to live happily ever after.

Well, that was it for his past. And his present and future. Gray mostly liked his life. He had a great job, neither too much work nor too little, a place in the community, lots of friends, and if, every once in a while, he became infatuated with a woman whose name he'd never know, he knew how to deal with that.

So what if every once in a while he felt a faint twinge from the place he imagined his soul had been. He knew where it was now, safely packed in cardboard boxes and living on his card table. That was more than most people knew about their souls.

The widow Mrs. Suzuki—Gray thought of her that way because she still wore black from head to toe fifteen years after her husband's death—had opened the door and raised the blinds by the time he arrived at the office.

"Have we got any applications?"

Mrs. Suzuki was convinced her job—answering the single telephone line, selling and typing up ads, writing the occasional obituary or story about the high school play, making coffee and chatting to the visitors who saw Gray as a source of free coffee—was too much for one person.

The subtext was that her daughter and son-in-law were expecting their first child and she desperately wanted to be available to babysit every afternoon. But Gray had given her a job when she needed one, and she wouldn't desert him, not even for her first grandchild.

Her expectant face fell when he shook his head.

"The ad's been in for three weeks. We're never going to get anyone. Maybe we should advertise in the city."

"Don't worry. I have a feeling about this. Something is going to happen, maybe not today, but very soon."

And Gray was telling the truth. He'd woken up knowing something extraordinary was going to happen. And it did. He met the weeping woman.

The minute he saw her he knew she would apply for the job. He wasn't sure how he felt about that. All the other women he'd been attracted to since his divorce had been spotted, fallen for and lost in a single sighting. He'd never spent any time with them. But Mrs. Suzuki needed an assistant and the weeping woman was his only choice.

"The baby's due in six weeks."

"Yeah, and the only other job in town is for a mechanic at the Esso station, so stop fretting. Someone needs this job and she's going to show up any time. You'll see."

They turned away to their respective desks, two sets of fingers crossed. Gray had suggested Mrs. Suzuki work mornings only and he'd still pay her full salary because she was so good at her job she could do it in half the time if she wanted to. She bridled at the idea.

He needed someone there, she said, in case he got called out to a story. Besides, she wasn't going to become a charity case, no way.

So both of them spent their days waiting for the bell over the door to tinkle, signaling the appearance of the perfect employee. Smart, well-educated, good-looking (that was Mrs. Suzuki's contribution) and able to start right away.

Gray had long since stopped racing Mrs. Suzuki to answer the phone. It was her favorite part of the job.

"Who may I say is calling?" Despite the fact that she almost certainly recognized the voice on the other end. She'd lived in Gibsons her whole life. She'd put her hand over the mouthpiece and yell across the room at Gray.

"It's Ron. Another car's in the drink at the bottom of Sunset Hill. No one's hurt but they're sending the tow truck to pull it up. Might make a good photo."

And Gray would nod and take her not-so-subtle advice.

Mrs. Suzuki knew exactly what people on the peninsula wanted from the *Sunshine Coast News*. He thought of her as his perfect reader. He'd watch while she scanned his headlines and front-page stories, grimacing when he saw two lines appear between her brows, smiling when they disappeared. He wanted to keep her happy. The weeping woman would have to come through for him.

All that day he watched for her through the window facing the street. She didn't show. He kept his butt in the chair and didn't disappear as he often did on slow days to wander the back roads looking at old logging sites, watching for animals and birds. He stayed in the office playing solitaire on his computer and drinking stale coffee long after Mrs. Suzuki had gone home and the sky had grown dark.

Infatuation. And this time he had it bad. Josie Harris... sad, scared Josie Harris, got under his skin and he didn't want her out.

Josie spent the day in bed, a box of tissues and a garbage pail next to her, the box rapidly emptying and the pail filling with wet tissues. The crying didn't hurt. It didn't even make her sad, at least not any sadder than she already was. But she couldn't stop.

She tried pinching her nose, closing her eyes, lying down, sitting up, jogging in place, even standing precariously on her head. She tried meditation but couldn't concentrate because she kept getting wet. Nothing worked. So she gave up and drank liters of water to replace the lost fluids, hoping the flood would somehow stop of its own volition.

She watched afternoon TV with equal parts of horror and delight, something she'd never done before. Marlene didn't believe in television, especially in the afternoons. She flipped indiscriminately between soap operas, judge shows and talk shows finding she could still laugh even through the tears. She loved the characters, unable to believe they weren't actors.

They were too good (or maybe it was too bad) to be true. They were caricatures of the spurned wife or cheating husband, of the rebellious teenager or bad neighbor. No one was that much of a good thing.

And the best part was that it didn't matter what channel or show she watched, somehow it connected itself to all the others. If she saw a cheating husband on *Judge Judy*, when she turned the channel she found his ex-wife and her new lesbian biker lover. If she caught a dog trainer on *Oprah*, she found a child who'd been mauled by vicious highly trained attack dogs somewhere else.

How did they do it? How did they put the dozens of shows together so that it didn't matter when or how often you switched channels, they became part of one megashow? Who planned it that way?

Josie finally turned off the TV when they started to show reruns of *Seinfeld*. Enough was enough.

She sat at the table she'd moved across the room next to her luck and opened the newspaper—the *Sunshine Coast News*—that Mercedes had given her that morning. She turned to the want ads and stared in disbelief.

There were only two jobs: a qualified mechanic at the Esso station, and an assistant for the paper. She could tune up, change the oil and the tires on her car but that was it. That left her with the paper. And the reporter. Damn.

She didn't trust him not to turn her disease—for what else could it be?—into a story, but she needed a job. And she needed it right away.

The cost of the room for a week and a little food had taken almost all of her money. She might ask Fred, but Marlene had always controlled their finances and Josie was willing to bet she had given him no money at all and no access to their bank account either.

She would expect that to bring him back to her. And she couldn't (*wouldn't*) ask Marlene. That left the job.

She sat with the paper in her lap until the newsprint began to turn to papier-mâché in her hands and the phone number washed away with her tears.

Josie pointed at the luck strung out on the windowsill.

"You guys aren't doing a great job so far today. I can't stop crying, no matter what I do. I'm probably going to become the front-page story in next week's *Enquirer*. Maybe I can set up some kind of exhibition and charge admission. Because otherwise, I'm going to end up working for a reporter and you know how much I'll hate that."

There was no reply. Not from Mary, not from the leprechaun or Buddha, not even the corn doll. Not a word or a sign from any of them. Josie swore they turned their backs on her so they could watch the night sky instead of her weeping face.

"I thought you'd be the one to appreciate this," poking Mary in her sky-blue robe. "I mean, you're the star of this particular crying show. You started it all. How do you get it to stop? You can't spend your whole life weeping. It's just not fair."

Even bad luck couldn't take you that far. But Josie knew it was possible to spend most of your life in a state of grace. She had. So the opposite must also be conceivable. There must be people—and she was beginning to think she had become one of them—who spent their lives in a state of disaster, whose every move turned out badly. She knew how it would be.

Josie fell asleep with the lights on and the tears continued to fall, drenching the bed with salty liquid that warmed her throughout the night. In her dreams, she floated in an azure sea. Dolphins frolicked around her, and the sun shone through the water so she could see the sandy bottom. She was alone, except for the dolphins, but she didn't feel lonely. She felt safe.

The tears began to evaporate from the sheets and blankets and pillow cases as she dreamed, forming a blue mist around her body. The mist, too, was warm and Josie smiled at the dolphins and sunk deeper into sleep. The tears slowed.

When she first woke, she retained an almost imperceptible memory of another life in a beautiful, wet world but as soon as she blinked, it was gone.

She felt the difference. The tears were still falling, but they were manageable now. Maybe Rose was right. At nine-thirty—exactly twenty-four hours after they started—they'd stop as if they'd never begun.

Josie had never been a believer in miracles, she'd never needed to be. She wasn't a person who read the "Dog Saves Two-Year-Old" or the "Face Of Jesus Appears On Tortilla" stories. She didn't even glance at the headlines in the Safeway checkout line. She knew her sign—Aries—but only because people were always asking her about it, not because she read her horoscope.

She didn't. Or at least she hadn't. But she hadn't been superstitious before, either. She didn't have her palms or her tea leaves or tarot cards read. None of those things made sense to her until she lost her luck.

But she was willing to believe that the miracle thing was different. Miracles represented good luck on a huge scale, a life's worth of luck rolled up into a single event. Did that mean your luck got used up rescuing you from a well when you were two? Or a stranger happening to drive by the deserted lake where your car had just gone off the road? Or what if you were days away from being taken off the transplant list and a teenager killed himself driving too fast and you got his heart? Would you live happily ever after?

Josie wondered about the teenager, too. Had he been lucky before the accident or was his death the culmination of a lifetime of bad luck? Or bad choices? What if they were one and the same thing? But Josie knew otherwise. Her luck hadn't been the result of good choices and it had changed without her making any decisions, good or bad. It just happened.

She still couldn't understand the nature of it, why some people had it, good or bad, and others didn't. Why some people were the recipients of a single bolt of luck—of either kind—and others had only one kind of luck. They were lucky with cards or money or men. They always found a parking space right where they needed it to be or ten-dollar bills on the sidewalk. They found four-leaf clovers or perfectly shaped stones to skip.

They couldn't hold a job: the company went bankrupt, the accountant was a thief, yet they had a loving family. They dated men who turned out to be crooks and liars. They never won a single door prize.

Because if you had that one kind of luck, maybe from the very beginning, you knew it was going to last only so long. In a single instant—like Josie's—that luck would invert itself. Bad to good. Good to bad. But the thing was, the truly important thing was, you never knew when or how or why it would change.

Maybe it was because you were in the right place at the right time. Maybe you saved some billionaire's pet poodle from being run over by a cement truck. Or you stepped into a fight to rescue a lovely maiden and got offered a television show.

Or maybe, just maybe, you walked in on a bank robbery. Or you got hit by an ambulance while you were sitting at a bus stop. Or the company you worked for went bankrupt because DVDs replaced videotapes.

And maybe, Josie thought, the uncertainty of it was what bred superstition. You couldn't know when you'd lose your luck at bingo so you watched out for black cats. You collected four leaf clovers and carried a rabbit's foot. You did everything you could so you couldn't blame yourself for the change in your luck.

Josie made mediocre coffee in the tiny pot on the dresser and watched the bedside clock click over to nine, then nine-oh-one. She couldn't bear the waiting. The barely perceptible sound the numbers made as they changed got stuck in her head, a kind of *kchaw* sound. If she turned away she couldn't hear it, but she knew when it happened.

Her body stiffened and she held her breath, waiting.

What if Rose's mother had figured out how to stop her tears but never told Rose? Josie might be just waiting when she needed to be doing something. But there was nothing to be doing, at least nothing Josie could think of.

The clock *kchawed* over to nine-thirty. Josie lifted her hands to her face, to her eyes. She wiped away the tears and waited. She took a new tissue but even before she used it, she knew. She was still crying.

The odd thing was that Josie believed the tears weren't hers, not really. They came from somewhere or something or someone outside and they would stop only when that some-one or something decided it was time. Josie had no control over it.

She was disappointed, of course she was, but she had al-ready decided what she was going to do. Jump into the shower, get dressed, put on her dark glasses and go start her job at the *Sunshine Coast News*. She knew he'd hire her. She'd understood the look on his face as he watched her cry into her breakfast.

CHAPTER 6

Gray had been at work since dawn, and only partly because he was on deadline. He was drinking his second pot of coffee and beginning to shake when the door opened.

"Anyone here?"

He'd forgotten to turn on the lights. In between stories, he'd been writing letters to the weeping woman and deleting them by the eerie glow of the computer screen. He'd started to doubt the certainty he'd felt yesterday, but here she was.

He couldn't see her in the dark, only her silhouette against the clouds outside, but he'd been hoping she'd show so he had sent Mrs. Suzuki to cover the ex-mayor's funeral, a job he'd normally do himself. He knew it sounded weird, but he liked funerals on the Sunshine Coast. They were sad, but they were almost always lively. And a great source of stories. He collected the oddest tales. Maybe one day they'd turn themselves into a book.

Gray's words came out husky and hesitant. "Back here. Hold on while I hit the lights."

He stumbled to the front wall, turned on the lights and stood blinking like a shocked owl in the glare of a flashlight. He still couldn't see her and he desperately wanted to. Gray needed to know if she was still crying, still beautiful, still a damsel in distress needing rescue. He blinked until the light stopped hurting his eyes and then focused on her face.

He didn't say what he wanted to, which was, "I love you. Run away with me, I'll replace your tears with laughter," because he wasn't sure of his ability to change anything.

The dozens of letters now in the recycle bin of his computer said basically the same thing. "I love you, whoever you are."

Because he did. Just like he'd fallen for all those other once-seen women, but different, because he hadn't fallen out of love once she'd walked away, once he'd written about his feelings. It scared him. The same thing happened with his ex-wife and it took him twenty years to get over her. He didn't have another twenty years, not now.

Gray knew it wasn't real love, but, for the first time in more years than he cared to count, he wanted to explore a relationship, wasn't doing it just to keep the troops happy. Oh, he used the word love, but he knew it wasn't love, couldn't be. He hardly knew her. He just didn't know what else to call it. Lust? Definitely. Infatuation. Yep. But it might change, mightn't it?

So he kept the L-word to himself, left it in the trash where it belonged. Instead, he said, "Can I help you?"

"I hope so."

The dark glasses hid her eyes but no tears poured down her face. Then she raised a tissue and patted behind the glasses. So. She still cried. He held out his hand.

"I'm Gray MacInnis. I run the paper."

"I know. I've come about the job. I saw your name on the

masthead." She looked around. "Where's D. Suzuki? He's on the masthead, too."

"She, Mrs. Doris Suzuki, that is, is out covering the ex-mayor's funeral. She'll be back after lunch probably. And speaking of food, how about breakfast? I haven't eaten yet."

She ignored him.

She had the gift of perfect stillness, Gray thought. She didn't fidget, didn't shift back and forth on her heels, simply stood in the doorway and waited him out.

"Can you use a computer? Answer the phone? Will you stay for at least six months?"

"Yes. Yes—" and, after a slight pause "—I can't promise."

"Okay. Well, stay as long as you can. Mrs. Suzuki needs a break. Start tomorrow, all right?"

"Yes."

"Now can we have breakfast?"

"No. I have to go to the doctor. This has to stop—" Raised her glasses to point at the moisture oozing from her eyes. "It's better but it won't stop. And I can't wear dark glasses forever. Does the sun *ever* shine here?"

"Sure. But it's April. One day it'll shine and you'll see. Have you eaten? Maybe you're crying because you're hungry. I mean, look at me. I shake when I'm hungry."

He held out his trembling hands. Gray knew what he was doing, and it was something he'd never done before.

He was talking instead of writing and if he'd felt scared before at the depth of his feeling for this unknown woman, now he felt sheer terror. Because something had shifted inside, something deep and dark and fundamental, when he saw her standing in the door, when his reassurances to Mrs. Suzuki had proved correct.

Possibility shook him to his roots. A future, a woman, a different life than the one he'd settled for. It scared him to death but she'd showed up at his door and he had to admit that a possibility—of what he couldn't say—had arrived with her.

Gray wasn't a believer.

He collected odd stories for their absurdity, not because they proved anything about the human condition. His childhood had instilled in him a deep cynicism about the world and the people in it. All people were groping, not toward enlightenment but toward oblivion.

Alcohol, drugs, sex, rock and roll.

Religion, lottery tickets, psychics, astrology, even love (and Gray knew he was guilty of this) were a way to silence the voice inside that said, "You're nothing, you'll always be nothing."

People mostly picked their poison—and then they used it to drown the voice and make sense of their senseless lives.

Gray never told anyone about his feelings. He thought now that had he stayed in college he might eventually have spoken about them. Universities seemed to specialize in young men and women talking about the meaninglessness of their privileged existence and then finding a meaning, usually because they fell in love with someone totally unsuitable. Just like Gray. Although he hadn't thought of her as unsuitable, he'd thought of her as perfect.

Gray's cynicism was always bumping up against his love for old movies and books. He grew up alone, his only company the books he'd brought home from the library and the movies he'd seen on their flickering TV, watching late into the night, standing in the hallway on a chair so he could see over his father's shoulder.

The books and movies taught him he had a soul. He wasn't sure he believed that, precisely, but he worried that some part of himself that he called his soul was trapped in those letters in the boxes in his living room. That was the disadvantage to not believing, at least for Gray. He knew too much to believe but he also knew too much to take risks. So he tried to balance the two sides of himself, that which honestly did not believe and that which knew and loved thousands of stories about the powers of hope and faith and love.

When he'd woken up yesterday morning with the conviction in his mind about the job being filled that day, when he'd seen Josie Harris at the Way-Inn and knew she was the one to fill it, he'd put it down to wishful thinking and he'd repeated it to Mrs. Suzuki to make her feel better. But now it was coming true.

Did that mean there was such a thing as precognition? And if that, then what else?

Would he have to start believing in ghosts, in the power of astrology?

Would he experience an urgent desire to be baptized?

Gray ignored the question as being unanswerable and turned back to the problem at hand.

Josie Harris.

His communication skills were all in his fingers, not his mouth, and he felt as if every time he opened it, he made a mistake. Oh, not when he was doing interviews, or talking to friends, but when it was important, like now, with Josie Harris. Or with his father or his ex-wife.

If it was important, he had to write it down. It was as if the neurons firing in his brain bypassed his throat and tongue and headed directly for his hands. Yet here he was, talking, and he felt like one of those odd, wonderful people whose brains worked differently than the rest of the world. Gray knew that verbal communication was the way of most people, but it had never been his.

"The clinic doesn't open until noon on Tuesdays. You have plenty of time to eat. It'll be your first task as an employee of the *Sunshine Coast News*, okay? I'll fill you in on everything."

He herded her out the door and pulled it shut behind him, still talking. He assumed, rather than saw, her nod of acceptance.

Rose showed them to a booth in the back and poured coffee without asking.

"Your regular?" she asked, including Josie in the question.

Josie nodded and she felt the corners of her mouth tilt up, just a little, at the thought that after a single day she was a regular. In Toronto, that level of recognition took months, if it ever arrived at all.

Mind you, yesterday had been a pretty unusual day. No one in the Way-Inn yesterday was going to forget following her down the hill in the fog at the pace of a horse-led funeral cortege nor the nonstop tears once she got there. Instant small-town celebrity-ship.

The hash browns and poached eggs were every bit as good

as they'd been yesterday, maybe better, because today they weren't floating in tears. Gray's ramblings, the busy café, Rose's constant attention—all of them distracted her, took her mind away from the tears. Josie raised her hands to her cheeks.

They were dry for the first time in more than twenty-four hours. She blinked. No moisture spilled over her lids.

She didn't hear the crash of the coffee cup as it hit the floor, feel the bump of the table against her hip or the toe she bashed kicking the back of the booth in her rush to get to a mirror.

She didn't notice the roomful of interested observers, nor the sudden silence when she brushed past Rose to get behind the counter to the mirror over the cash register. But once there, Josie hesitated. She stood in front of the mirror in her dark glasses and she started to shake as if the entire building were caught in an explosion or an earthquake, even though everyone else was perfectly still and perfectly silent.

She hesitated so long that Rose finally stepped forward and enveloped Josie in her arms.

"I'll do it," she said, "I'll take them off for you." And she pulled the glasses from Josie's face. She turned her to the mirror. "Look. You're not crying. You're fine, love, really. No tears at all. It's as if it never happened. Just like my mom."

And Josie started to cry, really cry, at the relief. She felt a moment of panic—what if she couldn't stop?—but her eyes started to sting and her nose stuffed up, and she knew these were real tears, and that she could stop them and she did.

The walk back to the booth took forever. Each person she

passed stopped her to say "congratulations" and to introduce themselves.

She met the part-time librarian and the couple who ran the Esso station. She met half a dozen retired fishermen, and the three women who ran the summer craft market.

"What do you make?" they asked and laughed when she shook her head.

"You will," they said. "Everyone does, even Gray."

She had five people offer to buy her breakfast, two invitations to drop by for tea and fifteen heartfelt handshakes before she got back to the booth and Gray.

She pulled her last five dollars from her wallet. "I have to go up to Sechelt. I'll see you tomorrow." She didn't wait for his reply, just hurried out of the coffee shop and up the hill to her car. Josie felt an overwhelming need to see Marlene and Fred and Florence, to concentrate on their problems instead of her own.

It wasn't quite lunchtime when she pulled into the parking lot next to Marlene's condo. In her rush to get here, she'd taken no time to formulate a plan, so she got out of the car, sat on a bench and stared at the ocean, waiting for something to come to her.

Instead she drifted. The overcast sky turned the ocean to dull gray, overlaid with green and occasional patches of a deep, oily black. She'd never seen anything like it. It moved but the swells were like one huge piece of multicolored mercury, shifting heavily on an earth-sized platter. Long rolling waves caressed the beach, dampening the rocks over and over, leaving them with a temporary shine until the wind dried them and the process began again. The ocean matched her mood, lazy and aimless.

Josie knew in the back of her mind that something needed to be done about her situation—the house she'd left in Toronto, sitting empty and unloved, the job she'd abandoned without notice.

She felt a twinge of guilt at that thought but it quickly evaporated when she remembered John Johnson's voice firing her.

For all he knew, she might be lying murdered in her bed, or in a hospital with amnesia, or stolen off to the Far East by white slavers. She hadn't shown up, she was fired. He wouldn't even bother to check if she was okay. Josie left a whole life behind and she couldn't just walk away from it, leave it there like a pile of dead leaves. Or could she?

No. She was here, temporarily, to deal with Fred and Marlene. She'd do that and then go home. In the meantime, Josie decided, she could forget all about her other life. The house would be okay and if she was still here in a month (which she hoped not to be), she'd sublet it for the summer.

Her next-door neighbors would forward her mail, her bills that is, and mow the lawn once the snow melted. Josie would carry on with this life. Go to work, maybe find a furnished apartment or make a deal with Mercedes for a long-term stay, spend time with Marlene and Fred, together if possible, separately if necessary.

The only drawback to the whole scheme was the crying. Josie knew neither what started nor what stopped it and that meant it might happen again at any time. She'd have to ask

Rose if her mother continued to have crying fits, if it happened only once in a lifetime, or once a year or every decade. She needed to do some research. If it happened to Rose's mother, and to Josie, it had happened to other women.

Josie had convinced herself that the tears came from somewhere outside, like a virus or a cold. So was she now immune? Or was she more susceptible? Was it like measles—you get it once, it's over—or like bronchitis—you get it once, you get it over and over again?

Josie wished she'd brought her notebook with her. It was time to plan out her week. Work. Fred and Marlene. Research. Talk to Rose. Talk to Mercedes. Suddenly, she felt busy and full of purpose. Maybe she'd needed this change, and now her luck would return.

Because Josie continued to refuse to believe that luck, her good luck, could really change. It might go away for a while, take a vacation or sabbatical, but it would come back. She just had to do the right thing, carry the right combination of charms, say the right prayers or incantations, read the right self-help books or go to the right personal empowerment lectures. She simply had to find it, the one thing that would entice her luck from its hiding place.

Luck was personal, and it was finicky.

Josie knew luck wouldn't respond to pleas, it scorned them. When she lost hers, she lay in bed and begged for it to return. It ran farther away and her life got worse. Luck favored the strong, the prepared.

She knew her luck, knew just what it felt like to have it. Once or twice over the past two years she'd had a whiff of it, not enough to change anything, just enough to convince her it was still around, waiting for her to do whatever was needed to bring it back.

And she was willing, God knew she was willing, but she didn't know what was needed. She'd tried everything she could think of and it still evaded her. But she felt good today, felt strong and confident and competent and that might help. It was time to talk to Marlene.

Josie's confidence diminished, just slightly, just enough to allow a smidgen of doubt into her mind as she walked across the parking lot. She couldn't help but remember the Marlene she'd seen the day before yesterday and that woman—tough, unflappable, professional—made her nervous.

She hadn't seemed the kind of woman who would be amenable to a heart-to-heart chat about her absconding husband. Far from it.

Josie pushed doubt away into a closet somewhere and locked the door. She walked faster. She'd get to Marlene's place before the doubt figured out how to pick the lock. Once she knocked, she was stuck and so was Marlene.

She'd have to let Josie in, have to talk to her. She'd driven three thousand miles to get here and, damn it, she was going to have her say. A rush of courage washed over her, quickly replaced by a surge of apprehension. But it was too late to turn around, too late to tackle Fred first. She'd already knocked on Marlene's door.

When it opened, Josie checked the number to make sure she was in the right place. The woman in the hallway bore no resemblance to the Marlene who'd served tea and lemon pound cake. This woman might be her grandmother. And she smelled of age, a combination of unwashed skin and mothballs, with an underlay of despair, a smell Josie recognized from volunteering at the old age home.

Marlene appeared heartbroken, Josie thought, wondering whether she was crazy to be thinking it. Her mother never let anything get her down, she was the eternal optimist. But Josie couldn't deny the evidence in front of her. Marlene's heart was broken. Or at the very least it was dented.

"Marlene?"

The old woman raised her head. Her cheeks had fallen in and her colorless eyes sunk into their sockets. Her hair hung limp against her dingy neck and slumped shoulders. When Josie's eyes met hers, a bolt of bitterness passed through Josie as if a spear entered her heart.

"Marlene?" Her voice softer this time.

"Get out. Get out. I don't want you here. Not now. Not ever. You're ruining everything. Go home."

The door slammed on Josie's already bruised toe, but the pain was nothing to the anguish she felt at Marlene's words. She wasn't sure whether to feel sorrier for Marlene or herself. She returned to the car, turned the heat and Tom Jones on and her mind off.

"Just for a minute," she muttered. "I need a break. I'm not ready for this. Not yet."

Josie sat back in her seat and tried to ignore the throbbing toe but she couldn't, especially when it began to beat in time with "What's New, Pussycat." She shrugged. It didn't matter, not really. The toe was nothing compared to Marlene.

"Stop. Stop it right now."

Josie concentrated on the front door of Marlene's building. She watched it open and shut, counted the people who went in and out. It was lunchtime and she imagined the ones who went in at their kitchen tables eating chicken noodle soup with too many crackers, and the ones who went out at a coffee shop on the beach somewhere.

She concentrated on the spring colors they wore—pink and green and yellow, bright against the somber sky. Some of the women wore hats to match, and Josie amused herself conjuring up a freak wind to tear them from their heads. The men dressed for golf, red plaid pants and windbreakers, although Josie doubted they would get any farther than the clubhouse on a day like today.

And then Marlene appeared and Josie's carefully cultivated calm snapped. Marlene wore an egg-yolk yellow suit and a paisley scarf around her shoulders. Her hair shone, pulled back in a perfect French roll. Her high heels clacked importantly against the sidewalk as she hurried to a car waiting at the curb. Josie strained for a look at the driver but the tinted windows defeated her. Without thinking, she pulled out of the parking lot to follow, needing to reconcile the two Marlenes she'd seen this morning.

Because it was more than weird, it was downright scary. In less than half an hour the ruined old woman had been transformed. Kind of like Cinderella dressing for the ball. But Cinderella had a fairy godmother, not to mention the mice and the birds.

How had Marlene done it? Or was the woman in Marlene's

condo not Marlene at all? Josie clenched the steering wheel and examined her short-term memory bank. The woman had recognized Josie, or at least Josie thought she had, but even more than that were the eyes. Even faded and colorless, Josie recognized Marlene in them.

The two cars headed up the coast, the road curving through forest and around bays. Josie caught glimpses of sailboats and freighters, light against the matching grays of water and sky, and flashes of color hidden in the trees, new subdivisions flowering with the spring.

She saw For Sale signs and gas stations and abandoned barns.

She followed Marlene north and farther north, venturing into uncharted territory.

Josie had to believe there were dragons; she'd already confronted one of them. But she hadn't known dragons were capable of transformation; that was her incentive for this trip. How had young Marlene become old Marlene and back again? Mary Kay was good, but that good? She watched as the brake lights on the car in front of her flashed for the first time, then signaled a left-hand turn. Josie followed and then pulled over to the side of the road and stopped under a canopy of trees.

The sign at the road read, Lord Jim's Resort. Marina. Hotel. Restaurant. Open All Year.

Now what? If she followed Marlene down this narrow road, she would spot Josie and then…confrontation. She could wait here and follow her home, accomplishing nothing except the same door slammed in her face yet again. Or was it only the old Marlene who'd do that? The young Marlene had let her in the other day. Josie wasn't sure what would happen but her toe couldn't handle any more pain. Nor could she.

She could go back on down the highway and find Fred. Maybe he knew what was going on, and if he didn't, Josie was willing to bet that Florence did. Florence had struck Josie as smart and quick, if a bit shy, and suddenly Josie wanted, more than anything, to hear that sweet, tinkling voice again, even if it was telling her things she didn't want to know.

Before she knew it, she was on the highway traveling south.

"Wrong. Wrong. Wrong. I can't do the easy thing. Not this time."

She spun the car around, and this time, when she pulled into the driveway, she drove right down it to the resort at the bottom. She parked next to the car that had brought Marlene and limped into the restaurant, ignoring the view, the pain in her toe and the hostess hurrying after her, calling, "Do you have a reservation?" She headed straight for the yellow suit sitting at the best table in the house and didn't stop until she got there.

Marlene sat across the table from Florence. Florence who looked like a scared kitten and barely kept the tears in her eyes from spilling out.

Josie wondered how Marlene had convinced Florence to bring her to this out-of-the-way spot for lunch. Had she allowed her a glimpse of the old Marlene, teetering down the beach in her bare feet and nightgown? From what Josie had seen of Florence, it wouldn't have taken much of that Marlene to shake her. Florence was neck-deep in guilt and Marlene was a master manipulator of the guilt-ridden.

But Josie had seen Fred and Florence together, had felt the glow of their joy embrace her, had watched them walk away down the beach as happy as if they were teenagers heading to a secret place for their very first kiss. No woman would give that up. Whatever Marlene had planned for this lunch, it wasn't going to work. And Josie would stick around to make sure of that.

Marlene's face contorted with rage when she saw Josie, and she spat, "You again? What do you want?"

And Josie realized right then that Marlene truly didn't understand what she wanted or how she felt.

She thought of Josie as an interloper, almost a stranger. All the years of carefully planned phone calls, rushed visits and gift certificates or money instead of birthday and Christmas gifts took on a new meaning.

Josie heard, from a long way away, Marlene's voice, repeating, "Go away. Just go away," but Josie was rooted to the spot. Her body had turned to stone.

Cold and lifeless, the only parts of her that still moved were her eyes and they were uncontrollable, bouncing from the view of the ocean to Marlene's yellow suit to Florence's shocked face to the table settings, without settling on any of them.

The world moved by in slow motion. Josie saw the waitress arrive with a basket of rolls and more coffee, heard her ask if she should add another place.

"No," Marlene said, "she's just leaving, aren't you, Josie?"

She saw her slap a hand at Josie as if whisking away a fly. And then she proceeded to ignore Josie and practically ignore Florence. The waitress looked at Josie and shrugging, worked around her to bring the soup, then bowls of steaming pasta. When the dessert came, she tried again, but Marlene gave her the look and the waitress subsided.

Josie stood beside the table for forty-five minutes while the waitress passed fabulous food around her and Josie tried not to vomit. Forty-five minutes of complete silence except for a few words spoken by the uncomfortable waitress. "Would you like more coffee?" and "Here's the dessert menu."

Josie watched while Marlene ate every bite of her salad, her pasta, her soup and her dessert. Florence moved the morsels around on her plate.

The silence stretched out, Josie's urge to vomit grew until, for a brief and glorious moment, she almost let it go. She stopped herself but only because of the look on Florence's face. If Josie threw up, Florence would be right behind her.

Florence said nothing, not a single word. Marlene didn't say much, either; but unlike Florence's silence, Marlene's spoke volumes. Even Josie understood it. You were *my* friend, it said, and you stole *my* husband. But I forgive you. Josie wondered if Florence knew Marlene well enough to realize how untrue that was, and tried to break out of her stone prison to tell her about the Joan of Arc thing, but she couldn't. So she settled for thinking it at her, although from the look of terrified guilt on Florence's face, she was quite certain it hadn't worked.

The careful patting of a lace handkerchief to Marlene's eyes said, *You've hurt me, but I'm a better woman than you. Let's still be friends.*

That way I can punish you more conveniently, Josie added.

I want Fred back, said the quick vicious snap of a bread stick, *and I'm going to get him,* said the crunch of her teeth on a piece of red pepper. The delicate arch of her baby finger when she raised the cup to her lips meant *I'm a civilized woman, we're both civilized women. We can work this out.*

But when Josie's eyes reached the point on their endless circuit where she could see Florence's face, she knew they'd never work it out, that Marlene had already won. The ongoing punishment was overkill.

Josie watched the bones on Florence's face shift and become more prominent, the color she'd so carefully applied fade and her skin dull with pain. She would give up Fred and send him home to Marlene. Josie saw this on Florence's face as clearly as she had spotted the heartbreak. And she knew the cost of it.

Florence would have to hurt Fred to get him to return to Marlene. She'd have to lie and tell him she'd made a mistake, she'd never loved him. And Fred would look at her, his eyes as huge and sad as a whipped puppy's, and she'd have to hurt him again. And because she loved him so much, because she couldn't bear to see the pain on his face, she'd hit him and scream, "Get out, get out. Can't you see I hate you?"

But Fred would shake his head.

And Florence would finally collapse sobbing at his feet and say the one thing Fred couldn't resist, "Please, Fred. You have to go. Please." And she'd kiss his feet and, without understanding, he'd walk away.

And the only place he could go was home to Marlene. She'd be happy and parade him around like a prize cow and

Florence would waste away until one day she'd simply vanish, leaving nothing but a house filled to the brim with heartache and a tiny silver bell lying on the floor.

"Fred's coming to stay with me," Josie said, the sound of stones cracking in her voice.

CHAPTER 7

Josie raced away from Lord Jim's and back down the coast so quickly she didn't even notice the sun coming out, just squinted at the highway and willed away any radar or red lights. As a condition of the compromise, she had promised Marlene she would take Fred away before Florence arrived home.

It wasn't going to be easy. The agreement worked out by Josie and Marlene over coffee—Florence had simply nodded with relief at Josie's first words and then left the two of them to work it out—had as many conditions, strictures and quid pro quos as a contract merging two major conglomerates.

The one that was going to hang her up today said she couldn't tell Fred what had happened over lunch, couldn't refer to Marlene at all, only that Florence and Josie had agreed it would be better all around if he stayed with Josie for a while. She had no idea how she would convince him to leave before Florence arrived home, but she had to do it.

She had seen the look in Florence's eyes when Marlene spoke so harshly to Josie, had watched Florence grow more and more subdued as the lunch progressed. Marlene may have touted Florence as *her* friend in her phone calls, but Josie was willing to bet that Florence had never thought of Marlene that way.

But Josie laid that thought aside along with her other discoveries. What mattered now was what she owed to Florence.

Because she had watched Florence overcome her fear, seen the courage she'd found to accept the drive back down the highway with Marlene at her side, to spend an hour with that dark glass hiding her and the woman who hated her with a passion so strong it turned the air around her ochre. Josie hoped Florence couldn't see the color, couldn't smell the scent of burning rubber that erupted whenever Marlene looked at her. Even without that knowledge, the drive home was going to be hell.

Marlene would sit in the passenger seat as if she were a queen, her ankles crossed, her hands folded into her lap. The yellow suit would reflect light up into her face, highlighting her triumphant smile.

Her eyes would glow and if Florence broke down and took her eyes from the road to look at her, Marlene would appear to be encased in flames. Josie knew the drive back down to Sechelt would never be forgotten by Florence.

In years to come, no matter what happened now, whether she won and she and Fred stayed together, or she lost, Florence would wake screaming in the night remembering the beautiful spring day she drove the devil home. And when she lay in her bed in the dark chill hours after the nightmare, she would wonder what would have changed if she'd been stupid or courageous enough to speak to Marlene during the drive.

Josie had risked warning Florence while they paid the bill

and Marlene tidied up—her euphemism since time immemorial for using the bathroom.

"Don't talk to her," she whispered. "Don't look at her. Just drive, okay?"

Florence nodded, but Josie wasn't sure she was paying attention.

"This is important. Look at me, Florence."

When Florence turned her head to look at her, Josie was sorry she'd said anything. Florence's eyes were too bright, as if they had swallowed a lifetime's worth of tears. Her lips, with their brave seashell-pink lipstick bitten away, trembled. Her hair sprung out around her head, its hairspray no competition for the pain within. Josie felt sick but she had to tell her, had to make it clear.

"Florence—" Her voice softer, less urgent. "Be careful, please. Just drive her home. I'll leave a note at your place to let you know I've got him."

Florence nodded again. Josie had to be satisfied with that.

Josie, unlike Florence, never remembered much about that drive down to Sechelt. Mostly it was filled with plans, none of which seemed reasonable or even possible, to get Fred out of Florence's cottage and into Josie's car. There had to be a way to do it without pain.

She knew he'd come with her if she said, "Florence doesn't love you. She wants you out." But she also knew that she wouldn't be able to bear the way his grin would disappear and his shoulders would slump when she said it.

Josie's job was to get Fred out of Florence's clutches—those were Marlene's words—so he could think straight enough to decide between them. He was to have no contact with either Florence or Marlene, not a single word. That's why he was banished to Gibsons, with Josie. It was far enough away that he wouldn't run into them on the street and besides, Marlene said, it was time for Josie to look after her father. And Josie was happy to do it. She owed him.

Josie didn't remember much from her earliest years except that Fred had always been there for her while they'd moved from house to house to house, always searching for the perfect neighborhood.

She did remember being a teenager. Silence. No friends allowed over so basically no friends. Rules, lots and lots and lots of rules. Be on time. Always. No excuses. Keep your room clean. Marlene was a great believer in the white glove test and she'd used it every day in Josie's room.

Josie's life—her out of control, totally out of luck life—was a mess and reexamining the past wasn't tidying things up at all. In fact, she wondered if her new view of the past was a way of trying to take control of a life that seemed to be falling apart. Blaming Marlene for everything wasn't fair, but Josie couldn't seem to stop herself. Her ability to see shades of gray had disappeared along with her luck. If Fred was right, Marlene had to be wrong.

Josie stopped the car. "Damn," she whispered. "I absolutely do not need this kind of introspection right now." She banged her hands against the steering wheel. "Stop it, stop it right now."

Josie pulled up next to Florence's cottage without a plan. She didn't know what to say to Fred, only that she had half an hour to get him out of there. No one answered her knock; she hadn't even considered the possibility that he wouldn't be in the cottage.

Josie's ever-incipient anxiety flared. What if she couldn't find him? She didn't know Sechelt, didn't know where he might go. But she had to find him. And fast.

She ripped off her shoes and ran down the beach, ignoring the pebbles and shells digging into her soles, the throbbing of her toe. The sand was cold and her feet were soon numb, the pain replaced with nothingness. So she ran faster. It felt good running on the sand, the sun shooting sparks of light off the water, the seagulls rising up off the beach as she approached them, circling until she passed, then falling noisily back to the ground.

She almost lost track of why she was there. Maybe, Josie thought, she would just keep running. Maybe she'd leave them to work it out on their own and she'd just keep running. Up the beach until it ended. Then back. And up the beach again.

If she did that long enough, ran hard enough, she might transform herself. Into a water sprite or a selkie. And then her only worry would be to stay out of the sight of man, to stay a myth, and safe. Josie ran and tried to imagine herself into another being.

She thought about water, the feel of it against her skin. She thought about fish, the silvery shine of them rushing by, the way the water shifted around them.

She thought about light and the soft cool green of it filtered through ten feet of water. She thought about floating on the waves out of sight of earth, and feeling safe in the water's embrace.

She thought about seaweed dancing and floating and she thought about dancing with it. She thought about octopuses and eels and sea anemones.

She thought about the smell of the ocean, the wild sweet smell it had on summer nights, the faint salt of the winter air, the nostalgic scent of October.

She thought about not thinking, simply being, and for a moment she felt herself begin to shift.

The bones in her feet—she looked down at them racing through the sand—began to fuse. It didn't hurt, but she felt them expanding, growing to join one another. The same thing was happening to her hands.

Josie smiled and kept on running. It felt good and right and so she ran and thought about the ocean and imagined her hair turning green and growing thicker and stronger and gills sprouting behind her ears. She kept changing, little by little, until she was, she thought, as much as five percent not-Josie.

And she kept running and thinking and trying to change even more of herself. She wanted to be all not-Josie. All something else… all water sprite, all not thought. She ran and ran and ran until she ran right into Fred, crashed into him, sending them both sprawling on the beach.

"Josie? What…?" Fred squirmed out from under her and stood up. "The sand is wet. And it's cold. Are you okay?"

Josie thought more people had had reason to ask her that in the past three days than in her whole life up to now. She didn't know the answer this time any more than she had yesterday or the day before.

"I'm not sure. Do I look okay?" She was thinking of green hair and gills when she asked, scared to look for herself. And she wasn't sure what she wanted to see, what would be more frightening—to have changed or not. Fred hauled her to her feet and brushed the wet sand from her legs and shoulders just as he had when she was a child.

"You look cold, that's all. You must be freezing, your lips are blue. What are you doing, girl?" He pulled off his windbreaker and wrapped it around her. "Come on. Florence should be home by now. You need a hot shower and a cup of tea."

"Oh God. Florence."

"Josie?"

The collapse of Fred's face sprung Josie from her waterlogged state and she spoke quickly to forestall any further panic.

"She's okay, really. I just saw her."

"At home? Let's go then—" And he tugged at her hand. "She'll be wondering where I am."

And Josie suddenly realized the depth of her betrayal, though she still thought she had done it in a good cause. She let Fred tow her back along the beach toward the cottage. Her legs ached and her body cooled rapidly as the wind dried the sweat on her face and arms.

Her toe throbbed with every step, sending its insistent pounding of pain-pain-pain up her leg and into her groin.

"Fred," she finally said as they headed up the path to the cottage, "I need you. I've found a job in Gibsons and I need you to stay with me for a few days. Florence thinks it's a good idea." Josie crossed her fingers and prayed Fred wouldn't ask where she'd seen Florence or why she needed him if she had a job. She didn't have a backup story.

Fred's face, as always, reflected his thoughts. Joy—Josie had never *needed* him before, and hesitation—Florence needed him, too, wanted him in a way he found completely satisfying. But Josie, in her rush to come up with a story, any story, had fallen upon the only thing that might sway Fred. His love for his daughter and his guilt over abandoning her care to Marlene.

"Sure. I can do that. I'll just let Florence know and pack a bag. I can stay for a couple of days, no problem."

"I have to leave right away. I…uh…uh, need to do some research this afternoon before I start work tomorrow. Florence won't be back in time but she said it was okay. Phone her tonight when you get settled. She's going to do a little shopping this afternoon."

As they drove away with Fred's packed bag in the trunk Josie saw Florence pull up and Marlene step out of the car.

"I'm going to work at the *Sunshine Coast News*," she said to distract Fred and stop him from ruining all her work so far.

"I met the owner this morning, well, I sort of met him yesterday, but I had an interview today."

And it was the oddest interview she'd ever had, as if Gray MacInnis knew or didn't care if she'd work for him and simply walked through the formalities. If you could call his odd questions formalities.

* * *

The interview had started out well enough.

"What sort of experience do you have?" he'd asked, sounding as if the answer didn't matter.

"I've worked as an office manager for the past ten years."

"In Toronto?"

"Did I tell you I was from Toronto?" She looked down at the résumé still in her hand.

"No. Mercedes told Rose who told Doris. She told me."

Josie didn't even try to work out the chain of gossip.

"Yes. In Toronto."

"Why'd you come to the Sunshine Coast?"

Josie grimaced but answered as truthfully as possible. "My parents are here."

"Oh, you're close to them?"

"Hmmm. I'm an only child."

"Me, too. But my parents are both dead."

Josie pegged this as the exact moment that the interview went off track.

"I'm sorry."

"My mother died when I was a baby. I don't remember her. But my dad…"

Josie shifted in her chair, echoing the discomfort she felt from across the desk. His face closed in on itself, just for a moment.

"Your dad?" she asked.

"He just died a couple of years ago. I really miss him. I mean, he wasn't perfect, but he did his best. I didn't see much of him lately, but I always knew he was there, you know?"

Josie reached to touch his hand, just a light friendly potential employee to employer touch. His hand was warm and slightly calloused under hers. She snatched it back. Big mistake, she thought, even while the warmth lingered on her palm.

"That's kind of why I came out here, too." She couldn't lie to the man across the desk from her. For a moment he had looked like she felt—tired and sad and lonely and confused.

Josie sat up straight and put on her most professional face on. "Look, Mr. MacInnis. I won't lie to you. I've never worked on a newspaper before and I'll be going home as soon as I've worked out a few things with my parents. You should hire somebody else."

"No," he said, shaking his head. "You'll do just fine. You can start tomorrow."

She'd been working long enough, been on enough bad interviews to know what that meant. He was desperate. Either the job was terrible, or he was.

But Josie had a reason for taking the job that she tried not to admit, even to herself. She loved the way Gray MacInnis looked at her. It wasn't lust or even love, she thought, but it included a trace of both. Josie laughed at the idea of love at first sight. But possibility? Now that was a whole other thing.

Gray looked at her as if he wanted to know her. He looked at her as if his interest was without boundaries, wanted the good and the bad, the weird and the wonderful, the past, the present, the future.

When she'd hurried Fred out of the cottage and into the car, she found herself recounting the story of her interview.

She said nothing about the odd impression she'd had of Gray MacInnis but Fred picked up on it right away.

"Are you sure he's okay? He's not some kind of weirdo, is he?"

Josie laughed. "No, Fred, he's not." She thought for a moment before going on. "He likes me, and I like him. There's a connection between us. I don't know what it is but it feels good.

"But maybe I'm scared. My luck has been rotten—" she surprised herself by telling this to Fred "—over the past couple of years, and I guess I don't trust anything that looks like it might be good. Everything's been so bad, I suspect the dark lining inside of the silver cloud."

Fred grinned and touched her shoulder. "Is he a hunk?"

"I can't believe you asked me that."

Josie contemplated.

"He's not handsome. Definitely not handsome. But there's something…"

She blushed. She couldn't tell her father what she'd been thinking. This conversation was already way too embarrassing.

Fred ignored her red face, pretending to miss the implications of it. "Let's see if he can have dinner with us."

Josie shrugged. "Why not?" It couldn't be worse than spending the evening alone with Fred, trying to keep the deal they'd made a secret. It couldn't be worse than that. Could it?

CHAPTER 8

Gray spent the rest of the day after Josie's abrupt departure accomplishing nothing. He glanced over Mrs. Suzuki's story on the ex-mayor's funeral, cut one paragraph for show, and hung around the office driving Mrs. Suzuki wild with his fidgeting.

He told her, "I've hired someone. Her name is Josie Harris and she's starting tomorrow morning."

Mrs. Suzuki had asked to see her résumé which, of course, he'd forgotten to keep.

Gray MacInnis had forgotten a great deal since his first sight of Josie. He was pretty sure he'd forgotten to eat except for breakfast, he hadn't even thought about the résumé until Mrs. Suzuki slyly reminded him about it, and he'd almost forgotten the way home last night.

But he remembered her face without even thinking about it, her eyes, filled with tears, her mouth, her hair. He remembered precisely how she looked and was tempted to draw her face except he knew he'd never get it right. The tears would make it impossible; she'd look like some black velvet Venus.

Josie Harris was locked in his brain. He could conjure her image, her scent, even her aura, without thought. He didn't even have to close his eyes.

Gray knew he was in serious trouble. Unparalleled trouble. And he didn't care a single iota. He felt better than he had in years and that was going some, because he was pretty sure he'd been enjoying his life on the Sunshine Coast, completely unconscious of anything missing.

He had thought he might fill the void with the paper, with news and stories about his neighbors, but even in the winter it wasn't enough. Once he'd lost his wife and his father, he'd stepped back from life. Meeting Josie Harris had forced him to see that he needed more and maybe, just maybe, Josie Harris would provide it.

He wrote to her because he couldn't draw her. Or talk to her.

"I wish I could," he typed, "wish I could capture the look in your eyes when you realized you couldn't stop crying. Wonder and despair—a volatile, impossible to capture mixture. Or when Rose took the sunglasses from your face."

Gray wished he'd been the one to do that, the first one to see her eyes without tears.

"I wish I could have drawn you when you started crying for real. The thing is, I can draw, really I can. I can draw anything but your face. I wish I could."

Gray spent much of the year doing thumbnail sketches of people and places up and down the coast, tiny portraits in black and white with a wash of watercolor that he framed and sold at the craft market. The craft ladies raised his prices every year and still tourists and residents alike wanted more. But Gray liked his routine.

He drew on Saturdays, rain or shine, every Saturday, all year. Two or three drawings completed, then framed on Sundays and put in the box for the craft ladies who collected them once a month.

The craft ladies loved Gray. Before he'd trained them, they were at his house every week, oohing and ahing at his new drawings. Even worse, they would pile in their new Jeep 4x4—they bought a new one every second year and emblazoned it with the craft market logo and a plethora of shells and plaster seagulls—and follow him around. When he stopped, thinking about drawing, they stopped too and jumped out of the Jeep to stand around and silently watch as he pulled out his pen and paper.

After six months of this—Gray was new to the peninsula and didn't want to offend anybody—he finally took a stand.

"If you want to sell my work, you have to leave me alone."

It didn't work the first time, or even the second, but it did work once he stopped drawing at all.

"I can't work like this. You have to go away." And he stalked back to the car without putting a single line on the page. He wasn't sure who was more hurt—him or the craft ladies—but it worked.

They stopped following him around and even ostentatiously turned their backs and left when they accidentally happened upon him on a Saturday, even if he wasn't working. They picked up the drawings the first Monday of each month while he was at work, using the key under the geranium pot on the front porch.

It had taken Gray a while to get accustomed to this habit but now he didn't worry about locking his door. If he did lock it, he forgot his keys and climbed in through the window. If he didn't, the only things of value—the boxes of letters containing his soul—were something no one would want to steal.

That's not to say there weren't thieves on the Sunshine Coast. Of course there were. But they mostly preyed on the summer crowd—the people who doubled the population in June, July and August and deserted when it turned cool. They were the ones with the new CD and DVD players, the ones with the collections of good wine and liquor.

Those kinds of burglaries, the kind that didn't hurt anyone Gray knew and liked, were perfect stories for the paper. Because everyone, including the RCMP, believed the thieves as well as the victims were from the mainland. Great story, especially in the *Sunshine Coast News*; no one who counted got hurt.

But Gray sympathized with the police, especially because the sergeant was one of his best friends.

The sergeant shrugged when he talked to Gray about it.

"I'm not blaming the summer folk, but if they'd talk to us, we'd tell them to use Ace. His system is as good as anybody else's and he calls us right away. That's how we caught that gang of kids at the dock last month."

Gray nodded. Everyone on the coast knew the sergeant's frustration with the robberies. How could they not? Since the burglaries began in the fall, his once-perfect crew cut had sprouted wings, hundreds of them, soaring up off his sunburnt head. He spent all his time pulling his hair out.

And his perfect uniform looked mussed, not anything obvious, just slightly askew. A button undone, a smudge on his shining boots, a wrinkle in his trousers. Everyone tried to

make him feel better but nothing worked. Not an extra helping of hash browns, or a smile from the most beautiful woman
in town, Mercedes's daughter, Julie, the one he'd been mooning over ever since his posting here two years ago.

Everyone in town except the most beautiful woman—
who believed her love for the sergeant unrequited—knew
about that as well, though the sergeant thought he hid it re-
markably well.

The sergeant and Julie Jones were a staple of conversation
in Gibsons. Rose, Mercedes, Mrs. Suzuki. As soon as the
three of them knew something, it spread out through the peninsula like ripples in a pond.

But not ripples from a tiny pebble. This gossip was like ripples from a honking big rock, a giant stone weighing hundreds
of pounds, thrown into a tiny little pond. Microseconds from
the drop zone to the edges of the pond.

Gray had occasionally tried to calculate the speed of transmission but all he could say for sure was that it moved faster
than he did.

The gossip about the love life of Julie Jones should have
been as clear and as easy as the water in the gossip pond, given
that Rose was her godmother and Mercedes her mother—but
it wasn't.

If Gray had to guess, he'd guess that the gossip queens felt
a conflict of interest and were staying out of it. Gray thought
they were wrong.

He liked Julie and Ron. He liked them a lot and it hurt
him to see their unhappiness. It was as if their separation was
draining the life from them. Oh, Ron still worked as hard as

anyone Gray had ever met, still cared about the people he worked for, but something was missing.

The exuberant good cheer characteristic of the sergeant was no longer automatic. Gray watched him reach for it, dig for the smile and the cheery hello, where before it came without effort.

The same something was missing in Julie Jones.

The faint hint of sorrow, Gray thought, made her more beautiful than ever. Smudges of palest blue highlighted her eyes and a shimmering of tears often brightened them. She moved more carefully, turning her once rapid stride into the graceful slow glide of a dancer. To Gray, she looked as if her bones ached. Maybe the beauty and grace were what made the women miss the underlying pain.

Gray wanted to get them together. He spent hours in the Way-Inn, nursing a pint of beer on the table in front of him, thinking of ways to do it. And he'd come up with some doozie plans. But in the end, he refrained, bowing to the greater wisdom of Julie's mother and her friends.

He resisted the urge to shake Mercedes and say, "Think back to grade school. Write a note—Tommy loves Julie. Or vice versa." And the romance would be assured, problem solved.

But people respected true love in Gibsons. It was the one thing they wouldn't mess with. Oh, they'd try to fix Gray up, but now Josie was in his life—they would have recognized the sparks the minute Rose saw him with the weeping woman on that first day—they would leave him alone. They'd talk about him, about her, about the progress of their relationship, but they wouldn't interfere, not unless it was necessary.

The same went for the sergeant and Julie Jones. Mercedes might ask Rose if she should talk to Julie, especially after a weekend filled with daydreams and sighs, but Rose always counseled waiting.

"Julie's a smart girl. She takes after her mother—" a grin at Mercedes "—and she'll figure it out eventually. Besides, they're both young yet."

Mercedes would nod and remember Julie wasn't even thirty and leave it for another week. But she watched Julie, and the sergeant, and so did everyone else in town. There were no secrets in Gibsons. Maybe there were in Sechelt or Pender Harbour, but Gray doubted it.

When he'd first moved up here, he'd been astonished by how quickly he'd learned everything about everybody. It wasn't malicious, it was simply something to do in the off season. Gossip slowed down in the summer when everyone got busy. And Gray missed it then, missed knowing who was feuding, who won a little money at bingo or on the lottery, who was sick and who was courting. He missed knowing the little things about his neighbors. He was always happy when Labor Day arrived.

When he went to the Way-Inn after Labor Day, Rose might sit down and tell him about the fight between Mrs. IGA and Mrs. Safeway over a produce department manager one was trying to steal from the other or about who danced all night at the Legion on Friday—with a woman who wasn't his wife.

She'd tell him how the hospital drive was going, how many cats and dogs the shelter had picked up after the summer residents left—that was always good for a story—and who was spending the winter in Arizona. In the summer all he got was a quick hello and a cup of coffee. He was so used to the gossip he was like an addict in withdrawal in June.

Because there was nothing to fill the emptiness. He'd tried various things—newspapers, radio, even television talk shows—but what he wanted was personal. He didn't care about people from somewhere else. He cared about his friends and neighbors, the ones he saw every day. He thought Mrs. Suzuki—with her connections to Rose and Mercedes—might fill the gap.

The first summer he had realized what the missing thing was—it took him almost five years to figure out why he walked around all July feeling like he'd lost something—he would talk to Mrs. Suzuki. He'd bring it up casually.

"What's happening in town?" he'd ask.

"Oh, not much," she'd answer without taking her attention from her computer screen.

After a couple of weeks of that, he resorted to direct questions.

"What's up with Mrs. IGA and Mrs. Safeway?" Thinking that if she knew he had heard about the feud, Mrs. Suzuki would consider him worthy of a response.

"They're fine. The stores look great with the new paint jobs, don't they?" And she'd turn back to her work.

When Gray thought about Mrs. Suzuki's refusal to keep him plugged into the gossip, he realized it was exactly the same as the would-be lovers. Mrs. Suzuki was conflicted about telling him anything. Employer, employee, newspaper owner. Of course.

Gray tried other ways to get his fix. He stopped at the Way-Inn at odd hours but it didn't matter if it was 5:00 a.m. or midnight, the Way-Inn was always packed with tourists. Rose would smile at him and race away to serve another table of sunburned foreigners. He didn't know Mercedes as well as Rose and Mrs. Suzuki, but she was the third member of the gossip triumvirate so he stopped in at the Sand Dollar Motel.

"Hey, Gray. Can't talk now, got four rooms to clean by noon. Drop by in September, I'll make you a coffee."

Even the craft ladies, once his shadows, were too busy to give Gray the time of day. So each year he prepared himself for the desert of summer and looked forward to the arrival of Labor Day when he again felt part of the ebb and flow of the town.

Maybe it was more obvious because he was single, an anomaly in a town where there were only two bachelors over forty—Gray and the hermit of indeterminate age who lived in an illegal windowless shack on the beach and made his living as a beachcomber.

The hermit fascinated Gray but he hadn't talked to Gray, at least not much. And Gray, despite his years of experience and his abilities as a journalist, had never even found out the hermit's name. People knew it, Doris and Rose and Mercedes knew it, but important secrets got kept in Gibsons with as much enthusiasm as gossip got forwarded.

Gray saw him often—on the beach mostly. He wasn't certain he'd ever seen him anywhere except on the beach or in the Way-Inn. Which was weird, because Gibsons was a small enough town that Gray saw everybody (unless they were out of town)—and that included the shut-ins—almost every week. It was as if the hermit existed in those two places, the beach and the Way-Inn.

He was polite, always nodded hello when he passed Gray on the beach. He even stopped occasionally to check out Gray's drawings or paintings, smiling, Gray assumed, to indicate his approval.

He smiled a lot, the hermit. Gray respected that cheerful smile, worn in the face of what must have been a hellish life. No money, no family, only a rough shack on a beautiful beach which was deserted seven months of the year. Gray couldn't understand that kind of isolation. And he wondered if once in a while even the hermit rebelled against it.

There had been one day when the hermit had talked to him. It was a winter day with the water dark and as still as ice, with the sky melting into the ocean. It was almost impossible to distinguish one from the other except for the faintest smudge of almost-pink at the horizon.

Gray muttered to himself. "I can't get it. It's too pale, or it's too dark. It looks like a wash of gunmetal gray. Damn." He threw down his brush, stamping his feet against the cold. "I can't get this right."

"It's right, boy," a raspy voice said over his shoulder. "It's just not beautiful."

The hermit looked at the painting. "Sometimes," he said, "things are sad and sometimes you just have to live with it.

"This," his wave took in the beach and the water and the sky, "is sad. And so is your painting."

Gray, speechless, handed him the painting. "Be careful, it's still wet."

Gray didn't know what that conversation meant but he had taken some consolation, on his loneliest days, in imagining his painting on the hermit's wall. Not cheerful, he thought, but true.

There were a few other single men in Gibsons, but like the sergeant, they were young and wouldn't remain that way for long. But if Gray had a partner, he'd have someone to talk to at night besides his laptop. The summers made him realize just how alone he was. He didn't even have a pet.

He could get one from the shelter in September, though. Pretty much every pet on the peninsula had come up with summer residents in June and then been abandoned when they went back to the city.

After the Labor Day weekend, the shelter hired kids to patrol the beaches and logging roads looking for filthy, shivering, starving dogs and cats. They found dozens of them. The shelter spayed or neutered them, gave them their shots, washed and brushed them to get them ready for the grand and official opening of the real season in Gibsons.

The Shelter Ball and Auction was held annually on the last Saturday of September. The townspeople danced and drank and at ten o'clock they began to bid on the animals. The money they raised paid Julie Jones's salary for the entire year and all the abandoned pets were adopted.

Julie was so beautiful, committed and convincing that every single year a few people did something they swore they'd never do and bought a dog or a cat, paying way more than they were worth in the excitement of the auction and under the spell of Julie's beauty. Petless households quickly became a thing of the past. Even the sergeant bought a black-and-brown mutt after swearing for months he couldn't have a dog.

"I'm always on duty," he said. "How can I give a dog the attention it needs when I'm at the station or on the road twelve hours a day? Every day. Besides, I don't like pets. They're messy."

And looking at the sergeant's hair and uniform, his spic-and-span condo, his excruciatingly tidy office, Gray had to agree with him.

He wasn't sure who was the most surprised when the sergeant took the mutt home. But once he took her home from the ball, no one was really surprised when he began taking Aska to work with him and when she showed up in the backseat of his squad car.

The women nodded knowingly. The sergeant needed something to love until he and Julie Jones figured out what was going on.

And so Gray continued to fidget, Mrs. Suzuki to grin behind her computer screen and the rest of Gibsons to carry on with their real lives for another month. But the pace was picking up, everyone felt it, felt the increasing sense of urgency as the days grew longer and warmer. Summer was on its way.

CHAPTER 9

Fred felt a moment of panic when Josie pulled into the Sand Dollar Motel. Mercedes was sure to know about Florence and he didn't want to talk about it. He wanted the more than forty years he'd spent with Marlene to vanish. He hated remembering the man he'd been, but spending time with Josie was an insistent throbbing reminder in his head. He remembered all the times he'd deferred to Marlene, the years, decades, he'd pretended to be best friends because that's the image she wanted them to portray.

"Not lovers," she said. "Love fades, but best friends are forever. That's what I want."

And Fred went along with her. And now with Josie he couldn't help but remember every time he had said to someone new, "We're best friends, have been since the first day we met."

He even remembered, in excruciating and perfect detail, the few times they'd had sex, the most memorable being the night Josie was conceived. He remembered it because of Marlene's expression of complete and utter distaste when he'd been foolish enough to open his eyes and look down at her.

He quickly learned to recognize that expression. She used it when anything or anyone seriously displeased her—a fish improperly cleaned, a rotten egg, a workman late for an appointment, Josie appearing at dinner with a grubby face. Or Fred, early on before he completely gave in, questioning one of her pronouncements about Josie or their life together. It was, he now thought, the expression her face settled into most naturally.

Her eyes closed, almost to slits, her eyebrows raised, her mouth pursed, her nose wrinkled. She was still beautiful, always beautiful, but she looked mean and cranky because that's what she was. And he couldn't help comparing her with Florence, with the way she taught him to love, to caress, to kiss and suck and lick and touch, to do things he'd only ever imagined before.

But Fred, not wanting, never wanting to rock the boat went along with Marlene's excuses over the years. The pregnancy, the baby, the busy life she led, and then, we're too old to do this anymore. Fred wondered if Marlene was totally uninterested in sex or just in him. Didn't matter, really, it came to the same thing in the end. And he was used to it, didn't miss it, or at least he didn't think he did. Not until he met Florence and realized what he was capable of. Without Viagra.

He stood beside Josie while she talked to Mercedes. Mercedes had taken one quick look at him, said, "Hey, Fred. How's it going?" and turned back to Josie. He was grateful for her discretion. Josie didn't need to know the sordid details he was sure were being bandied about—even here in Gibsons. He wasn't sure he wanted to hear them either, but a tiny spike of temptation contradicted his better judgment.

"Can I buy you lunch at the club tomorrow?"

Mercedes smiled. "That'd be great."

Josie looked from one face to another. Fred couldn't miss the perplexity in her eyes and he laughed.

"Mercedes and I play crib together almost every week. I walk the five miles down to the club and she drives up for the weekly tournament. Almost all my friends are there and you know Marlene. She never really liked the same people as me."

"Yeah, and I beat you nine times out of ten, old man."

"You're lucky not to get skunked." He turned to Josie. "We haven't seen each other since, well, in a while. I miss whooping your ass, Mercedes Jones. Noon okay?"

And he surrendered himself to the lengthy explanations and rehashings and Marlene-bashing Mercedes was sure to indulge in. She'd never liked Marlene, although Fred had been careful not to say anything bad about her. He guessed he hadn't needed to, almost anything he said about his life would say more than enough about Marlene.

Fred settled into the connecting room to Josie's. Once he'd put his boxers, socks and T-shirts in the top drawer of the dresser, he stood at the window and looked out at the water. It looked the same, exactly the same, as it did from Marlene's condo. It looked the same as it did from Florence's cottage. He pondered that, but it meant little except to make him feel at home and homesick at the same time. Not for the condo; he'd never felt at home there.

Marlene used the spare bedroom for an office and she'd turned the entire place into a… What? Fred thought it looked like a stage set from one of those Fred Astaire–Ginger Rogers movies, her apartment, all pink and fluffy and dainty. He was scared to move. And Marlene, for the first time in their life together, had dropped the pretense of being the perfect wife. She smiled when he left for the library or the club, glad to get his masculine presence out of *her* space.

No, he was homesick for the cottage. And Florence. The cottage was tiny; Florence couldn't afford anything else after her husband died. But it was filled with books and paintings and crafts and magazines and photographs and flowers and plants all jumbled up together and presided over by two imperious cats. It was friendly.

Fred had forgotten if he ever knew that a house could feel that way. He belonged there. He didn't have to worry about banging into things or where he sat or where he put his paper.

Mercedes's presence had the same effect as did Joseph's. Whenever he showed up at Joseph's rickety shack on the beach, Fred felt welcome. They played chess. Fred always lost. They listened to Joseph's store of old 45s, picked up in thrift stores and garage sales, and played with the aid of his tiny portable generator. Fred had enjoyed dozens of sunsets, each one unique, from Joseph's windows.

It was odd, Fred thought, that he'd been on the Sunshine Coast for only two years, yet he'd found three people—three amazing people—to share his life with. And in the other fifty-eight years of it, he'd found only one. His daughter, Josie.

Now Fred wasn't stupid. He didn't know the details, but he did know that somehow Marlene had convinced Florence and Josie that Fred needed to be separated from Florence. Convincing Florence wouldn't have been hard, his sweetheart carried a huge hunk of guilt around on her shoulders. And Josie's compliance might be laid directly at Fred's door.

He could imagine the conversation, if not the scene. Florence would retreat into the shell her jerk of a husband had built for her. Josie would try, but she'd spent all her life believing Marlene.

No, Marlene, as always, would have all the words. First. Middle. Last.

"Fred's lost his mind."

Maybe a bit too harsh, Fred thought. Florence might not react to those words but Josie definitely would. How about...

"Fred needs some time to think about his future. I know him better than anyone."

She was wrong about that. Four people, count 'em, four people knew him better than her. Too bad for him that two of them were silenced.

"Let's give him a few days away." She wouldn't say it, but "from evil influences" would be implicit in the sentence.

And Florence, unable to do anything else, would nod and Josie, his smart foolish daughter would agree, thinking that all it would take would be time. Just a little time for her to figure out a way, for the first time in her life, to get the better of Marlene.

It made Fred uncomfortable knowing that Josie, the light of the years he spent with Marlene, was in the room next door. The feeling went deeper than discomfort, almost as far as dread.

He waited for her to unlock the door between them. He

didn't know what he would say, how he would explain what had happened to him.

He needed her to understand about all the years he'd allowed Marlene to rule both their lives. He needed to make Josie understand why he'd allowed Marlene to be in charge, why he hadn't stood up to her. The trouble was he didn't know why he'd done it.

He'd talked to Florence about it a little. That's what began their friendship. Her husband had been a bully, too, telling her what to do, when to do it and who to do it with.

"I couldn't even do the dishes right," she told him. "One day he threw a tuna salad sandwich at me because I put too much mayonnaise on it."

When he died, Florence said, she started doing the things she'd always wanted to. Walking on the beach, playing bingo on Friday nights, hanging out at the local coffee shop. She started volunteering at the library and that's where Fred met her.

He'd seen her before, but her husband didn't like her talking to anyone else so he'd never really spoken to her until those days at the library. And at the beginning they mostly spoke of their spouses. Fred, as always, was careful to lay the blame on himself.

"Marlene's a wonderful woman, so strong and confident. I'm not good enough for her. I can't keep up." And the thing was, even now he believed that he *wasn't* strong enough for her.

Marlene knew with absolute certainty how life should be lived. Fred wasn't sure about it at all. So he went along. He knew now that even bad choices were better than no choices at all—he just hoped it wasn't too late to show that to Josie.

Florence had nodded and smiled and sympathized. It took Fred months to figure out why she was so understanding. He'd heard what she said about her husband, but hadn't equated him to Marlene.

He was so wrapped up in himself, in the courage it took even to talk to her about his life, that it was six months before he figured out he was talking about her life, too. Florence was so open, so easy, so caring, all the things Marlene had squelched out of him. He'd fallen in love with Florence the day he figured it out.

Because she understood why he'd lived a life he hated with a woman who frightened him. She understood why he pretended everything was fine, why he did whatever Marlene wanted, including moving three thousand miles away from his daughter.

But it took Fred another twelve months before he told Florence how he felt. He'd never have left Marlene if it wasn't for Florence's support. He wished he had it now. She'd know how to deal with Josie. Fred didn't.

Josie stood with her hand on the door to Fred's room. The lock was on her side, but that made it her decision and she wasn't ready. She'd been an idiot to agree to Marlene's scheming. Josie knew she'd have to tell Fred the whole story, she just wasn't keen on seeing his face while she did it.

Maybe she could phone him. They'd always had their best conversations that way. Josie in the big old comfortable chair in her living room, Fred on the phone in the bedroom. They'd talk for hours, late into the night, as long as Josie was paying for the call. If Fred phoned, Marlene would interrupt after five minutes, "Money doesn't grow on trees, you know." She didn't care about Josie's money.

Josie knew Fred would be disappointed in her. He should be. She was almost forty years old, and her mother still told her what to do. And once she'd told him, she'd have to convince him to stay, and she knew that wouldn't be easy. There was something different about Fred. It wasn't something Josie could define, at least not clearly.

It was as if someone had removed a veil, kind of like the ceiling of the Sistine Chapel. She'd seen a documentary about the restoration of the paintings and marveled at the clarity and color revealed. It was the same painting, only younger and fresher, healthier. Just like Fred.

He was the man she'd always known, only more so. More clear, maybe. Josie realized she'd known this even from the short conversation they'd had the day she arrived, otherwise she'd never have consented to take him away. Because no matter how crucial the situation, he wouldn't have been able to make the decision to leave Marlene. Not without Florence.

Josie thought about the change, thought carefully about it with her hand still on the doorknob. She'd agreed with Marlene's condition—don't tell Fred why he's with you—because she thought Fred wouldn't be able to cope with the truth of it. Now she wasn't so sure. And because of that uncertainty, she knew she had to tell him what had really happened over lunch.

And to do that she needed to be a different woman. One who could walk away from a hairdresser she didn't trust; who could snub a rude salesperson; who might even demand her money back if she got ripped off.

Josie walked away from the door and picked up the shell Fred had found for her at the beach the year she'd turned seven. It had broken on the trip across the country, and was faded to a pearly grey, but she still loved the feel of it in her hands. Because Fred had found it for her, because every time she looked at it she thought of him, because of what she'd learned from it.

"Listen," he'd said when they found it, holding it to her ear, "you will always be able to hear the ocean, no matter how far away from it you are."

Just like your love, she thought. No matter how far away Fred was, she could feel it. It was always there.

She put the pieces of the shell back on the windowsill and looked at the damn door another minute. Finally, her heart pounding, she knocked.

"Josie," Fred's voice rumbled, responding through the hollow door between them. "Don't you have something you need to do this afternoon? 'Cause the library closes early in the winter and you only have an hour or so. We should get going."

Josie was tempted to leave Fred at the Sand Dollar Motel, and go away. To the library, to the beach, or even back onto the ferry and home. She could pretend this had never happened. There were lots of jobs in Toronto, or she could sell her house and work part-time at Starbucks or Chapters. She had lots of options; she didn't have to do this.

She leaned her forehead against the door and took a deep

breath. Fred was going to be royally pissed-off. She'd never seen him angry so she didn't know what to expect but she knew it would be big. Because she'd learned one important thing from Fred...*keep your nose out of other people's beeswax.*

So she didn't blame him for being mad, he was entitled in more ways than one. She'd forgotten the one thing he'd thought crucial enough to sneak behind Marlene's back to teach her, and that wasn't to mention that she might be ruining his life. Of course he would be angry.

Josie unlocked the door. "Come on in," she said. "We need to talk."

She told Fred the story, the whole story, with the exception of the tears and the water sprite thing. She didn't tell him about the crows, or losing her luck and her job, either. They didn't have anything to do with it.

Fred didn't say a word, not even when she finished the story. He didn't look at her. Josie sat in the ugly uncomfortable chair and looked at her luck on the windowsill. In the bright coastal sunlight, it didn't appear to be worth much. The Virgin had dust marks on her cheeks as if she'd been crying. The leprechaun's paint was faded and cracked. The elephant had turned his back on the room and his companion, Ganesh, had obviously retreated to some other world. The rosary had fallen behind the radiator and the shell lay broken in the sunlight.

Fred picked up the two pieces of the shell and the agate.

"I can't believe you still have these. I remember when you found the agate. It was the same summer I found you the shell. You were so excited and I couldn't bear to tell you it was only a piece of an old beer bottle. You thought it was a jewel from a pirate ship. And maybe you were right. You've kept them all these years. They must be very precious."

He handed the soft-edged piece of brown glass to Josie and she curled her fingers around it.

"We'll work this out. I need to phone Florence now. I'll be back and ready for dinner in an hour."

Josie hadn't expected that response and all she could do was nod as he went back through the connecting door. She heard it click behind him. What would he say to Florence? What would he decide to do? What would she have to do now?

She bent over and pulled the rosary from behind the radiator, the beads warm in her hand. They gave her no more comfort than they had when she'd first bought them, but the ritual of running them through her fingers, the warm softness of the beads and the cool rough chain in between was a kind of mantra, calming her, taking her mind off Fred.

The light was beginning to fade outside the window, the shadows lengthening, growing deeper and more distinct. They might be pathways—clear and sharp-edged. And Josie longed to be on those pathways, to be anywhere away from her increasingly messy life. But she couldn't go. Josie had never been a quitter.

She'd stayed and finished her degree despite bouts of homesickness so severe she appeared to be the victim of a greedy vampire. She'd done well, too, sticking it out, going to classes, handing in her papers on time, studying diligently for exams. She'd stayed with John Johnson for months past the day she felt she couldn't stand it anymore.

She kept paying her bills, getting up and into the shower, going to work every day. And Josie thought that might have been the hardest thing she'd ever done. Because what was the point of it?

She had known fairly soon after the haircut that the rest of her life was going to be hell. This room, Fred next door, her bout of uncontrollable crying, were all evidence of her ruined life. But she carried on; she would carry on. She wouldn't quit.

Josie had given herself this same pep talk most days since her luck disappeared. It didn't change anything, just got her through the next task. And once in a while, once in a very long while, she felt a ray of hope pierce the despair that overwhelmed her most days.

It never came to anything, never translated into something concrete, something she could pin down and say, "Aha, there it is, that's the thing," like a ten-dollar win on the lottery or a parking space, but it felt good, maybe good enough to keep her going. Those rays of hope reminded her of what her life used to be like.

They weren't *like* her old life, Josie was confident of that, but they were something. She thought of them as tiny clues in a mystery novel—a piece of carpet fiber, a smudge of dirt—unidentifiable but ultimately capable of distinguishing one villain from another. The brief flashes of hope weren't her old life but they reminded her of it.

Fred banged on the door between their rooms.

"Come on, Josie. I'm starving. I want Swiss steak and hash browns and a beer. Let's go."

Josie wrinkled her nose at the thought of that particular combination of flavors but picked up her purse and car keys.

"Okay," she yelled. "Meet you at the car."

"We'll walk," Fred said when she got there. "It's a perfect evening."

The hill down to the Way-Inn might have been in a different world than it had been the first time Josie drove it in the fog. The setting sun lit up the windows along the route like beacons glowing gold in the fading light. The grass was green and the trees wore the faint blush of new leaves. Crocuses and tulips caught color from the sky. People stood on their front porches enjoying the sunset and called hello as Fred and Josie passed.

"Hey, Fred, good-looking daughter you've got there. My son's coming up for the weekend, maybe they should get together."

"Don't eat all the hash browns, Fred Harris. I'll be down later."

"Haven't seen you at the club for a few weeks. Don't forget you owe me a rematch."

Fred grinned and waved as if there were nothing more important in his life than this walk with his daughter on a spring evening. And perhaps, Josie thought, that was true.

He had somehow transcended, at least for the moment, the mess his life was in. Fred's world was crumbling around him—his ex-wife wanted to ruin him, his daughter had tricked him away from his new love, he was stranded without transportation and, Josie suspected, without much money—yet here he was looking like he was having the time of his life.

"That's the secret, you know," he said, reading her mind. "What good does it do to worry about the future? Just makes you feel miserable and doesn't solve anything. All this," his wave included the whole world, "is still here. Might as well enjoy it."

He grabbed her hand and swung it as if she were six years old again.

"Come on, Josie, give yourself a break. It's not the end of the world."

He gave a little hop and twirled her around on the sidewalk.

"You'll love the Swiss steak. And you need a beer. I can tell."

Four beers later, Josie agreed with him. She did feel better, much better. The Way-Inn was hopping. Old Johnny Cash and Elvis tunes poured from the jukebox and although people sat in booths, it was as if they were all members of one big party. They yelled back and forth over the music, occasionally bounced up to demonstrate a dance step or the size of the salmon they caught last week.

Everyone passing in or out stopped to kiss Fred's cheek, to say, "How are you?" Nodding sympathetically. And they all commented on Josie, calling her beautiful, wishing her luck in her new job—everyone knew all about it—telling her about apartments and cottages for rent.

The beer was cold and Josie sat in the booth and smiled at the strangers. There was nothing to do tonight except enjoy herself.

CHAPTER 10

Gray spotted Josie the minute he walked into the Way-Inn. She was sitting alone in a booth near the back, smiling to herself, swaying a little to the old Floyd Cramer tune playing on the jukebox. None of the regulars had picked that music. Josie? Or her father?

He recognized Fred right away from his resemblance to Josie. Older, taller, thinner, but with the same freckles and sparkling green eyes. He even had her smile, transformed in Fred to a full-out grin.

Gray stopped at the jukebox and plugged in a dollar. He punched A11, C9 and D4. All love songs. Elvis, Louis Armstrong and Patsy Cline. All dead, too. He wondered if that meant something. Nah, of course not.

He waggled his fingers at Rose and mouthed, "a beer," pointing at his chest, "and whatever she's drinking," waving over at Josie. It'd be all over Gibsons by morning. Love songs. Gray buying Josie a drink.

By the time he reached her, he was laughing so hard there were tears rolling down his face. He tried to spit out, "Oh my God, it's my turn," but it was clear she hadn't understood a word he'd said.

"Gray? What's so funny?" Josie's nose wrinkled. When he wouldn't stop laughing, she poked her fingers at his shoulder. Hard. He might have a bruise tomorrow. Which only made him laugh harder.

"Gray MacInnis, tell me right this minute. Why the hell are you laughing like a hyena? Tell me or go sit somewhere else."

He managed to choke out a few words between the bouts of uncontrollable laughter.

"Give. Me. A minute. Please."

He held out his hand and, reading his mind, she placed the beer in it, holding his hand within her two smaller ones so he could lift the glass to his mouth.

He took a drink, and then another.

"Thanks, Josie." He grinned at her.

"Don't thank me until you tell me the joke. And if I don't think it's funny enough to warrant your hysteria, you're outta here."

Because he wasn't sure she'd find it funny—and why would she?—he stalled. He drank half of his beer and turned around to catch Rose's eye. He gestured for another round.

"Now," Josie demanded. "Tell me now."

Gray gave in.

"You." He pointed at her. "Me." He touched his chin. "The town's favorite let's-find-him-a-date bachelor. A single dollar in the jukebox to play three of the world's best love songs."

He smiled and raised his glass to her.

"And all done in the presence of two," he pointed at Rose

behind the bar and Mercedes playing pool with Fred, "of Gibsons three gossip queens. It'll be all over town by morning."

Josie's eyebrows rose until they almost disappeared into her hairline.

"You're telling me…" She stopped dead.

"Yep. We're an item. In fact, by lunchtime tomorrow they'll probably have us engaged and be ready to start planning the wedding. I hope you're partial to fall weddings. No one will have time to plan anything until after Labor Day. Unless you'd rather elope?"

She shrugged, but humor lit up her face.

"Not me," she said. "Big wedding all the way. Hundreds of guests, three course meal, expensive champagne, live band. The whole shebang. Of course, there's one small problem you might want to consider. I'm flat broke so you'll have to cough up the dough."

She leaned back and smiled like a cat with a mouse, assuming she'd beaten that mouse to death.

"I've got a few dollars stashed away. Whatever you want, you get." And he knew he wasn't kidding when he said it.

He chuckled to himself, careful not to let Josie see his glee at the win. He watched her shift uncomfortably on her seat. Maybe he'd scared her. He backed down.

"Hey, listen. We'll just tough it out. They'll talk about us but we'll ignore them. Okay?"

Josie nodded at Gray's comments and glanced over at Fred enjoying himself with his friends. His face glowed and he laughed and grinned and joked. Even after she'd told him the whole story. Even without Florence. She'd never seen him so happy. She wasn't getting out of the Way-Inn anytime soon. She'd let him have his fun.

Gray sat quietly across the table, his eyes steady on her face. She should be uncomfortable, she thought, after all the talk of marriage, but she wasn't, not really. The conversation had felt frivolous but she'd sensed an underlying seriousness on both their parts.

"So tell me about these people," she said. "If I'm going to be here for a few weeks I might as well get to know them. Start with," she looked around the room, examining everyone, "her."

Josie gestured with her chin at the most beautiful woman she'd ever seen. "Tell me about her."

Gray's smile pulled down at one side and Josie knew without even thinking about it what that meant. He knew exactly what she was doing—distracting herself—and he was going to let her get away with it.

"I'll do better than that," he said, and stood up. "I'll go get her." And he did.

He arrived back at the table towing the tall blonde. Close up, she was perfect. Even in her ragged jeans and grubby T-shirt. Even smelling of wet dog. Flawless skin, big blue eyes and a smile that Josie imagined could change the world. But Josie also saw a deep-down sadness in her eyes and, despite the beauty, despite the fact that she must have everything she'd ever wanted, she was obviously missing something.

Gray said, "Julie Jones, this is Josie Harris. She's just moved here from Toronto and she's starting work at the paper tomorrow."

"I know. And she's staying at the Sand Dollar and her mom and dad are involved in a messy breakup," she glanced apologetically at Josie. "And she's not crying anymore."

"Not fair." Josie laughed, starting to feel the beer she'd been drinking. "You know all about me and I don't know anything about you."

"Not much to tell, really," Julie said, settling into the booth. Gray faded away.

"I'll give you the short version. My mom runs the Sand Dollar, I've lived here all my life, I run the animal shelter. My life is an open book."

Josie was pretty sure the last wasn't true. She'd caught a tiny shift of Julie's eyes when she said it. She tucked the thought away in the back of her mind and hoped she'd get to know Julie well enough to find out what she was concealing.

"It must be weird to live in the same place all your life. Do you like it?" She asked the most innocuous question she could think of.

"I love it. Even if everybody knows every single move I make almost before I make it."

"I grew up in a big city," Josie replied. "This scrutiny feels uncomfortable, but you know what I do like?" She waited for Julie's questioning shake. "I like being a regular. I enjoy Rose—" she smiled up at Rose as she dropped two beers at the table "—knowing how I like my breakfast and bringing me another beer without asking. I feel at home here."

Julie grinned. "Yeah, if they like you—and they'll love you, you've already given them a whole bunch of new things to talk about—you're a part of the community right away." She took a drink of her beer and settled back against the wall, swinging her legs up on the bench.

"So tell me," she said. "Tell me about the weeping."

Josie took a deep breath and said, "There's nothing to tell you. It started. It stopped. And I don't know why either thing happened."

Julie looked disgruntled. "I'm not going to tell anyone," she said. "I'm not planning on taking over my mother's position as a gossip queen. You can trust me."

"It's not that. I just don't have any answers. Rose told me the exact same thing happened to her mother. I want to ask her about it. Can we offer to buy her a beer?"

Julie looked around the room, obviously assessing the number of people in it. "Maybe. Everyone seems to be playing pool. I'll go get her."

Josie watched Julie cross the room like a parade on a street full of kids. Faces lit up when she passed. Old and young, men and women, didn't matter. Julie walked by and everyone smiled. She said a few words to Rose and Josie saw Rose nod.

Rose must know more about the whole weeping gig than she'd told Josie those two mornings at breakfast. But she didn't.

"Josie, I don't know any more than I told you. My mother told the story just like this. 'One morning I sat down at breakfast and I started to cry. And I couldn't stop. I cried all day and all night. But the next morning at exactly the same time as it started, it stopped.' That's all she ever told me. Sorry I can't help, but thanks for the beer."

"Did it ever happen again?"

"Nope. At least she didn't tell me if it did, and my mother loved to tell stories. I'm sure she would have told me if it did."

"That's a relief." Josie almost felt the weight lift off her shoulders. She wasn't going to have to spend the rest of her life worrying about whether or not she was going to start crying and not be able to stop.

"Josie. Julie. Come on, you two, the pool tournament is about to start and I need some partners."

Julie stood up. "I can't stay. My night-shift worker needs to leave at…" she looked at her watch. "Whoops, I gotta run. Two sick dogs. Bye, Josie, great to meet you. Let's get together. Soon, okay?" And she was gone.

"Josie, you're it." Gray grabbed Josie's hand and pulled her from the booth.

"You really don't want me on your team. All my luck is bad luck."

"Doesn't matter. No one cares who wins. It's just a game, Josie."

So she and Gray played against Fred and Mercedes and lost. And just like that they were out of the tournament. But it didn't matter a bit. They laughed and drank beer and kibitzed with the rest of the players.

Fred and Mercedes won the tournament, high-fiving each other and laughing until they were rolling on the floor.

"We won, we won, we won." Fred grabbed Josie around the waist and danced her around the floor. "We won. Damn, we're good." And Josie agreed.

When Gray pulled her aside to say good-night, Josie had leaned against him for a moment and felt his lips touch her hair.

CHAPTER 11

Gray wondered if Josie remembered her ride home in the squad car last night. He'd said good-night to Josie and then watched her and Fred being escorted to the car by the sergeant, Rose hovering anxiously in the background. He'd seen it coming in the way Rose had watched the two of them throughout the night.

The same thing had happened to him the night his father died. He'd consumed way too much beer and begun sobbing in his booth. Rose phoned the sergeant to take him home.

It was a privilege riding home with the sergeant instead of in a taxi. Rose only phoned him for people she believed in. Gray had watched over the years, learning Rose's pecking order. It had nothing to do with money or worth to the community—he'd seen her call the sergeant on more than one occasion. It seemed to be about the level of despair Rose felt in her customers.

And so Gray had begun paying attention. Rose had a form of desperation radar; she spotted it coming in the door, even if it was buried under layers of smiles and laughter. She let the despairing ones drink just so much, let them cry on her shoulder for just so long, and then she called the sergeant.

Gray hadn't remembered the ride, just waking up the

next morning in his own bed with a bitch of a hangover and without a car. Mrs. Suzuki, when he finally got into the office late in the afternoon, loudly informed him of his mode of transportation.

"You got a little carried away last night, huh? First time in the squad car?"

He'd spent the next couple of days cringing every time he passed the station, wondering if he'd be arrested for being drunk and disorderly, worried even more about what kind of fool he'd made of himself that night. But Mrs. Suzuki never mentioned it again, the sergeant didn't slap the handcuffs on him, and everyone else treated him as if nothing had happened.

He sensed a slightly heightened level of sympathy for the week or so following that night but he might have imagined it.

After he'd gotten over his embarrassment and returned to the Way-Inn, he began to watch. Sometimes it was months in between phone calls and sometimes twice in a week, but Gray learned to identify those people deemed worthy of the sergeant's help. It had never happened to Gray again. In fact, he seldom saw it happen to the same person more than once. The sole exception was the hermit.

Rose called the sergeant to take him home once a month, always at the full moon. The odd thing was that the hermit never spoke, not a single word, at least that Gray heard. He didn't cry either; he just sat in the back booth and sipped rye and water. The sole indication of his consumption was the way he began to slouch into the booth, his head falling lower, his shoulders rounding, his hands traveling a shorter and shorter distance to get the glass to his lips.

Just when his head looked as if it would hit the table, Rose picked up the phone. She'd serve the hermit one more drink and then slide into the booth across from him, holding his free hand until the sergeant arrived. Gray never heard her speak to the hermit, only to the sergeant.

"He'll be fine now," patting the hermit on the back and handing him over to the sergeant's care. "He'll be all right."

Gray was tempted, more than once, to head down to the shack on the beach and learn the hermit's story. Maybe even write about it because there was a story there, a big one. Gray was sure of it. He read it in Rose's solicitousness, in the sergeant's care, in the way the hermit never featured in the town gossip. He saw it in the way the mayor ignored the breach of town regulations. No one else had a shack on the beach. He knew it because of the bags of groceries he saw unloaded from so many different cars and left next to the shack. There was a story and a good one.

But Gray couldn't bring himself to disturb the hermit's solitude. Some great tragedy had brought him to this place, had forced him to leave his life and land on this beach like a piece of driftwood thrown onto the sand by a fierce winter storm. Gray respected that overwhelming desire for solitude. Though it wasn't in him, it had been in his father and he knew the price of it. Because Gray had paid it along with his father.

His reporter's instincts insisted on the story; his personal history refused to search for it.

That was why he'd been so insulted by Josie's suggestion that he might turn her crying into a story. He'd learned discretion since his arrival in Gibsons, learned there were stories that should not, could not, be turned into articles.

They might be talked about, mulled over, ruminated on. They might be tucked into the back of his mind to haunt him on a rainy day in the middle of November. They might even be input into his computer and kept there, password protected, so he could read them again. But they were not for publication. They were private.

The hermit's story was one of them. The not quite relationship of Julie Jones and the sergeant was another. The resident of the seniors' home who ran naked down the lane two or three times a month. The teenager who had tried to kill herself and failed. The kleptomaniac who stole only condoms and pregnancy tests. Josie Harris and her tears. All stories Gray MacInnis would never write.

He felt that way even more strongly once he had heard the hermit's story late one night when the sergeant was in Winnipeg for a training session.

The hermit—his name was Joseph Kennaday—had showed up at the Way-Inn at his usual time. Gray had been sitting in his usual booth at the back, his laptop on the table, and his second (and last) beer in front of him. He was thinking about packing up and going home but something about Joseph had tempted him.

He had a face the likes of which Gray had never seen. A face so strong and yet so tragic that Gray always wondered what had caused such a man to end up in a shack on a beach, living a subsistence life and depending on the goodness of others for his welfare.

He pondered the question, ordering another beer without thinking.

Rose leaned over when she brought it. "Don't drink too much, Gray. The sergeant is away and I need you to drive Joseph home."

Flattered, Gray traded in his beer for a coffee and settled back to wait. He was pretty sure he'd be able to tell when the ride was needed, but he was wrong.

Rose didn't come by to get him until almost an hour after he thought the time had come for Joseph to go home.

"It's time," she said. "I'll help you get him out to the car."

"He's not very big, Rose. I think I can handle him."

"Oh, Gray, I'm sure you can, but he's got his pride. He'll be okay if I walk out to the car with him. Come on, let's go. I've got customers."

She brushed aside his twenty-dollar bill.

"You're doing me a favor," she said. "The least I can do is buy you dinner."

The hermit settled into the back of Gray's car without trouble and Gray drove carefully along the coast road to the beach turn-off.

"Joseph?" he asked, stopping the car. "Do you need me to help you home?"

No answer.

"Joseph?"

Gray walked around to the back door and opened it. Joseph stared straight ahead, as if he saw nothing or everything.

"Joseph?"

Gray reached into the car and touched the thin arm.

"Come with me," he said. "I'll walk you home, okay?"

The hermit shook off Gray's hand and crawled out of the car. In all the nights he'd sat in the Way-Inn watching him, Gray had only heard him speak once. Silence enveloped him like a winter night.

Not even a grunt came from him as he stood swaying on the pavement.

"This way, Joseph," Gray said, his arm hovering protectively over the man's shoulders. "Be careful, the path hasn't been cleared yet for the tourists."

Gray thought he heard a chuckle, but it wasn't repeated.

The walk down to the beach shack was slow. Gray moved as quickly as he could in the darkness. He was nervous and getting more so.

"You're home, Joseph."

Gray stood at the front door of the shack and waited for Joseph to disappear inside of it.

"This isn't home."

The voice was soft, and Gray strained to decipher the accent. Irish, he thought, or a Newfoundlander. But away from home a long time.

"Where is home?"

"You own the paper, don't you? I've seen your picture."

"I do," Gray reluctantly admitted, figuring the admission would put an end to the speech.

"I used to be a journalist, you know. You might even have heard of me. Joseph Kennaday."

"Joseph Kennaday?"

Gray sat down on the sand with a bump. Joseph Kennaday, *the* Joseph Kennaday, the man who'd disappeared at the top of his game? The man he'd studied once he decided to buy the paper? The publisher of the best small independent paper in the country? *That* Joseph Kennaday?

"Yes."

"But…but…"

"What am I doing here? It's a long, sad story, Gray Mac-Innis, and one I'll not be telling to the likes of you."

"Joseph Kennaday. I'll be damned."

Gray fell back into the sand.

"You're Joseph Kennaday. *The* Joseph Kennaday. In a million years I would never have guessed it."

The old man sat down on the sand beside Gray.

"No one would guess it. That's why I'm here and not anywhere else."

Gray glanced at the door of the shack.

"Do you still?"

"No, I don't. There's nothing in there but books and a bed and a stove. No story. No newspaper clippings. No writing. I've given that up."

"But you were the best. The very best. You could have gone on forever."

"I couldn't. Too many changes, too many sorrows. I had to give it up. This," the thin arm flung wide to encompass the beach and the ocean and the sky, "is all I need now. It comforts me."

"Family?"

Gray was embarrassed. He had practiced the art of leading questions for years, but he was having difficulty putting more than a few words together. He was shocked and saddened and curious and practically unable to think.

"I have no family. Not now."

"I'm sorry," Gray said, sensing the sorrow in those few words.

"Don't you be sorry, young man. It was nothing to do with you. It was something that couldn't be helped, an accident. A terrible accident."

Joseph Kennaday repeated those words as if he'd memorized them to stave off something more honest. Or more horrible.

"I should have died with them, really," he continued without emotion. "But I was at work, my ever so important job, and so they traveled by themselves that Christmas. Going home for the holidays.

"I was too important, of course, to take two weeks off so I was to follow them a few days later. The plane crash wasn't anyone's fault...not manufacturer's error, not pilot mistake, not even the weather.

"Birds killed them," he said. "Even I couldn't believe it. And I couldn't report it. Nor anything since. It's not fear, you know, not even loneliness anymore. All of us need to find a way to cope with pain. For me, solitude works."

Gray nodded. "I need people," he said in response, surprising himself with the words.

"I have no family," Gray continued. "No tragedy, really. My father died from liver disease a couple of years ago, my mother so long ago I don't even remember her. No wife—I'm divorced—and no kids. But," Gray almost crumpled to the sand with the force of the realization, "I have friends, good ones, neighbors, a community."

Gray waved his arms at the lights up the beach. "This community is what keeps my pain at bay."

Gray cringed, hearing himself equate his pain with Joseph's.

Joseph stood up, swaying while he spoke. "Pain is pain, Gray MacInnis. It all hurts."

Gray reached out his hand but stopped himself before Joseph Kennaday slapped it away, saying, "The whole story is a cliché, and it's embarrassing to tell it."

Gray didn't see embarrassment in the face across from him, he saw sorrow. But he nodded anyway.

"You won't print anything about this."

It wasn't a question, but a statement. Gray nodded again and waited while Joseph Kennaday opened the door to his shack. He turned before disappearing and smiled at Gray.

"Good night, young man," he said. "Perhaps you'll drop by for tea one day."

The tender sadness of that smile might have felled a lesser man, but Gray found himself smiling back and looking forward to tea.

Picking his way among the rocks and logs walking back to the car, he thought of Joseph Kennaday and how he'd made one decision, not even a wrong one, just an ordinary kind of decision, and his life had been forever altered.

Gray wondered if he would have had the courage to walk away from such a life even in such circumstances. He smiled, a little tentatively, and realized that it wouldn't matter. His life was changing, he could feel it.

He wondered whether it was Fred or Josie who had garnered Rose's sympathy last night.

Gray had heard the gossip about Fred and his geriatric love triangle. It was a seven days' wonder—Fred had dared to leave Marlene. The rumor mill buzzed with speculation about Marlene's form of reprisal. Gray listened, as always, and waited with the rest of Gibsons for the denouement.

Everyone was disappointed when nothing happened. After a few days of anticipation, they moved on to something else but the possibilities popped up regularly in conversation.

"What's she going to do?"

"She'll never let him get away with it."

"If I were them, I'd move away. A *long* way away."

And ideas would bounce around the table and then die from lack of oxygen. Gray wasn't sure that anything gossip-worthy would actually happen—he'd never met Marlene—but he kept his ears open, following the story because he'd been there for the beginning.

Right there. He'd been sitting next to Fred and Marlene in the fish-and-chips shop on the beach at Sechelt when Fred, his face as bleached as a starfish stranded by high tide on a hot summer's day, said to Marlene, "I have to leave."

"Is your stomach bothering you again? I've told you a hundred times not to eat fried foods." Gray watched while she raised a forkful of batter and fish and chips to her mouth. "You'll have to wait until I'm finished."

Gray hadn't figured the white face to be the result of an upset stomach but he was satisfied with the explanation and turned back to his own lunch when he heard a voice so full of emotion, it haunted him for days after. He heard it in his sleep, while he drove to work, when he picked up his pen to draw, when he was doing the dishes or eating breakfast at the Way-Inn. Even now, when he thought about that day, Fred's voice was clear in his mind.

"No, Marlene. I'm leaving you. Permanently."

The voice wasn't loud, didn't tremble, had no tears accompanying it. The level didn't vary, nor the tone. Gray was accustomed to listening—he did it in interviews, in courtrooms, in homes where some terrible event had occurred. He had thought until that day that he knew all the nuances of a human voice under stress. He was wrong. He had never heard anything like this one.

Steady, low and full, it should have been satisfying to hear, instead it was frightening. It was as if the man had distilled decades of some fierce emotion in a bottle and then spilled it out onto the table where it ate away at the plastic tablecloth and into the wood beneath. Gray never did figure out what emotion could produce a voice like that—at once completely controlled and desperately wild—but he was forced to acknowledge its power.

The beautifully groomed and self-possessed woman sitting across from the man flinched as if someone had struck her. No, different than that, Gray thought. Her body quaked for a moment, as if for the very first time in her long life someone had dared to contradict her, to raise a hand to stop her. She was obviously upset, but it went deeper than that. Those few words, spoken in that particular voice, set off a seismic shift in her view of the world.

They'd been married a long time, that was clear. And he'd

seen the aftermath of divorce a million times over. It was devastating. And some people never recovered from it.

But Gray believed he was seeing more than that. It was about power. Because the woman's face reset itself long before she spoke, returned to wearing its bland, sweet mask. Gray wondered if he'd imagined the rage he'd seen, because that's what it was. He was certain of it. He didn't wonder for long.

"Oh, Fred, you're having a midlife crisis." She laughed a charming, disdainful little laugh.

"Come on—" holding out her perfectly manicured hand "—let's go home. I'll make you a cup of coffee and we can talk about this."

She sounded so reasonable, so confident, that Gray didn't understand how anyone could refuse her. But the man found the courage to do so.

"I'll take you home, Marlene, but we won't talk about this. There's no need. I'm leaving. This afternoon."

Her mask slipped again. Gray caught it this time only because he was watching for it.

"Well, okay." Her voice ever-so-slightly sulky. "Maybe you do need a vacation. You had that flu and you've been out running around in the rain all winter. A couple of weeks in Arizona, playing golf and you'll be right as rain. I've been wanting to paint the bedroom and this is my opportunity. By the time you get home, it'll be done. I know you hate the smell of paint."

Yeah, thought Gray, and by the time this guy gets home pigs will fly, too. They got up from the table, leaving Fred's meal untouched, and walked out to their car, she inching ever nearer, and he moving away, a kind of sliding vee making its way across the parking lot.

Gray hadn't seen either of them since then, though he'd heard plenty about them from gossip central. And he, like almost everyone he'd talked to, was firmly on Fred's side. He had been pleased last night to see Josie with her father. Because after that one glimpse of her mother he hoped never to meet her again.

Two things had stuck with him from that day—the sound of Fred's voice and the look on Marlene's face in those few exposed moments. She had seemed to Gray to be capable of anything and she had confirmed it by so quickly attempting to repair the damage, by so obviously asserting her power.

If Fred had a few too many drinks last night, if he gave in to the fear and despair, Gray couldn't blame him. Gray would have fled in terror years ago rather than live with that woman.

CHAPTER 12

Josie's alarm clock rang and rang and rang. It rang its little heart out. It tried varying the tone, ringing up, then down. It rang louder, then softer. It stopped and started again. It rang until its bells ached and still no response, no testy snap at its buttons, no fumbling hand knocking it off the bedside table. It didn't know what to do so it kept on ringing. And ringing. And ringing.

A voice roared from somewhere outside the room.

"Josie. Turn the damned thing off. It's been ringing for half an hour and it's driving me crazy."

The alarm clock bristled at the criticism—it was just doing its job, after all. But it agreed completely with the voice. It could feel its power leaching away, the ring losing its beautiful clear tone. Turn me off, it pleaded silently.

The voice yelled a bit more, the doorknob rattled, but no one appeared for what felt like a very long time. Its bells hurt.

Fred threw on his clothes. The sound of Josie's alarm was unbearable. *Ring. Ring. Ring.* Damned thing. He remembered her as a teenager. She could sleep through anything, and did.

Getting her up for school had often involved devices as barbaric as pots and pans, ripping off the covers and flinging open the frost-patterned window, a jug of ice water. An alarm clock had never been enough. He spared a minute to wonder how Josie had managed to get herself up for work or school when he hadn't been there to help her.

Mercedes gave him the key to Josie's room and he shut off the alarm—thanking God for the silence—before turning to Josie. She was curled up in bed, the covers snarled and twisted, looking as if she were twelve years old. Fred's heart skipped a beat. His beautiful daughter. He reached out to touch her shoulder.

"Josie, honey. Time to get up. Come on, honey." He shook harder and she wriggled away. "Josie. Get up. You're going to be late."

"Hmmm," she mumbled. "Leave me alone." She burrowed deeper under the covers, no longer quite so beautiful.

Fred's years of experience with the teenage Josie stood him in good stead. He made sure she was wearing pajamas and then ripped away the covers. She curled up tighter. He got a glass of water from the bathroom.

"God, what's that?" Josie's scream would have woken her next-door neighbor if he wasn't already standing beside her.

"Get up. You're going to be late for work. You have to be on time your first day."

"Who do you think you are? My father?"

Fred grinned at that. Josie hated to get up; hated it more than anything in the world, but once she was awake she was as cheerful as could be. No transition for her. She was either asleep or awake. Even without a cup of coffee.

He didn't know where she'd gotten that from. He was an

early bird but he could barely speak until he finished his third cup. And Marlene? She demanded a pot of tea in bed every morning and stayed in bed with her eyes closed until every drop was gone.

Josie leaped out of bed—once you accomplished the extraordinary feat of waking her up—immediately ready to face the world. Fred marveled at her ability, envied it in fact.

"I don't know what time I start work. He never said. Never said what the salary was, either. I don't even know what I'll be doing." She smiled up at Fred. "But thanks anyway."

"Get dressed. If you don't know when you have to be there, you have time for breakfast. I want scrambled eggs."

Josie's stomach churned at the thought of scrambled eggs. And once Fred left her alone, she noticed the headache running rampant behind her eyes. Ouch. She sat gingerly back on the bed and took a survey of her body parts. One head, throbbing outrageously. Two eyes filled with some sort of powdered glass. Mouth, dry and foul. Upset stomach. Thousands of muscles, most of which she didn't know she had, aching. Ouch again.

Forget the eggs. She wasn't even sure she could drink the glass of water she needed to swallow the Advil. And she knew the Alka-Seltzer would make her puke.

"I remember…" careful to whisper and avoid setting off the drummers waiting inside her head "…I used to be able to drink better than this. Really."

Josie remembered the first four beers. They'd tasted great. And made her feel better than she had in days. Maybe years.

She'd pretty much given up drinking when her luck ran out. She didn't have much money, but even more than that she'd felt the lure of it.

She'd dreamed about losing herself in a bottle of red wine, going to a place where it didn't matter that her charmed life had been sliced away with her hair. She'd succumbed a couple of times, early on, and then she stopped. She knew what would happen if she kept drinking.

First, not often but maybe once a month, she'd be unable to get up for work. She'd start phoning in with tales of the flu or a cold, her raspy hungover voice making it sound perfectly legitimate. When those stories ran out, she'd have to resort to bigger stories—a dead aunt, a sprained ankle, a minor car accident. It would take some time for her employer to get suspicious, but he would. And then he'd warn her and she'd promise to behave. And then, inevitably, he'd fire her. As would the next one.

And she'd keep drinking, because now she'd really need to. Her life would be an even bigger mess. Her jobs would begin to pay less, carry less prestige, and she would eventually end up working at Wal-Mart until they fired her too. She'd sell her house and live on that money for a while. And then she'd have to go on welfare.

She would already have been forced to drink Thunderbird most days or Calona Red on special occasions. Now she'd be drinking absolutely anything. Cooking wine, cough syrup, homemade hooch. She'd get thinner and thinner because all her money went to keeping her alcohol level up.

She'd end up on the streets, a thin, disheveled woman old

long before her time, begging passersby almost as badly off as she for the few dollars she needed to buy the next bottle. She'd die in a back alley one night, cold and lonely but oblivious to the way her life had changed.

That scenario held little temptation for Josie, and mostly stopped her drinking at all. So the four beers last night had contained more than enough alcohol to kill the exact number of brain cells required to quell any inhibitions about drinking she'd learned over the past two years.

Sometime after those four beers, she thought, she might have switched to Jack Daniel's. She wasn't a hundred percent certain, but surely this hangover couldn't have been caused by beer alone. Something much more serious must have contributed to this level of pain.

She wondered how they'd got home. She didn't think she'd been in any state to walk back up the hill and she did have a vague recollection of riding in some backseat. Gray? She was pretty sure she'd remember being in his car. But Rose? Or Mercedes? Some other friend of Fred? Didn't matter, she was here. And she'd have to do something about getting up, dressed and ready for her first day of work at the *Sunshine Coast News*.

A half hour later, a long half hour later, Josie Harris had showered, dressed and had barely avoided vomiting as she brushed her teeth. She spent the thirty minutes moaning each time she moved and trying to figure out what she could put into her abused stomach that wouldn't come right back up. After lengthy deliberation, she thought a cup of weak tea and a piece of lightly buttered toast might be okay as long as she didn't have to watch Fred put ketchup on his eggs.

* * *

The door was open when she arrived at the *Sunshine Coast News* promptly at 10:00 a.m. Papers swirled around like whirlwinds in the desert. Computers hummed and the phone rang without hope of answer. Lights blinked furiously on the answering machine. Josie pulled the door shut behind her and watched the whirlwinds collapse in on themselves, paper fluttering to the ground all around her. She surveyed the empty room. It appeared as if a bomb had exploded or a very messy burglar had just walked out the door. A ripple of not-quite-fear passed over Josie.

She cleared her throat.

"Anybody home?"

Her voice echoed in the stillness.

"Hello? Gray? Mrs. Suzuki? Anybody here?"

There were no hiding spaces in the main room, no bodies sprawled behind the counter or beside the desks, nothing except paper. Everywhere. And the phone. Ringing. It sounded angry.

Josie walked to the back of the room, picking her way around desks and through piles of multicolored paper. It might have been confetti for a giant. She opened a door at the back of the room. A storage closet. Reams of paper. Boxes of pens and staples and paper clips. Lurid piles of Post-It notes. Towers of yellow lined pads. No humans. She opened the other door. A spotlessly clean bathroom.

"Ah," she said, walking back out to the main room. "I get it. A big story. They're out on a story. Someone just forgot to close the door."

She sat down in a chair behind the counter, grateful for the respite. She wasn't quite ready to face anyone, especially a new employer who was also a potential lover (she gulped when she thought that word) and a brand-new coworker. She closed her eyes to enjoy the sun on her face and opened them again in annoyance. The phone wouldn't stop ringing. She picked it up in sheer exasperation.

"Sunshine Coast News."

She searched around for a pen to go with the paper littering the room.

"Who is this?" a husky voice demanded.

"Josie Harris. I just started this morning."

"Oh. Well. Can I speak to Doris?"

"There's no one here right now. Can I take a message?"

A pause.

"No. It'll be too late. I know the deadline is noon and what if she doesn't get back in time? Write this down. And don't forget to put the time on it. It *has* to be pulled."

Josie wrote down the time—10:17 a.m.—and the date—April 14—and waited for further instructions.

"This is Rowena Dale. R-O-W-E-N-A space D-A-L-E. Got that?"

"Yes, Mrs. Dale."

"I want to cancel the announcement of my engagement. Cancel it, you understand? Tell Doris it can't run. Just make sure it's pulled."

The voice at the other end of the phone sniffed.

"Are you all right?"

"I'm a fool, that's what. A damned fool. You just make

sure Doris sees that message the minute she gets back. It's important."

Josie started to nod, and then stopped as quickly as possible. Despite the toast and the tea, it still hurt to move her head.

"Of course, Mrs. Dale. I'll give the message to Doris—" she assumed Doris equaled Mrs. Suzuki "—as soon as she gets in."

"Thank you." Another sniff accompanied the words. "You're a good girl, Josie Harris. Thanks for your help."

Josie hesitated, almost scared to ask, but in the end she couldn't resist.

"Mrs. Dale? What happened?"

More sniffs resounded through the receiver and then the most subtle of sobs.

"Rowena?" Josie whispered the name. "Are you okay?"

"No, I'm not okay. I have spent the past six months making an ass of myself. Of course I'm not okay."

Josie's tentative response was swallowed up by the onset of what she was later to know as the Dale tantrum.

"How old are you, girl?"

"Thirty-five."

"Well, I'm damned near eighty and I should know better by now. Do you?"

"Do I what?" Josie wondered out loud, not really expecting an answer.

"Do you know better than to be drawn in by some sweet-talking, perfumed, lazy, pretty boy? Do you know enough about men to figure out when they're up to no good?

"When they're trying to con you out of something?

Doesn't matter if it's sex or money or favors—all those cons are the same."

"I'm not sure if I do know better."

Josie was confident that she didn't know better about her mother or her father or her own life, so why should men be any different? And she thought back to her immediate and intense attraction to Gray MacInnis.

Was it foolish?

She knew nothing about him except that he was irresponsible—after all, he'd left the office wide open for anyone at all to walk in—and impulsive—he'd hired her without a resume, a reference or an interview.

"Mrs. Dale? How can I learn to know better?"

"Not from me, that's for frigging sure. I've lost track of the men who've ripped me off. Four husbands, half a dozen fiancés, not including the most recent one. Two stockbrokers, one lawyer and one weasely brother-in-law. And those are only the ones I can remember. I can't help you at all."

"You haven't learned anything at all from those bad experiences?"

"Oh, sure, honey, I've learned a lot. The trouble is that the things I've learned are the kinds of things that fly right out of a woman's head when she sees a smile lighting up a man's eyes when he looks at her."

"Tell me anyway. Maybe I'll be able to remember them. I'll try to, I really will."

Josie leaned back in the chair and pulled a yellow pad and a red pen toward her. She would memorize Rowena Dale's words. She'd be safe from the charms of Gray MacInnis.

"I'm ready."

"Okay, here goes.

"One. Always pretend you're poor, even if you're not.

"Two. Don't trust extremely good-looking men.

"Three. Time is important, time to get past the immediate attraction, time to get to know the man."

Josie interrupted her.

"How much time?"

She thought of Fred and Marlene. They fell into something (Josie no longer thought of it as love or even friendship but wasn't any closer to figuring out what it really was) at first sight and stayed married for more than three decades. She thought again of Gray MacInnis.

"Lots of time. Years would be best." The raspy voice quivered with rage and a hint of sadness.

"Four?"

Josie broke in to stop the flood of bile she sensed was coming.

"Four. This one's not so easy. Self-respect."

Fred and Josie both needed to learn this one, she thought, and put a dozen exclamation marks next to it.

"Five. Sex isn't love, although it often feels like it.

"Six. Learn from your mistakes.

"Seven. If a man much younger or smarter or better-looking than you is falling all over you, don't forget to ask yourself why.

"Eight. Never, ever put up with rudeness in a partner. Look at how he treats waiters and salespeople. That'll tell you what kind of man he really is.

"Nine. Women aren't perfect, either.

"Ten. You don't get smarter just because you get older."

Josie snickered, couldn't help herself, and didn't get her hand over her mouth fast enough to hide it.

"Are you laughing at me, Josie Harris?"

Rowena Dale demanded an answer.

"No, Mrs. Dale, I'm laughing at myself. I'm pretty sure I'm getting stupider as I get older. Every single thing I thought I knew has been proven wrong over the last couple of years. I know less now than I did when I was thirteen."

"Me, too." Mrs. Dale sighed.

"Do you think that's true of everyone or are we just more foolish than the rest of them?"

With that question, Josie and Rowena lost whatever composure they'd managed to retain through the conversation. Laughter and hiccups engulfed Josie until she wasn't sure if they were laughing or crying. Both, she thought.

"I've got to go, Josie. Thanks—" hiccup, hiccup, sob "—I enjoyed talking to you."

"No more engagements, Mrs. Dale, okay? Call me if you feel one coming on and I'll read you the list."

Josie hung up and looked around the room, wondering where to put Rowena Dale's message, where it might go that it wouldn't be lost amongst the debris. She folded the list and put it in her bag. She'd keep it with her.

She settled on a spike on the front counter for Doris's message and sat back in the chair. The sun felt good on her aching bones. Josie drifted, almost asleep, until the phone began ringing again. This time she didn't hesitate.

She spent the morning taking messages. She soon figured out that Doris and Mrs. Suzuki were the same person and that all messages were for her. The spike quickly accumulated a dozen pieces of paper though none of the messages or the conversations were as heart-rending as the first.

Lost dogs; white elephant sales; a 1987 Buick, only three hundred thousand kilometers, no rust, new tires, for sale, cheap. An invitation to a fiftieth birthday party. A query about advertising rates. A man selling timeshares in Hawaii.

Josie took care with her spelling, her handwriting. She put the exact time—taking it from the clock above the door—at the top of each page. No one except Rowena Dale did more than leave a message but Josie began to feel needed.

So she picked up the papers from the floor and put them into piles on the empty table beside her. She weighted each pile with a book—a dictionary, a thesaurus, a jumbo book of crossword puzzles. The door hadn't opened since she entered it, but Josie wasn't risking another whirlwind, not after she'd picked everything up.

Hours passed and still no one appeared. Josie made coffee and began to think about her empty stomach and the possibility of a late lunch. She watched people walk by the front windows carrying brown paper bags which surely contained sustenance. But she couldn't leave because she couldn't lock the door. She would be responsible even if no one else was. The phone rang again.

"Sunshine Coast News."

"Josie? Is that you?"

"Who's that?"

"Gray MacInnis."

All Josie's pent-up anger and hunger escaped.

"Where the hell are you? I arrived to a mess, no one here, no one to tell me what to do, and I've been answering the phone ever since. And I'm starving."

"God, Josie, I'm sorry. I'm on the mainland with Mrs. Suzuki. Her daughter had to have an emergency caesarian this morning."

"Oh." Josie's face heated with shame. "Is she okay?"

"She's fine. The baby's fine, just a few weeks early. I can't get back until tonight. The next ferry's not till five."

"What do I do?"

"There's a key under the mat at the front door. Go on home, just lock up behind you."

"But what about all these messages? One of them is urgent."

"Is it about the paper?"

"Yeah."

"Well, however urgent it is it can wait until tomorrow. If the paper's a day late, so be it. Everyone will understand."

"Why don't I stay until closing time? Five o'clock, right? I'll just run out and get a sandwich. I'll leave a note on the door. Someone has to answer the phone."

"Thanks, Josie. I'm sorry I forgot about you, but you've been a big help today. I'm glad I hired you."

"Thanks."

Josie hung up the phone and looked around at the room. This was her place now, her paper. She'd done what needed to be done and she'd done it right. She smiled as she taped the handwritten sign to the door—back in fifteen minutes—

and locked it behind her. Tuna salad on whole wheat with plenty of mayo and pepper and green onions that's what she wanted. Tuna salad and a Diet Pepsi. Maybe two or even three Diet Pepsis.

CHAPTER 13

Gray stood shivering at the bow of the ferry slicing its way from Horseshoe Bay to home. He was oblivious to the mountains rising out of the ocean, didn't see the sun setting flamboyantly behind the islands, nor the sailboats flying by in tight formation.

He had raced along the Upper Levels Highway to the terminal, hoping the RCMP were too busy doing something else to have radar out, cursing the people who left work early to clog up the road. He desperately wanted to be on the ferry going home. He even more desperately wanted to forget the morning.

His phone had shrilled in the darkness. His eyes opened involuntarily and he saw the red lights on his clock radio informing him it was four fifty-three. The phone kept ringing. Gray knew what it meant and he contemplated pulling the pillow over his head and ignoring it. The sergeant could do this accident without him. But his reporter's instincts overruled his sensible side.

"Yeah?"

A voice responded, but it wasn't at all who he expected. "Gray? It's Doris. Doris Suzuki."

"Doris? Are you okay? Has something happened at the paper?"

"It's Tonika. She's in emergency. They were in Vancouver buying furniture and she got hit by a car. I have to catch the first ferry."

Gray didn't ask any further questions, instead he said, "I'll pick you up in half an hour. You pack your bag and I'll take you down there. You shouldn't be driving, anyway."

After a few minutes of obligatory refusals, Mrs. Suzuki accepted and Gray hung up the phone. The shower took five minutes, the drive to the paper another ten. He figured he had five more before he had to leave for the motel to drop off a note for Josie with Mercedes. She could start tomorrow instead of today.

He squelched the resentment welling up in him. She was coming to work with him, for heaven's sake. It wasn't the last dance in some cheesy country bar in some small town he was leaving forever first thing in the morning. He'd basically done that last night. He still felt the weight of her against him and smelled the fresh sweet scent of her hair when he breathed.

He'd see her every day for months. Or at least weeks. The urgency he felt was unnecessary. But he sat down at the computer anyway.

The letter he began said this:

Josie,

I won't see you this morning and it's all I've thought about since you left the restaurant last night. I made it through the night by remembering the look on your face when you leaned against me last night.

You looked like you'd just seen the most amazing thing in the world, like Burton finally seeing Victoria Falls, or Neil Armstrong stepping off the lander and onto the moon. You looked as if nothing could ever equal that moment.

I want you to look at me that way.

He'd gotten that far when the phone at his elbow rang, startling him out of his reverie.

"Where are you? I can't miss the ferry, Gray, we have to get going."

"I'll be right there."

He'd raced out of the office without any idea of what he'd done before he left. He obviously hadn't locked the door if Josie Harris walked right in. He hoped he'd deleted the letter.

The rest of the morning went downhill from its beginning. Mrs. Suzuki kept her face turned away from him but he saw her red-rimmed eyes and the pain that made them so. He didn't even suggest breakfast in the cafeteria, just left her in the car and ran upstairs for coffee and donuts to go.

When he handed her the coffee, the chill of her hands shocked him and he pulled the blanket from the backseat, shook most of the sand from it and wrapped it around her.

The trip to the hospital felt endless but nowhere near as long as the time in the waiting room. It was only a few hours by his watch, but it was forever in terms of pain.

"You can go, Gray MacInnis. You're on deadline."

"The paper can be a day late for once. Besides, I want to put the baby notice in, so I can't go yet."

His clumsy attempt at cheer fell flat. They waited in silence. Tonika's husband Richard paced, his head swiveling as nurses and doctors passed through, then dropping when they paused to talk to someone else. Mrs. Suzuki sat primly in an orange plastic chair, her trembling hands grasping a crumpled napkin from the ferry. Gray stood by a window overlooking a parking lot and counted cars.

"We'll hear something when the fourteenth blue car goes in," he mumbled under his breath. "When the third Beetle goes out. When the one hundredth car goes through the barrier."

And still nothing. Counting cars hadn't worked any better when he was a child waiting on the front porch for his father to come home but he still found it oddly comforting.

Five rotten cups of coffee later and he, too, was trembling. When the doctor finally did come in, he was smiling.

"Mr. Margate? Everything's fine. Your wife has a broken leg and some bruises but she's going to be okay. And your daughter is perfect. We have her in an incubator but that's just a precaution. They can both go home in a few days. You can see them now."

And just like that the world blossomed. Mrs. Suzuki laughed out loud and wrapped her arms around Richard.

"I'm a grandma. And you're a daddy. Let's go and see our baby."

The two of them rushed away without a word. Gray didn't care. His view from the window had somehow transformed itself from a gloomy parking lot into a spring garden. The sun peeked around the clouds, lighting up the cherry blossoms and the daffodils and tulips lining the walkways. He had no idea how long he stood there before Mrs. Suzuki came back bearing a Polaroid photograph and a piece of paper.

"Thanks, Gray. Thanks for coming with me." She handed him a Polaroid of a wrinkled baby and the piece of paper. "Here's the announcement. Her name is Emily Doris Samantha Margate. It's nice, isn't it?"

He smiled at her. "It sure is. And she's beautiful."

"I won't be back at work for a while. I know we talked about a month, but now…"

"I know. Don't worry. The new woman will be fine. You look after Emily and Tonika and come back when you can."

He didn't know which of them was more shocked when she leaned over and kissed his cheek. "I'll call you when we get home."

Gray left the hospital with all the speed of a drunk heading for his first drink of the day. He'd managed to quell his nausea for Mrs. Suzuki's sake but hospital smells always made him sick. And the sounds. And the color of the walls.

His father wasn't a healthy man and most years he spent a piece of time in the hospital. In those days, in that small town, and because they were poor, it was the equivalent of a sanatorium. He went in a broken-down old drunk and came out clean and shaking and sober.

Gray learned to be careful of the stranger who came home from the hospital. He didn't even look like his father. Gray accepted his presence solely because he'd seen the stranger emerge from his father's body during the weeks in the hospital, like a moth from a pupae.

But the man who came home from the hospital was *not* his father. He was angry, full of rage and resentment. Gray stayed out of his way, walked softly through the house, and never, ever refused him anything. He ate foods which made him gag, did chores which got done only once a year, showered twice a day and did every single piece of his schoolwork every single day.

Gray hated to admit it, even now, but in those years he had waited impatiently for his father to start drinking again. He had sworn to himself that if one year the stranger remained in place of his father he would run away. Each time his father went into the hospital, he packed his emergency backpack and kept it ready underneath his bed. He never had to use it, but he was prepared.

So Gray knew about hospitals from an early age. He'd stood at his father's bedside year after year as he'd wrestled with his demons. Not much good came out of hospitals as far as he could see; either you died or you turned mean. He'd been happy to see that hadn't been true for Emily and Tonika—but he still hated hospitals.

The salty ocean air was clearing the disinfectant smell from his head and for the first time in hours he felt free to think about Josie Harris. He gave himself over to it.

Fred and Mercedes sat on the Sand Dollar Motel dock in rickety old deck chairs, blankets wrapped around their shoulders and steaming cups of coffee in their hands. When Fred showed up at the office to go to the club for lunch, Mercedes handed him a picnic basket and a bundle of blankets.

"I think we should have this conversation somewhere slightly more private than the club."

Fred respected that bluntness even though his life had been spent with the most subtle and devious of women. Mercedes never hesitated to speak her mind; Fred always knew exactly what she thought. It was a change.

The thermos was empty before he'd finished the story, ending with Josie's tale of the Lord Jim's lunch and its consequences. Mercedes had confined herself to a few grunts and nods. He felt her anger, though, simmering just below the surface, and he welcomed it.

He realized how much he'd wanted to talk to her about this, knowing she'd be wholeheartedly on his side and wanting her to express the anger he seemed incapable of venting. He'd spent too long containing his emotions for them to be easily released. Love had been simple; because of Josie he'd never lost his ability to express that, but everything else was locked inside.

"You're such an idiot. Really. I don't know how you survived this long. And it's going to take a miracle to get you and Florence and Josie out of this mess."

She reached into the picnic basket. "Here. Have a sandwich. I need to think."

They chewed companionably in silence. Mercedes's anger was coming in waves now. Fred saw it. It wasn't red, as he might have expected, but a kind of deep oily pink, full of violence. It rolled over her, transforming her features from the energetic cheerful cribbage player to someone far more powerful, more frightening.

She didn't scare Fred, after Marlene no woman could do that, but he did realize it was essential to be still. And so he ate his sandwich, and reached into the basket for another. Confession and cold and sea air made him hungry.

Mercedes ate her sandwich with tough little chomps, each bite distinct and vicious. Fred enjoyed watching her because he knew her anger was on his behalf.

"I don't have any ideas," Mercedes finally said. "My mind is a complete blank. But she's a real bitch, your wife, isn't she?"

Fred nodded in response. Even now he couldn't say what he knew about Marlene. Whenever he tried, it was as if a hand squeezed his throat, strangling the words so that he heard them in his head but couldn't speak them. He nodded again and saw Mercedes's face soften a little from the goddess of justice mask she'd put on.

The softening did what the fierce anger had been unable to accomplish. It allowed Fred to speak words he'd barely even articulated in his own mind. They were words he would not, could not speak to Florence or Josie, because he knew without understanding why that the mere voicing of them would be dangerous.

"There is something wrong with Marlene."

Fred started slowly, fear making him cautious, though even saying those few words caused him to tremble.

"Something besides being a world-class bitch?"

"Hmmm." Fred took a deep, choking breath. "Yes, something else, but I don't know…"

"Fred. Wait here for a minute. I think we need

Fred clutched the reprieve to himself like a frightened child with a beloved toy and then began talking to himself.

"I don't have to tell her. Not really. No one needs to know. I'll just have a drink and say nothing."

But Fred knew, even as he continued to mumble to himself, that someone needed to know the truth. No one would be better than Mercedes as the keeper of that knowledge.

"Have a brandy," Mercedes said, sitting down beside him. She handed him a tumbler full of alcohol.

Fred took a sip and began.

"Marlene is evil, I think. I don't mean that she's cranky or vicious or even spiteful. There is something in her that is deeper than maliciousness or mean-spiritedness. And it's worse because she's so good at hiding it."

Mercedes nodded.

"I know. I can see it in her. But you're safe now, Fred. You've left her and you've made this deal. Everything will be fine if you just stick to your guns."

"No, it won't."

He smiled sadly, knowing that if Mercedes didn't believe him, no one else would either. He tried again.

"She wants to hurt me," he said. "She wants to hurt Florence and she wants to hurt Josie. And she will figure out a way to do all of those things."

Mercedes patted him on his shoulder.

"Why don't we wait and see what happens? We'll think of something. Josie has given us a bit of breathing space. Marlene will keep to her end of the bargain, won't she?"

"As long as she doesn't find out that Josie told me everything. As long as she doesn't know I'm talking to Florence. Yes, she'll keep her end of the bargain as long as there's something in it for her."

Fred contemplated that statement and then nodded emphatically.

"She looks like the good guy in this mess and that should be enough to keep her in line for a while at least."

He abandoned his attempt at truth telling and went back to what he did best. Ignoring the obvious.

"Okay," Mercedes said. "Pick up the basket. No point in fretting. The solution will come faster if we don't think about it too hard and there's nothing more distracting than a good game of crib, especially against someone I always beat."

Fred snorted and followed her up the dock. He spared a thought for Josie and hoped everything was going well at her new job. She was smart, he thought, it would be fine.

CHAPTER 14

Of course Josie had read Gray's letter to her. She'd been drawn to his computer screen. She'd tried to ignore the pull, tried keeping busy tidying up. But every time she passed his desk a siren sang to her.

"Read me," it sang. "You know you want to see these words."

Josie managed to resist for most of the day but the song grew more enticing and less resistible after she spoke to Gray. And finally, just after she turned off the lights to go home, she caved in.

She'd never read anything so beautiful, she thought, and memorized the phrases so she could take them away with her.

She could not talk or even think—as if it were possible for her to ignore it—about the letter. Not to Fred, and definitely not to Gray. She wanted to forget she'd seen it, but his words were locked in her head, tingling on her skin. Josie knew the trouble acknowledging those words would cause. It didn't mean, though, that she wasn't attracted. She was.

But Josie wasn't sure if her attraction to Gray MacInnis was simply her mind's sneaky way of distracting her from everything else that was going on in her life, helping her cope with the stress by conjuring up another, more enjoyable thing to worry about. And because that might be true, Josie was even less inclined to think about the letter. Because she'd seen the look in his eyes when he looked at her and she didn't want to hurt him.

She told herself, quite clearly, that there were all sorts of sensible reasons for not even thinking about getting involved with Gray MacInnis. She worked for him. She would be going home soon. His attraction to her would fade as quickly as it had blossomed. But most of all, she was a mess. Her life was a disaster. A relationship was out of the question.

By the time Josie locked the door of the *Sunshine Coast News* behind her at five o'clock she'd learned more than she ever expected to know about the Sunshine Coast and its inhabitants. She'd learned about broken engagements, weddings, anniversaries, birthdays, births. She'd learned about cancer and deaths and beloved lost pets.

She'd learned about divorces—the fire sale of a house and its contents a pretty clear clue—and poverty—selling a car cheap to get the money to pay the rent.

When she told callers Mrs. Suzuki and Gray were both away, they immediately adopted her as a substitute. They told her the story and asked her to write the ad.

"We met over the Internet. He's moving up here next week and we're getting married. He's wonderful. It's not really an engagement so what do I say?"

"He just disappeared. He's never done that before. We were walking down to Joan's for a nice cup of tea—he loves her vanilla cookies—and he ran off into the bush. We looked and looked and the sergeant looked, too, but we couldn't find him. His name is Pepe, after Pepe le Pew, you know.

"Maybe I should have called Julie Jones. She and Pepe really love each other. I bet she can find him. But put the ad in anyway, dear, just in case."

"The funeral is at two o'clock on Saturday. She let go at the end, as if she was too tired to go on. The doctor said she could have lived for months but she wasn't interested. She stopped eating and refused an intravenous. She'd had enough. I couldn't blame her."

In between phone calls, Josie cleaned up the papers remaining on the floor, and wandered around checking out the blackboard covered in notes, the piles of old issues of the paper, the time line printed on continuous feed paper and taped around the top of the wall. She studied the cork wall pinned full of photographs and articles.

A few of them were from the *Sunshine Coast News*—she was beginning to recognize its down-home kind of style—but most of them weren't. There were missing people, crop circles, political essays and cartoons. Photographs of actors, politicians, burning cars and houses. Josie kept circling back to it, looking for a clue about the man who made it. She knew Gray MacInnis had pinned these pieces of paper to the board; she wanted to know why.

She glanced at the two desks, one neat, one a mess, then tried to avoid them. They were private. Except, of course, for the damn computer sitting on Gray's messy desk. She wouldn't walk into someone's office and rummage through it and she wouldn't sit down in either Mrs. Suzuki's or Gray's chair. That was another thing she'd learned today, almost everyone called her Mrs. Suzuki and him Gray.

As the day went on, Josie became more and more worried about working at the *Sunshine Coast News*. Oh, not the work itself, from what she'd seen so far she'd have no trouble with that. She was worried about Mrs. Suzuki.

The motel was silent when Josie drove up. The neon sign—bearing a misshapen sand dollar and a No Vacancy sign—wasn't lit. No cars, not even the beat-up old Mercedes that Mercedes drove as a joke. Josie pulled into her regular spot, turned off the car and the lights and took a deep breath.

"Just don't let it be another problem, please. Just not another problem. I don't think I could bear it. They're just late back from lunch, right? That's all. Fred hasn't convinced Mercedes to take him up coast to see Florence. They're not missing, they haven't been in a car accident, they're just having fun."

Josie listened to her voice as if she were outside the car looking in. She saw her own face begin to wrinkle up in preparation for the tears that invariably accompanied the panic. It was the oddest sensation, floating above herself. She'd heard of it happening in operating rooms and hospital beds, on street corners after accidents. But she wasn't dying, her body wasn't lying somewhere having released its spirit. In fact, it was still in the car spouting off.

"Maybe they're still at the club. Is there such a thing as a crib marathon? Or maybe they ran out of gas. Should I go look for them? But I don't know where the club is. But they're okay, I know they are. They're really okay. Just a tiny bit late. They haven't seen each other for a long time. They've got a lot to talk about."

Josie realized that it was possible to talk herself into a panic. She listened as her voice got higher and higher, listened as she wound herself up in knots trying to figure out something she didn't know how to control. She saw her face get redder and her hands begin to flutter.

"Stop it, stop it right now, Josie Harris. You are not going to do this. It's silly, it's debilitating and besides, it's useless. Just go on inside and turn on the radio or the TV. They'll be home soon."

It worked. The panic died down as quickly as it had flared up.

Josie laughed and remembered Fred saying once that one kiss did not a romance make. Well, with everything else falling apart around her, one averted panic attack did not a cure make. But she crossed her fingers just in case.

She sat in the chair by the window, the broken shell in her hand, and wondered about the last few days.

Josie's self-control, for most of her life firmly cemented in place, had been slipping, no, way more than that, it had collapsed since she'd been here. There was the crying fit, being turned to stone at Lord Jim's, trying to turn herself into a water sprite and almost succeeding.

And look at Fred, leaving Marlene after all these years. Where did he get the courage to do that? If anyone had said to Josie two weeks ago that Fred would leave Marlene, she would have laughed and told them they were crazy. It would never happen. Maybe, she'd say, Marlene might leave Fred. But Fred? Never happen. Yet it had.

And Marlene herself. She'd managed to be two people—the old, wisened Marlene and the regular one. How did that happen? The more Josie thought about it, the more she wondered.

Her family, her solid perfect family, was falling apart and Josie couldn't do anything about it. She'd tried and just made things worse. Marlene's problems, Fred's problems, weren't hers. Not anymore. Josie wasn't certain how she'd come to that conclusion, nor certain about what it would mean to her, but…

"They're not my problems." Saying it out loud felt good. "Not my problems. Marlene and Fred's problems are not my problems. Not. My. Problems."

Josie spoke to the luck on her windowsill and the broken shell in her hand.

"I've got problems of my own. Fred and Marlene can't solve my problems. And I can't solve theirs."

The shell didn't answer, although she thought the Ganesh might have winked at her. She smiled back at him.

"Maybe this is the right place for me. I'm getting to know people here." She ignored the picture of Gray which flashed into her mind and thought about her day.

Almost everyone who'd phoned the paper had sympathized with her about her crying spell and congratulated her on its cessation. Many had mentioned Fred, or Marlene, though seldom both. And three people had asked about her ride home from the Way-Inn last night. Josie had assumed they were asking if she'd driven home drunk, but that wasn't it.

Finally one woman said, "Isn't he a doll? That uniform drives me wild."

And Josie, usually a discreet and private woman, couldn't help herself. She asked a complete stranger for information about herself.

"What are you talking about? What man?"

Julie Jones, who had phoned to place an ad for the animal shelter, said, "The sergeant drove you and Fred home last night."

"Why?" Because Josie couldn't think of anything else to say.

"Because, oh because of a whole lot of things. It's Rose, really. She started it with the hermit. It's a privilege." Josie heard a sigh. "I wish he'd drive me home. But not like that."

"But why me?"

"Rose has hunches about people she likes and who are really unhappy. Instead of calling a cab for them she calls the sergeant. Me, I'd rather go home on my hands and knees than have everyone in town know how sad I am. That's why I mostly drink at Oysters. No one there cares how sad you are."

"But I'm not sad. I'm fine. Rose mistook those tears for sadness but I'm perfectly happy. Really. Now what do I do about the sergeant? Do I send him some money or thank him or something?"

"I don't think so. He does it for Rose. Everyone knows she's always right about people. You may not be sad right now, but for sure you were last night."

"No, I wasn't. It was probably Fred. I was just along for the ride."

Josie had hung up the phone feeling… Well, she didn't know what she was feeling. And she hadn't had time to think about it until now. The phone had kept ringing, the cork wall fascinated her and, although she'd managed to restrain herself for most of the day, the messy desk kept calling to her.

She'd gotten close enough to see an unfinished letter on his computer screen and a pen-and-ink sketch of a sailboat in a small wooded cove sitting on the single unpapered spot on his desk.

She glanced at the letter, saw her name and quickly averted her eyes but a voice inside kept pushing her toward it. Curiosity was Josie's besetting sin, but she'd learned early to keep out of other people's business. She wasn't her father's daughter for nothing.

So what if Gray MacInnis was attractive? So what if he obviously liked her? He was writing a love letter that meant he was committed. She'd made a fool of herself more than enough times in front of him. And she had one inviolate rule about men: Do not date the boss. Ever.

She'd seen it screw up dozens of lives, create havoc at work, and lose friends their jobs. Oh, maybe once in a hundred times there was a happy ending but those were terrible odds. And Josie needed this job. Besides, she was going home in a few months. And… And a lot of things. So she resisted the desk's siren call and told herself that tomorrow would be easier. *He* would be there and she wouldn't be tempted anymore.

Josie admitted that it had been nice to think about something other than Fred and Marlene and Florence for a while, but now it was time to get back to the mess at hand. Something had to be done.

"Fred?" The connecting door sounded hollow beneath her knuckles. She unlocked it and thought she might as well leave it that way. "Are you there?" No answer.

He wasn't back from the club yet. She shivered with a relief so great it scared her. She didn't have to face him, didn't have to deal with anything. Not yet. Josie sunk into the chair by the window and closed her eyes. Her headache had settled to a dull pain behind her forehead and her stomach had succumbed to the lure of Diet Pepsi and tuna salad. The sun shone directly in the window, warming her, and she fell into an uneasy sleep, peopled with images and situations racing by so quickly they were impossible to catch. Except one.

Josie stood in the window of a tall dark building. It was black outside, the windows unreflective, capturing light and eating it. It was dark inside, too. The fluorescent tubes on the ceiling hummed as if they were on but Josie saw no light.

She looked down through the open window at the unrecognizable city below her. People rushed about their business in cars, buses and on foot and the sun shone on them. Josie wanted to leave the dark building but the flowing red exit signs had all vanished along with the doors.

The crows came. But they didn't fly around the building as they used to; they flew right into it. The dark building had somehow turned itself into a rookery. The windows opened and the crows flew in, filling the building with the sounds of their wings and their voices. And they spoke in a language Josie could understand.

They spoke of food and flight and fear and fury. They spoke of the warmth of the sun and the dark coolness of their home.

Josie looked down at herself and found her body transformed. She wore glossy black feathers and a beak. She lifted her wings and stepped out of the window.

The crash of Fred's door banging against the wall echoed the scream of longing and fear she'd begun as she launched her crow self into flight.

Josie heard the water running and then Fred's voice through the connecting door.

"Hey, Josie, open up. How was your first day at work?"

Fred was the perfect listener. His face and body reflected his responses to everything. His eyes grew sad when she told him about Tonika, then sparkled when she told him about Emily. He laughed out loud at the failed engagement.

"That's Rowena. She's always meeting these great guys who want to marry her, says yes, then convinces herself it's only about her money. God, I'd marry her myself if I hadn't met Florence first. She's a wonderful woman. Maybe one day she'll say screw the money and go for it. I hope so."

Josie thought back to her conversation with Rowena Dale and reevaluated her take on it.

Fred's voice had slowed as he finished talking about Rowena, slowed to a dead stop and then brightened.

"What'll we do for dinner? I have to call Florence and then we can go. I'll tell you about my day."

He disappeared back into his own room, shutting the door behind him. Privacy. There was precious little of it in either of their lives right now and Josie wasn't sure how she felt about that. She liked the feeling of being a regular at the Way-Inn, even with the whole sergeant thing and the crying thing.

She'd have to remember to ask Fred about the sergeant. She needed to make sure he was the despairing one, not her.

And she especially liked the way everyone talked to her and called her by name. She already knew as many people here as she did in Toronto and she'd lived there most of her life. She liked Rose and Mercedes. She thought she was rapidly falling into adoration of Julie Jones and was delighted (although kind of shocked at the same time) with the new Fred. Then there was Gray MacInnis. She was sure that she shouldn't, but she liked him. A lot.

She liked his face, thin but round at the same time. Beautiful lips, teeth slightly crooked and strong. His eyes were brown with speckles of green and gold and they looked right at her. No glancing away, no distraction. He had great hands, too, long blunt fingers with big fingernails, showing pink. She wanted to run her fingers through his short curls, to touch the mustache and beard he wore. Okay, she definitely liked Gray MacInnis.

But she didn't like what was happening with Marlene.

She didn't like the things she continued to discover about Marlene and liked even less the things she discovered about herself. She wondered if she'd begun to know some of these things a long time ago, if her subconscious had been sending out signals long before her consciousness turned on the receiver. That might explain a lot of things. But it worried her.

She worried that the changed world she lived in now would change again. Not back to her old life but to something even worse than this one. She worried that she'd too quickly taken sides between Fred and Marlene. She worried about Marlene. What if she was sick, really sick with some form of madness? And once she started worrying, she worried about money.

Her world had changed too much in the past few days. Every step felt as it had to be taken on shaky ground—quicksand, the deck of a ship, a rope bridge. Josie felt split in two.

The first woman was strong and smart and funny and brave; the second was an idiot. They were layered inside of Josie and she couldn't be sure which one was going to end up on top.

She replaced the broken shell on the windowsill and shook her head.

Josie listened to Fred's voice in the room next to hers. She thought about Jill, about Rowena Dale, about Florence. All of them brave enough to change their lives, to step out into a new and frightening world.

Josie smiled to herself. Okay, it wasn't going to be easy. It hadn't been easy for Fred to leave Marlene but he'd done it. Nor for Marlene to be left behind. But she was learning, Josie hoped, to do it. Nor for Jill to move halfway across the world. She got on the plane and flew away into a new life.

And Florence? And Rowena? They were trying something they'd never done before.

"Maybe I can do it, too," Josie whispered. "I'm going to try."

Before she allowed herself time to think about it, Josie picked up the phone and dialed Marlene's number. She sighed in relief when the machine picked up.

"Marlene? Just calling to see how you are and to let you

know I've got a job. In Gibsons. So I'll be around for a while at least." Josie hesitated before going on. "Maybe we could get together for lunch. I need someone to show me where to shop. And I desperately need a haircut. You're sure to know where the best salon is. Call me. I'm at the Sand Dollar. Or you can call me at work. The *Sunshine Coast News*."

Josie had a completely new life and she was going to live it. Time to go to dinner. Time to hear about Fred's day. Time to deal with some of those damned problems.

CHAPTER 15

"Josie? Can I come in?" Fred stepped through the door. "How was work? What'd you do? I had a picnic with Mercedes and then whopped her butt at crib. I had one hand..."

Josie smiled at his enthusiasm and when the crib stories slowed, she spoke.

"I'm hungry. Let's eat and then we need to think about what we're going to do."

"Oh, no need to worry about that. Mercedes is working on it. She'll think of something."

Josie's jaw landed on the floor. At least it felt that way.

"Mercedes? What does she have to do with this?"

"This isn't your mess, Josie, it's Marlene's. It's mine. Maybe it's Florence's, but it's not yours. You are not responsible for this mess and you can't fix it either. Maybe no one can. But Mercedes is my friend. She's smart and she's an outsider. Your ideas, my ideas, even Florence's ideas—they're all biased. Mercedes can see it all with a clear eye."

"But, but..."

"No buts. It's my life...and Florence's. I've talked to her and she agrees there's no real rush. As long as Marlene thinks I'm staying down here, as long as she sees Florence staying put, she'll keep to her part of the bargain. We just need some time."

Josie wanted to argue, but Fred and Mercedes and Florence were right. They needed time and they needed a plan and Josie was fresh out of plans. She settled for food.

"Where shall we eat? I'm starving and I'm exhausted. Somewhere cheap and cheerful, okay?"

Fred brightened immediately.

"I know just the place. The Way-Inn."

Josie sighed and wondered if the Way-Inn was to become her local bar, coffee shop, family dinner table.

Josie contemplated living at the Sand Dollar in this small, clean and extremely bright room, eating at the Way-Inn where every single person knew her, and Fred. They knew about her job, about Gray (and they would soon, if they didn't already, know about their mutual attraction).

Everyone within a ten-mile radius would know what she had for breakfast, lunch and dinner and who, if anyone, she had it with. Mercedes would know when she left the Sand Dollar and when she returned. If she returned alone, Mercedes would know. If not, she'd know that, too.

Josie wasn't sure whether to laugh or cry at the transformation in her life, but she was certain of two things. She wanted at least a little privacy and she wasn't going to get it here.

She thought of the list of furnished apartments she'd pulled from the want ads in anticipation of her first paycheck. She liked the Way-Inn, even though it had been the site of two great humiliations, but she wanted to make peanut butter and banana sandwiches, cheese and crackers and chicken noodle soup. She wanted to eat in front of the TV wearing her oldest T-shirt and her slippers. She wanted to be alone.

Josie walked up the hill after dinner by herself. She'd abstained from beer and left Fred in the back room at the Way-Inn playing darts. She turned off the road and down a path with a sign that read: To the Beach.

Her shoes sank into the sand before she realized she'd stepped off the asphalt, and the sneakers quickly filled with sharp damp granules.

"Ouch." Her voice rang in the silence.

She sat down on a log and pulled off her shoes and socks, shaking the sand out of the shoes then placing them on the log beside her. She wriggled her feet deeper into the damp sand, allowing it to massage her soles, her toes, right up to her ankles. Bliss. She might pay hundreds of dollars for a day at a spa yet here she was getting the same benefit—bliss—for free. And she noticed another thing. For the first time in two days, her bruised toe had stopped throbbing. Josie settled back on the log to enjoy the absence of pain.

But other things intruded. The slight breeze blowing off the water cooled her face and brought with it a myriad of scents. Josie identified some of them: a faint hint of some sweet flower, maybe a wildflower blooming farther down the beach. A toxic undertone from the pulp mill across the water on the island. The Christmasy aroma of pine trees, and firs, and cedar.

The salty wetness of the spring air, the salt temporarily stolen from the sea, to be returned at a later date. And over and under and around it all lay water.

What did water smell like? Josie knew it had a smell, knew it to be distinct from the air, and the salt, and the other flavors carried on its waves. It was heavy, ponderous and old and powerful—frighteningly so. Because it held the fate of the world in its depths.

She knew if she could say to her empty room that this is what the water smells like on a moonless April night, she could banish all her demons, her eyes would close, and she'd drift into a dream filled with sunlight sparkling on water.

So she concentrated harder than she had in years, and allowed water to invade her nostrils, to permeate the membranes in her nose, up into her sinuses, into her brain. She opened her mouth to allow it more access, as if water were a man and she wanted the kiss to deepen, become more intimate. And water took advantage.

It swarmed into her mouth, playing over the taste buds, tickling her lips and her tongue. It entered through the pores in her face, her neck, the backs of her hands. Josie was filled with it.

She took a breath, then another, but the smell eluded her. It felt too big to define. Too full of things and places and people and plants and animals and fish and tiny plankton and protozoa and the past and the future and memories and everything that had ever touched it to distill into recognizable words.

Water kept everything, gave nothing up, took it all and combined it with all other things into one huge smell that encompassed everything. But Josie kept trying because the naming felt crucial to her, as if success in this one thing meant success everywhere.

Life, she thought finally. Water smells like life. And that satisfied her, felt exactly right. But she knew if she said that in the night it would convey nothing, would feel lifeless and empty and she would be left with her demons. And then it came to her.

The water here smelled like passion, the scent of a summer room after lovemaking, the way sex lingers on bodies, on sheets, in the air. It touches everything, scents it with its own indefinable aroma that smells like nothing else. Josie knew she could close her eyes and think of passion and she would have water to banish the nightmares, this water, this specific night, this exact moment.

Because water might smell differently in the winter or in the daytime, or on another beach. Josie knew she'd try it, smell the water in other places, at other times, but she also knew it would never be as good. She'd learned something here. This memory would be the one she'd return to.

"Josie?" A voice came from the path behind her. She wondered if she'd conjured him up with her dreams of passion.

"How's the baby?" She asked the question quickly, trying to dispel the image of the two of them together that threatened to overwhelm her.

"She's fine. You want to see her picture?"

He sat down on the log beside her. Too close, she thought, he's way too close. But she welcomed the warmth and instead of shifting away from him, she did the opposite. Josie moved closer until their bodies were less than an inch apart.

She heard him sigh and then felt, how she had no idea, his heart begin to beat in time with hers. It felt oddly comforting.

"Josie?" He cleared his throat before going on. "The baby?"

She reached for the photo but touched his hand instead. And when their fingers intertwined she knew he felt the same things she did. Hearts beating together, blood pounding through veins, minds and bodies yearning for each other. Josie took two deep breaths and pulled away.

Too fast.

Too soon.

"What's her name again?" She took the photograph from his hand and waited while he shone his flashlight—she'd forgotten hers—on the picture. "She's so lovely. Mrs. Suzuki must be over the moon."

"I need to talk to you about that." Gray sounded serious. "Mrs. Suzuki won't be back at work for a long time—maybe three months, maybe more. Tonika, that's her daughter, broke her leg so she needs a lot of help with the baby."

Gray smiled hopefully at her.

"Will you be okay without her help?"

Josie couldn't help laughing. "I've worked in places a thousand times worse than the *Sunshine Coast News*. I'll be fine."

She crossed her fingers when she spoke the last sentence. She'd be fine except that she was working with a man whose heart beat in tune with hers. Now that could be a problem.

CHAPTER 16

Josie slept that night without crows, far away from the cityscape which had been haunting her. The soft susurration of the waves on the beach reached into her sleep and banished the worries trapped in her mind like bees in a jar. Marlene disappeared, the wishful counting of the bills in her wallet, even what to say to Gray MacInnis in the morning. All gone, swallowed up by the water.

The morning came too soon, for Josie it always did, but the alarm clock's ringing didn't bother Fred. Josie shut it off immediately. She contemplated rolling over and going back to sleep, gave it serious thought, but decided against it.

She was almost ready to head out the door when the phone rang.

"Hello?"

"Josie? Is that you?"

"Marlene?"

Josie took a deep breath and dropped into the chair by the window. She wasn't ready for this conversation because in order for it to work she had to ignore everything she'd learned about Marlene since she arrived on the Sunshine Coast. She needed to forget Fred and Florence and the sad old lady and the wicked witch. She cleared her throat but Marlene got in before her.

"Why are you staying at that terrible motel? The woman who answered the phone asked me who I was."

Josie knew Marlene hadn't told Mercedes who she was, because Mercedes would have lied and said Josie was out. Or gone home to Toronto. Or something.

"I'm sorry, Marlene. I think it's just policy. You know how hotels are."

"Whatever. You called me?" Her voice sounded like the Marlene Josie had known all her life.

"I did. I wanted to come up and have lunch with you. I need your advice."

Josie was going to pull out all the stops, use everything she'd ever known about her mother. Marlene *loved* to know more than other people.

"About what?"

"I need a hairdresser. Desperately." And that was the truth. "And I need you to tell me where to shop."

"Shawn's the best hairdresser on the peninsula. I go to the city, of course, but Shawn cuts my bangs when I'm in a hurry."

Josie smiled to herself. Of course Marlene wouldn't get her hair cut on the Sunshine Coast. Josie had seen the salons—if you could grace them with that name—in Gibsons. They were all called something like Brenda's Buzz'n'cut or Hair Today, Gone Tomorrow. Marlene would get her hair cut at a place called Antoine's or Opus.

"Where's Shawn?"

"He works out of his house. I'll e-mail you his phone number."

Josie gave her the e-mail address at the *Sunshine Coast News* and then got the heart of the conversation.

"Do you have time for lunch? I miss you." And Josie realized as she said it that it was true. "I haven't talked to you for days."

"Oh, Josie, I can't. Not right now."

"Why not?" Josie couldn't help the little hitch in her voice and knew Marlene would hear it and know exactly what it meant.

"It's complicated, baby. Soon, though, okay? I promise."

"I don't understand." Now she was whining and Marlene hated whiners. But she didn't slap Josie down like she'd expected.

"I know you don't understand. And I'm not sure I do, either. I'm just trying to figure things out. I need some time to myself."

For the first time in her life, Josie heard tears in Marlene's voice and that, more than anything else that had happened since she'd arrived on the Sunshine Coast, scared her.

"Marlene? Are you okay? Please let me come up and see you."

And just like that the wicked witch was back.

"No. I don't need you. I don't want you. I wish you'd go back to Toronto, but if you won't, stay down there in Gibsons. Josie, I don't have time for you right now. Stay away." She slammed the phone down so hard it hurt Josie's ears.

Josie wasn't sure what to think. She had expected the witch but had found a woman just trying to work out how to deal with the changes in her life. Changes she hadn't chosen. She'd found a woman just like her. And that was more than confusing, it was an epiphany.

But it was an epiphany she didn't know what to do with. So Josie did what always worked for her, she carried on.

By the time she'd pulled herself together and stood at the door of the *Sunshine Coast News*, it was eight forty-five. She'd had a quick breakfast at the coffee shop two doors down— not the Way-Inn—and had done so without Fred. He'd headed for the Way-Inn once she told him her plans for breakfast and before she talked to Marlene.

Gray had been watching Josie standing on the sidewalk. He wondered what was keeping her out but he liked observing her when she couldn't see him.

He'd been in the office since dawn doing damage control. The printer was pissed—one day's delay put him on the hot seat—but Gray reminded him of all the money he'd made and would continue to make from the *Sunshine Coast News* and assured him it wouldn't happen again.

A concession in time from the printer, in dollars from Gray, and the paper would be twenty-four hours late instead of three days. He'd read Josie's messages and finished the classifieds, laughing at this month's failed engagement.

By the time Josie showed up, the office was in pretty good shape. The paper had been shipped to the printer and the Monday edition was mapped out. If things went well, he'd have everything back on track by the end of the day.

He'd reread the letter on his screen when he first sat down

and grimaced, thinking of Josie reading it. But after last night, he thought, it really didn't matter if she'd seen it. His feelings were obvious.

No one, not a single person, had read a letter from him since his ex-wife stopped opening the envelopes. He'd written hundreds, but sent none. Maybe they weren't even letters, maybe they were... What? The desperate cries of a lonely, middle-aged man?

Gray laughed out loud at that. "Yeah, maybe that's what they are," he said to his computer. "And maybe you're just wallowing in self-pity. Give yourself a break and lighten up. A beautiful woman will be arriving any minute to spend the day with you. There is absolutely nothing to complain about. Nothing."

He saved the letter and got on with his day, radio blaring, coffee steaming in a cup on his desk. The computer cooperated. Words flowed from his hands without prompting, almost without thought. Everything was easy. One of the perfect days.

Made even more perfect by seeing Josie standing on the sidewalk, outside in the sun.

"I've been thinking that you and Fred might need a place to stay." He spoke to Josie as if she'd always been there and they were in the middle of a conversation. "The Sand Dollar Motel is nice if you're a tourist but you need a kitchen and a balcony and some space of your own. Besides, it's expensive. An apartment would be cheaper."

He noticed the hesitation in her nod. He'd been right, then, she didn't have much money. He'd seen the signs— checking the menu, calculating prices, then ordering the cheapest thing; the careful counting of the few remaining bills in the wallet; the hesitation over the obviously maxed-out credit card.

"I've found the perfect place for you. Cheap as can be because the woman who owns it rents it out mostly so she'll have company."

Josie's face pulled in on itself.

"Not like that. She lives quite a ways out—for Gibsons, I mean. About a fifteen-minute drive. And she works a lot. She likes to have someone else there."

"Sounds okay but I don't have a deposit." She fell silent. He could see how hard it was for her to say that, could see her thoughts race across her face. "And neither does Fred. At least I don't think he does. And I don't have furniture."

"Don't need either. I talked to her this morning and she'd just be happy to have someone there. She'll give you the rest of the month as a move-in allowance and you can pay rent with your end of the month check."

She wasn't sure whether to laugh or cry, Gray could tell, so he rushed in before she could get her defenses in order.

He saw the stubborn set of her jaw, knew what it meant because he had experienced it himself. He'd lived all his life in a state of stubborn self-sufficiency and he couldn't forget how much it had cost him. Sleepless nights, headaches, endless antacids, but it was much more than that.

It had taken Gray years to realize that people liked to help each other. It made them feel needed. So now, whenever he caught himself starting to say, "I'm okay, don't need any help," he tried to think of the person offering that help.

He forced himself to think of how good he felt when he helped someone else and said instead, "Thanks, I really appreciate your help."

But because he knew how helpless Josie must feel, he gave her an out.

"It's Julie Jones. She's been without a tenant for almost six months. She's very picky so it hasn't been easy since Joan and Dave moved back to Alberta. She really needs you. I have the key—she dropped it off this morning—so we can check it out later on. Okay?"

She hesitated but finally said, "Okay."

He took advantage of Josie's hesitation, racing to the door before she could step inside.

"Come on," he said, pulling the door shut behind him. "We've got to get over to the beach." He thrust a camera case into her hands and turned to lock up behind him.

"Doesn't someone need to answer the phones?"

The doubt on her face was undeniable and, rather than upset her, Gray gave away part of the surprise.

"No one will phone for a couple of hours. They'll all be on the beach.

"Hurry up. We don't want to be late."

Josie couldn't believe she'd got to the office without even noticing the people—on bikes, skateboards, Rollerblades, feet, in cars and buses and trucks—heading down the street toward the water.

"What is it?" she asked, as Gray towed her through the crowd like a tugboat guiding a boom.

"It's summer. Well, it's almost the beginning of the tourist season, so we celebrate the summer we won't get to enjoy. We celebrate with our friends and neighbors."

Josie tried to catch her breath. Gray was enough taller than her that she was moving pretty fast to keep up with him.

"Why not do it in the summer?"

"I keep forgetting you haven't spent those months here. Okay, I'll catch you up. But keep moving." He pulled at her hand. "Our population increases by at least fifty percent over the summer. Everyone's busy, frantically busy, because we need to make a year's worth of income in four or five months."

Josie got it. "So you don't have time to socialize?"

"Right. This is a way to wish our friends a safe journey through the months when all we have time to do is pass each other and smile. And even the smile might get lost round about August.

"We're here."

Everyone Josie had seen or met was on the beach plus hundreds she didn't recognize. But they recognized her.

A tall redhead in jeans and cowboy boots came up to her.

"Hi, I'm Rowena Dale. Thanks for taking the message for me."

When she winked, Rowena's age lines appeared but Josie had trouble seeing this vibrant woman as elderly.

"She's not," Gray whispered, reading her mind.

"I want to grow up to be like her." Josie smiled up at Gray. "She's amazing."

"Yes, she is."

Josie saw the rest of that sentence in his eyes, "And so are you," and reached for his hand. She enjoyed every minute she spent with him, because when she was with him, she stopped worrying about Fred and Marlene and her lost luck.

She waved at Fred and Mercedes, Rose and Sam, and dozens of others whose faces she recognized and whose names, if she'd ever known them, were gone.

People danced through the throng, waving and smiling and hugging. There was no agenda, no rule, it appeared to Josie to be a giant love-in. No children cried for their mothers, no teenagers whined about being with their parents, no one complained about the crowd or the weather or sore feet.

After an hour, Josie found a log and plopped herself down on it. A moment later, Fred sat down beside her.

"It's good, isn't it?"

"It is. Dad?"

"Today's not the day, angel. We're got something to talk about but not today, okay?"

"Marlene?"

Fred shrugged then straightened his shoulders. She could almost see the thoughts whirling but she couldn't have anticipated what came out of his mouth.

"Don't be too hard on her. She thought her life would never change."

Josie gulped. "So did I."

"Things change, angel, people change. We have to learn to roll with it."

He patted her hand and headed back into the crowd, looking as if he'd been a part of this place his whole life. He belonged here in a way that Josie wished were possible for her.

"I'll do it," she said out loud. "I can."

"Do what?" Gray asked, coming up behind her.

"Sell my house," she said. "Move," she smiled. "Change my life," she whispered.

After a couple of hours on the beach, Gray steered them back to the office where the rest of the day flew by for both of them. Josie answered the phone and began exploring the contents of the new computer and desk Gray had set up for her. He'd taken Mrs. Suzuki's desk and moved it, exactly as she'd left it, over against the wall.

"Tell everyone that Mrs. Suzuki will be back in a couple of months, I think, but for the mornings only," Gray said in response to Josie's question. "I've told her to take as long as she likes, but that's what she told me and that's what you can tell everyone else."

And that's mostly what Josie did for the morning, tell people where Mrs. Suzuki was and tell them the story of Tonika and Emily and Richard to explain why their paper was late—a whole day late.

Most phone calls began not with a greeting but with, "Where's my paper? It's that damned paperboy again. I know he steals it."

Almost everyone calmed down when they heard what happened and the front counter quickly began to pile up with brightly wrapped baby gifts "For when they get home."

Gray smiled when Josie pointed out he'd have to deliver them.

"I'm used to it," he said. "The paper's the collection point for the Scouts raffle, the United Church white elephant sale and almost everything else at this end of the peninsula. And at least once a month I end up doing one of the delivery routes. Newspaper publishers in small towns do everything."

Josie could vouch for that. In the few hours left in the day the publisher and owner wrote articles, sold ads, laid them out, went to a christening and took photographs, developed them in the dark room at the back, spoke to half a dozen potential customers and advertisers, and helped a small girl with an ad about her lost bike.

And while all this was going on, he kept up a running commentary for Josie's benefit, telling her who the people were, what they liked and disliked, how to deal with the difficult ones and which ones to simply pass along to him.

She watched him sit down to coffee first with the mayor, then Ed from the Esso station, and a straight-backed elderly woman from the apartment block two streets over. He had time for everybody.

It didn't seem to matter how busy he was, he never acted rushed, never looked or sounded impatient. He concentrated just as hard on his conversation about Diana Gabaldon and her sex scenes—were they maybe a little too much? asked the old ladies with a blush—as he did talking to the mayor about the water supply and spring run-off.

And Josie, without the help of Mrs. Suzuki, figured out precisely what her job really was: to keep the paper running while Gray MacInnis dealt with all those people. So she kept the coffeepot filled and the cups clean, she answered the phone and quickly felt confident enough to take and input ads. She figured out the billing system and the banking. The big picture gradually came into focus.

Josie knew it would take weeks to really understand the place, but by the end of the day she knew enough to satisfy the customers.

"Gray? Josie?"

And the most beautiful woman in the world appeared at the door. Josie took a closer look at Julie than had been possible in the dark bar the night before. Julie Jones might have been any age between twenty-five and thirty-five but it didn't matter. She had long dark hair tied back in a braid hanging to her waist. Her olive skin glowed with health and her dark eyes reflected light so it looked to Josie like they shone in the sun. Her smile, when she saw them, was as big and bright as the harvest moon. Josie couldn't help it. She stared. The woman laughed.

CHAPTER 17

Julie Jones had had a lifetime to get used to the eyes staring at her. She'd won a national "most beautiful baby" contest and she'd only improved over the years. But the admiration hadn't even come close to spoiling her—she wasn't Mercedes's daughter for nothing. Julie was as down to earth and as practical as a potato.

She knew people liked to see her smile so she smiled a lot. She knew people—men, women and children—liked to look at her, so she learned to control her shyness and her blushes. She knew people would do almost anything for her so she turned that desire toward a good cause.

Julie Jones could do anything. She could have anything.

Except the only thing she'd ever truly wanted. Ron. From the first minute she'd seen him talking to a lost child on the beach she'd wanted him.

Oh, she'd fallen into lust a few times before Ron, but this was different. It was forever. She knew that because she'd been watching him for almost three years and he'd not said more than ten sentences to her in all that time. Ignoring someone in Gibsons wasn't easy; he'd had to work really hard to keep it up.

Julie Jones remembered every word he'd said to her, every

single time she'd seen him. She'd memorized the tip of his hat and the slow "ma'am" if he passed her on the street. And she'd dreamed for months about the time he'd bid for Aska at the Shelter Ball and the way their hands touched when she passed him the dog in exchange for his check.

Julie had cried a whole oceanful of tears over Ron, but she hadn't given up. She couldn't. He was the man for her. If not Ron, then no one. She was slowly getting accustomed to the idea of ending up like her mother and Mrs. Suzuki—old and alone—but she was mightily pissed off that she couldn't have him for at least a little while before she lost him.

She squared her shoulders and ignored the shaft of envy that hit when she saw Gray MacInnis look at Josie MacInnis.

"You look like your mother," Josie said. "I see the resemblance now I see you in the sunlight."

"Isn't my mother a doll? I think I'm the luckiest woman alive having her for a mom. So, anyway, I need to put an ad in the paper. I've got to find a volunteer to help me with planning the Shelter Ball."

Josie, like all the residents of Gibsons who'd acquired pets they weren't sure they wanted, couldn't resist Julie Jones.

"I'll help." And just like that, Josie acquired one more tie to the Sunshine Coast.

Julie's smile showed her pure delight.

"Why don't you go now?" Gray said, breaking in on the smile fest. "Go look at the apartment. We're done for the day."

"I'll drive," Julie smiled at Josie. "I have to come back for dinner anyway. You can leave your car here and I'll drop you off on my way to Mom's."

The apartment was much more than Josie had expected. The top floor of a big old farmhouse, it looked out over acres of gnarled fruit trees down to the ocean. It only had one bedroom, but a small alcove contained a single bed and dresser. Josie could sleep there for now while Fred had the bedroom.

The furniture was worn but comfortable and clean. There were vases of wildflowers on the kitchen and coffee tables and the windows were open. It smelled like spring.

"Do you like it? Sorry, I know I said I'd be quiet but I'd like to have you here. Really. And Fred for as long as he's staying. I'm not scared or lonely. It's not that. It just feels more homey to have someone else around. I grew up in a motel, always someone buzzing in the middle of the night, the phone ringing, the cleaners singing and arguing and laughing, the tourists asking for directions. Always something going on. Guess I'm used to it."

She looked at Josie. "Please take it. I'd be so happy."

"It's exactly what I wanted," Josie said. "When can we move in?"

When Josie got back to the Sand Dollar she felt she'd accomplished something, had a productive day in a way she hadn't done since she lost her luck. Her neck felt stiff, her eyes gritty, even her feet hurt, but none of those things mattered. She felt great.

She burst into Fred's room through the connecting door. "Fred. Fred. I had a great day. Let's go…"

No Fred. And not just no Fred, but no sign of him either.

No jacket hanging over the back of a chair, no dirty socks on the floor by the bed, no half-read newspaper on the table.

"Shit."

Josie sat down on the chair against the wall and carefully scanned the room. No Fred. No remnants of his presence.

"Shit. Shit. Shit. Oh Fred, not now."

She knew where he'd gone. There was nowhere else for him to go. But she wished he'd waited until she got home from work. He left because he didn't want her to change his mind— she knew that. He'd still go, she knew that, too. But he'd been unhappy about Josie and her misgivings and perhaps he'd spent too much of his life being sad to willfully choose it again.

She wondered where he'd put the letter. He wouldn't worry her by leaving without telling her why he had to go. She wandered around the room, touching the surface of the table, smoothing out the bedspread, opening the drawers in the dresser and the bedside table. No note. She checked the bathroom. Nothing there either.

Josie's room had been cleaned, as it was every morning although the process did little to obscure the clutter Josie brought with her. Books and papers and stuff on every flat surface. There wasn't a note. She checked. And then checked again.

"He's left it with Mercedes. That makes perfect sense. He thought it would get lost in the mess."

But Mercedes simply looked puzzled when Josie asked about it.

"I didn't see him go. Are you sure?"

Josie nodded, following behind as Mercedes hurried down to Fred's unit. She did the same search Josie had done with the exact same result.

"Do you mind?" A quick look at Josie for confirmation— even though it was her motel and she'd already been in the room that morning to check on the cleaners—and then into Josie's room.

Still nothing, although Josie felt a moment of anticipation hoping Mercedes might spot something she'd missed. A note saying, "I've gone to stay with Jim in Pender Harbour for a couple of days. Here's his number." Or Vancouver. Some indication that he'd gone anywhere but back to Florence.

When Mercedes finally stopped searching and turned to Josie, her face looked like Josie felt. Worried, pissed-off and maybe just a little scared.

"There isn't one, is there?" asked Josie.

"Nope."

"So now what?"

"Now we wait for all hell to break loose. We'll hear it, even down here we'll hear it."

Josie tried a smile but it didn't work very well, wavering on her face like a brand-new ballet student en pointe.

"I'll phone Florence."

Mercedes didn't comment, just looked out the window at the fading sunlight.

When she turned, Josie was shocked at the anger on Mercedes's face. Although she didn't know her well, Josie was sure this wasn't a normal expression. She looked, Josie thought as

Fred had thought earlier, like justice personified, like an avenging angel, like nothing or no one could stop her.

Josie stepped back, an involuntary reflex. She raised her hands to her chest.

"Mercedes? You're scaring me."

The goddess mask broke.

"Hell, honey, I'm sorry. I guess you can tell I'm mad, huh? I really thought he'd listen to me and stay put while we figured something out. But I should have known he'd say okay to placate me and then do whatever he was going to do anyway. I know your dad well enough to know he always tells you exactly what you want to hear."

"He does?" Josie was offended by this image of Fred.

"Oh, yeah. I bet he never once in all those years said as much as boo to your mama."

"Once. He did once. But it didn't work out very well."

Mercedes laughed. "Hell, Josie, you don't have to tell me that. So what do we do now?"

"I'll phone Florence and then we'll decide."

The phone rang six times before a frail voice answered.

"Hello?"

"Florence. It's Josie. Are you okay?"

"I'm waiting to hear from Fred. He hasn't called yet today."

Josie's heart slammed into her ribs. Neither here nor there.

Josie felt stupid, but she asked the obvious question anyway. "Fred's not there with you?"

"No. And he hasn't phoned."

The frailty had left Florence's voice. It was replaced with fear and a taste of anger.

"I don't know. He's not here…"

"Ask Mercedes," Florence ordered. "She'll know where he is."

"Mercedes?" Josie turned to her across the room. "Florence says you'll know where he is."

Mercedes scrunched up her face. "Let me think about it. Maybe…"

"Josie?" Florence interrupted. "He's not up here. I can see Marlene. She's on her way out to dinner with Bert so Fred's definitely not with her."

Bert? Who in the hell was Bert? Five minutes ago, Josie couldn't have imagined being more confused and put out than she was, but this news put her over the edge. She ignored the new player and asked, "What do we do?"

"Wait, I guess. He's probably gone off with a friend. We'd know if something was wrong so we have to assume he's okay."

The words were brave but Florence's voice had tightened into a thin almost-wail.

"Shall I come up there?" Josie wanted something to do, anything that might take her mind off the Bert news.

"No," said Florence. "Stay there. Who knows where he'll turn up?"

Before Josie could hang up the phone Mercedes spoke.

"He's with Joseph on the beach. Give me the phone." And she grabbed it out of Josie's hand.

"Florence, it's me, Mercedes. I know where he is. He's at Joseph's."

Josie heard Florence's sigh of relief all the way from Sechelt and then heard her say, "Of course he is. Where else could he be?"

Josie heard the further murmur of a voice from the phone but could no longer hear the words.

Mercedes said, "No problem. I'll run down there now and make sure he's there." A pause. "I'll call you as soon as I get back. Bye."

"Joseph?" Josie asked.

"He's a friend of Fred's. They play records and chess together. He'll be fine there. And it's cheaper than the Sand Dollar."

Josie shook her head. There was so much she didn't know, so much she'd refused to see. She picked up the Ganesh from the windowsill.

"Maybe you're today's answer. Creator and solver of problems. Just like me. I create 'em and then I solve 'em."

She rubbed the dusty brass with her fingertips. It still held some warmth from the sun beating in the window and Josie enjoyed the feeling for a moment.

"There's nothing for it," she whispered. "I'm just going to carry on."

Three boxes and two suitcases later, she was once again at Mercedes's door.

"I'm off now," she said.

"Drive carefully. That little road is full of potholes." Mercedes handed her a grocery bag. "Here's some stuff to get you started."

"Thanks, Mercedes. You'll call me?"

"Of course."

Josie shrugged off the guilt she felt at leaving the motel

without Fred and drove out to her new apartment. It was even more perfect than she remembered. The trees in the orchard were crowned with light from the setting sun—reds and oranges and pinks and all right outside her window.

Julie appeared from the porch. "Let me give you a hand."

"I hardly have anything," Josie replied. "When I left Toronto I wasn't planning on staying. I definitely didn't plan on a job and an apartment."

"No? Well, you got them, and good ones, too. It must be fun working at the paper." Julie's voice faltered a little.

"Did you want that job?" Josie was quite prepared to give it up; it might make her life less complicated.

"No, no. It's just that…"

"What?"

"Oh, come on down to my place once you get settled and I'll tell you. It's a long and boring and stupid story."

Julie pulled a bottle of wine from the fridge and put a plate of cheese and crackers on the table. A box of chocolates completed the array.

"Sit," she said. "Drink. You'll need it if you want to listen to *this* story."

"It started out with the two problems I've had since I was a kid. My mother's great, but she's a legend in this town and that makes it tough to be her daughter. Everyone expects me to be as smart and funny and know everyone and everything exactly the way she does. And I don't.

"I love dogs and cats and birds and pigs and goats better than most people. I understand animals and I don't really get people."

Josie reached for another chocolate and filled both their glasses. She said, "I bet I can guess the other problem. You're so beautiful, people expect you to be perfect. And because they expect you to be perfect, they stay away in droves."

Julie's blue eyes widened until Josie could see the whites all the way around. Her mouth dropped open and her nostrils flared. And despite all that, she was still beautiful.

"How'd you know?" Julie slapped her hand across her mouth. "Ohmigod, Josie, I'm sorry. I didn't mean to say…"

"You didn't mean to say that I wouldn't understand because I'm not beautiful? Please. If it weren't for this damn haircut, I'd be just as gorgeous as you are."

Josie giggled. "Okay, okay, maybe not quite as gorgeous, but pretty damn close."

Julie reached over and hugged her. "No, really, you are beautiful. You're vivacious and funny and smart, and people like you. It's obvious."

"Yeah, they like me because I give them something to talk about. Weeping. Gray MacInnis. Florence and Fred and Marlene. I'm a one-woman gossip column. *And* all my luck is bad luck."

"You have bad luck? I don't think so. You found a great job, you found a fabulous apartment with cheap rent, a perfect landlord…" she waved her arms around the room and then pointed at herself "…a new friend, and a lover. I don't think a woman could get luckier than that."

Julie's eyes filled with tears. "You've got one problem. Your mom and dad. But them splitting up won't ruin the rest of your life. You're lucky."

Josie got up and headed for the fridge. "I'll get another bottle," she said. "We're going to need it."

She sat back down and passed Julie the chocolates. "Okay," she said, pouring more wine into their glasses. "You have two problems. You're too beautiful and you're not your mother. Got that. But that's not all. It has to be a man."

Josie curled her feet under her and leaned against the back of the couch. "I'm ready. Just don't tell me it's Gray, okay? That's all I ask."

Julie laughed. "I like Gray. He's a great guy, but it's not him. No, it's much more complicated than that."

She pulled a pillow to her chest and clutched it tight. "Have you met the sergeant? The RCMP officer? He drove you and Fred home from the Way-Inn?"

Josie thought about it for a minute. "Does sitting in the back of the squad car trying desperately not to throw up all over the seat count as an introduction? I don't even remember what he looks like. It is a man, right?"

Julie laughed again. "Yeah, Ron is definitely and completely a man. And he's not interested in me at all." Her eyes filled with tears again.

"Hang on, hang on." Josie tried to leap from the couch but she'd had just enough wine that leaping didn't work. She carefully placed her feet under her and levered herself up from the cushions. "I'll be right back, wait here." She opened each of the three doors leading off the living room looking for the bathroom and some tissue. Of course it was the third door she tried.

Josie grabbed the box of tissue from the back of the toilet, and then hunted under the sink for another one just in case.

"Here," she said, plunking the two boxes on the coffee table. "Cry your heart out. I bet you're the kind of woman who looks even more beautiful when she cries. And that's totally going to piss me off. Me, I turn all red and blotchy and then I can't breathe and my ears start to ache."

Julie hiccupped a bit and the tears stopped. "I've spent way too much time over the past three years crying over that man. It stops right here." She straightened herself up and sniffed a couple of time. "No more tears."

Josie smiled at her. Julie Jones was kidding herself if she thought she wasn't going to cry over unrequited love. But Josie was having a lot of trouble imagining that her love really was unrequited. Julie Jones? Drop-dead gorgeous sweet Julie Jones?

"Tell me the rest of it," she said. "I'm sure we can come up with something."

"He won't talk to me. I see him on the street, he nods and tips his hat. He calls me ma'am."

Josie giggled and after a little while, Julie joined her.

"He calls you ma'am? He calls *you* ma'am? Whew. That's serious."

"I know, that's what I'm trying to tell you. He has to be at most five years older than me, and he calls me ma'am. What am I going to do?"

"What have you done? You must have tried something. Dropping into the station? Asking him out for a coffee? Stopping by his house on a fundraising drive? Come on, tell me what you've tried so far."

Julie looked sheepish.

"You haven't tried anything? Not one single thing?"

Julie shrugged her shoulders and shook her head.

"Julie Jones, I'm ashamed of you. You just finish telling me that your problem is that people are scared of you and you're surprised that he hasn't talked to you? Did your mother teach you nothing?"

Josie drank some more wine and popped two crackers loaded with cheese into her mouth. She spit the crackers back out into her hand.

"Wait," she said, "wait just a minute. I didn't learn anything from my mother. I learned everything I know from other women."

She looked across at Julie, her hair hanging into her eyes and her shoulders slumped.

"You don't have any girlfriends, do you?" Josie smacked herself on the forehead. "Of course you don't. I'm going to have to teach you everything."

Josie settled back into the couch and prepared to transmit all the things she'd learned. She would tell Julie everything: how to plant asparagus, how to know true love when you saw it, how to placate a jealous spouse. *Finally*, Josie thought, *I've made it. I'm one of those bright interesting women who knows all the important stuff*.

"You know you're going to have to do the work, don't you? You're going to have to ask him out."

"Uh-uh. Not me, no way. I can't ask him out."

Josie cajoled and pleaded and eventually threatened, but nothing worked. Julie was too scared to try anything.

"I'm stubborner than you are scared, Ms. Jones. You *will* ask Ron out. Maybe not this week, but soon."

Josie pulled the throw off the back of the couch and placed it over Julie.

"I'll see you tomorrow, okay? We'll talk more then."

Josie stumbled up the stairs to her apartment knowing she'd found a best friend. She looked at the boxes and suitcases piled in the living room, shrugged, poured herself a glass of water and fell onto the sofa. She'd sleep here tonight.

The moon above the orchard lit up the room and every time Josie opened her eyes she couldn't help but smile. At the trees and the window, at the curtains and tables, at the thought of having her own space.

She even smiled thinking of Julie and Ron. What man wouldn't love Julie Jones? Beautiful. Smart. Funny. Caring. Josie was going to figure out a way to knock some sense into his head come hell or high water. And she'd didn't give a hoot if he was a cop.

The next morning was hell, combining a slight hangover, worry about Fred and the stress of a new job. Not to mention the buzz she got from being in the same room as Gray.

Josie checked in with Mercedes.

"Yes, he's with Joseph and no, he's not going back up to Sechelt or moving in with you. He likes it on the beach."

And then she checked in with Florence. All three of them were angry, so the conversations went like this—

Florence: "Why isn't he staying with Josie? There's no damn phone at Joseph's."

Mercedes: "He's such an asshole."

Josie: "I'm going to kill him when he gets back."

Even though she knew where he was, she worried. She paced when she wasn't on the phone. Gray had told her early in the day that the only quiet days at the *Sunshine Coast News* were the days the paper was delivered.

"So enjoy it," he said. "It never lasts long."

Later that afternoon, if Josie'd had long fingernails they would have been bitten right down to the quick. As it was, she had little red holes around each of her nails where her teeth had ripped at her cuticles, pulling the skin from the nail. And then doing it again until the skin was down to blood.

Gray couldn't stand it any longer. Something had been bothering Josie all day and he was going to have to call her on it.

"Josie? What's wrong?"

He stood over her desk, the light at his back so he could see her face. He wasn't a reporter for nothing.

"I'm fine."

"No, you're not. Come on, tell me what's going on. Maybe I can help you."

She caved in much sooner than he'd expected. Gray thought that might be a good sign; maybe she'd started to trust him, even like him.

"What is it?" he repeated.

"It's Fred. He's missing."

Gray burst out laughing and then laughed even harder at the pissed-off expression on Josie's face.

"Fred's not missing. I'll bet you a hundred bucks he's at Joseph's."

"Yeah, yeah, so Mercedes says. Who's Joseph?"

"He lives on the beach. Come on." He pulled her to her feet. "Get your coat and we'll go find him."

Fred and Joseph sat on the bench facing the ocean. They hadn't said much over the past two days; not much more than "Pass the butter," and "Your move." That was the beauty of the time he spent with Joseph, Fred thought.

Joseph expected nothing from him. He didn't need talk or consolation or love or pity. All he ever wanted from Fred (if *want* wasn't too strong a word for Joseph's feelings) was companionship.

They ate the canned soup and crackers Fred brought with him. They used huge bowls and had a can each. They drank coffee and played chess. Fred always lost, though not by much. He was convinced if he kept playing, he'd start to win. Eventually. But he didn't care one way or the other. It was peaceful here on the beach, peaceful and stress-free. But he could see that was about to change.

He braced himself.

"Fred," Gray said. "It's time to go home."

Josie said, "Yeah. You need to phone Florence. She's not very happy with you right now."

CHAPTER 18

Josie couldn't believe she was heading into the weekend and Fred had disappeared again—back at Joseph's obviously. He'd refused to stay at her apartment for almost a week now. She was glad she'd missed his phone call to Florence. Josie was on Florence's side, but even so, she wasn't sure she could have listened while Florence tore a strip off him, even if he did deserve it.

Josie was settling into her new life, busy at work and spending time with Julie in the evenings. And every couple of days, she and Gray stopped at the Way-Inn for a drink after work. Even after spending the whole day in the office with him, she had plenty of things to say to him.

She heard more about Gray's father and his ex-wife. He told her about the letters and she couldn't help a little shiver of jealousy.

"Can I read them?"

"Are you kidding? They're bad writing and they're embarrassing." His face reddened. "Even I can't read them."

"But I want to." When Josie said that, she realized it was true. "I want to know who you were back then."

"I was someone else," he said decisively. "Just like you were."

Josie thought about that for a minute and then told him about losing her luck.

"See what I mean? We're both different people and if we'd met ten years ago—" he smiled and reached across the table for her hand "—we probably wouldn't even have liked each other."

Josie laughed. "Maybe. But I still want to read the letters."

"No." But his voice was gentle as he said it. "I'm not that man anymore."

"You're right," Josie said after a moment's contemplation. "I don't want to go backward, either. I'm just starting to like the new me."

Josie phoned Mercedes from the office during the afternoon lull, after the coffee drinkers were gone and before the last-minute ad customers arrived on their way home from work.

"Have you talked to him?"

"Nope. And no one else has seen him, not at the beach or at the club or on the street. I know he was there until a couple of nights ago, but I think he might have left."

"Shit."

"Yeah. He really *is* a shit. It's not like Fred to worry people."

"It's not like Fred to do any of the things he's done recently."

Josie heard the anger creeping into her voice and didn't even try to hide it. Worry made her madder than almost anything else. And she was worried, couldn't even deny it anymore.

"Where in the hell is he?"

"He's with Florence," Mercedes said. "Where else would he be? A pause. "Josie, I know you don't want to hear this but… Fred's happier with Florence than he's ever been in his life. Despite the threat of Marlene, without money or a job or any of the things he thought he wanted, even without you, he's happy with her. He wants to be with her more than anything. I've seen it."

Josie's eyes teared up and she quickly turned to face the wall so Gray wouldn't spot them. Once in a while she caught him watching her, waiting, she thought, for the tears to start. He'd been attracted to that weeping woman.

"I've seen it, too. Fred's a different man and I'm glad. But he could phone. If I don't hear from him today, I'm going up there tomorrow. I have to see Marlene anyway."

Josie felt Mercedes stiffen, even across the distance, through the telephone. She saw her face evolve into the goddess of justice mask and shivered a little at the rage Mercedes emitted. Josie waited for the pronouncement.

"You don't know how dangerous Marlene is. If you interfere now, you may do untold damage."

Josie cringed, but she persisted.

"I know she's scary. But she's my mother. She won't hurt me." Josie wasn't a hundred percent certain about this but after the phone conversation she felt more confident so she said it anyway. "And I'll be careful."

"Not careful enough. Not ever careful enough. Not with Marlene."

"I'm going."

Josie needed to see Marlene. She wanted to know about this Bert guy even though she knew Marlene well enough to know that a new more expensive model would never make up for the old broken one. Marlene never forgot and never forgave. She held a grudge like nobody's business.

Josie still remembered the month she'd spent in purgatory after she broke Marlene's favorite casserole dish taking it out of the dishwasher. Josie spent all of her allowance to buy a new and better one but, although it might have shortened the punishment, it certainly didn't eliminate it.

Josie knew if she didn't see Marlene this weekend, she might never go.

It had happened to her once before. Just after college she'd made friends with a coworker, a man, who had AIDS. It was as if they'd been separated at birth somehow—they laughed and cried at the same things, loved the same movies and books, craved the same foods at the same time.

Josie watched as Dennis got sicker. She visited him in the hospital every single day, but when his parents took him home to die she put off a visit. Just one day, she said, I'll go tomorrow. And then another day. Until a week passed and then it was too late.

She didn't go to the funeral because she was so ashamed of her behavior she felt she didn't deserve to be there. She didn't go, even though his mother called to ask her. She didn't go because she was punishing herself for deserting him at the exact time he needed her most.

Josie wouldn't let that happen again. Marlene might be scary, she might even be evil, but she was still Josie's mother. And Josie owed her everything. Life was *everything*, wasn't it?

Okay, Josie owed her respect and courtesy and… Damn it, Josie was going to confront Marlene for Fred, because she'd never before appreciated the sacrifices he'd made by staying with Marlene, trying to be a buffer between them, staying until it was almost too late to save himself.

Saturday morning she'd get in the car before she had time to think about it and she'd drive straight to Sechelt, park the car in the parking lot, and walk right up to Marlene's door. And she wouldn't take no for an answer, either. She was going to sit down with Marlene and talk about Fred.

She'd tell Marlene she was still a beautiful, youthful woman—which she was, at least most of the time. Josie tried to forget the fury who'd met her at the door the other morning. She'd lie if she had to.

"Fred isn't worth it," she'd say. "You're too good for him. Besides..." she'd be thinking of all the Berts over the years as she said it "...there's plenty of fish in the sea."

And only part of that would be a lie. Marlene was beautiful and funny and smart. She'd always had other men around her and now she seemed to have this Bert guy. Josie grew up with dozens of well-off, good-looking uncles. Marlene flaunted them in the same way she did new clothes or new drapes for the living room.

Josie sighed, slightly too loudly.

"Josie, are you okay?" Gray's eyebrows met in the middle, and his lips pouted, turning on his concerned look.

"I'm fine."

Gray had watched Josie as she talked to Mercedes. He'd catalogued the emotions crossing her face. She was so easy to read: concern, sorrow, anger, fear, stubbornness. He'd really gotten to know that last expression. Josie was as stubborn as a two-ton boulder. If she didn't want to move, nobody was going to make her.

The more time Gray spent with Josie, the more he wanted her. And he knew his feelings were reciprocated. It wasn't lust, though that was part of it. How could he help it? She was gorgeous, and when she laughed, he wanted to grab her in his arms and kiss her until she couldn't laugh anymore. She was the one, the woman he'd dreamed of for most of his life.

The funny thing was that she wasn't at all like his dreams. She was as stubborn as all get out; he dreamed of someone he could look after. She had all sorts of problems, none of which he could solve, which sort of canceled out the whole knight in shining armor thing. She was smart and funny and right now she was scared to death and she wouldn't let him do anything to help her.

Oh, she let him distract her from her problems and her fear, let him entertain her, but he wasn't allowed to help. It didn't matter. He knew she was the one.

He knew it so deeply his bones ached from the knowing. He felt them begin to vibrate when she walked in, every single one of them humming in her presence. The first day he spent half his time in the bathroom in front of the mirror, checking to see if the vibration showed. It didn't. Or at least he didn't think so. But it wouldn't stop, not while Josie was around.

It felt like effervescence in his bones, but Gray didn't compare it to champagne. It hurt too much for that. Maybe Alka-Seltzer, working away in his bones…little sharp bubbles scouring out his marrow. By the end of each day he ached so badly he worried he might be coming down with the flu. It was easier to blame it on that than on love. But Gray couldn't fool himself. The vibration began when Josie walked in and stopped when she left. So he asked again.

"Are you okay?"

Josie looked up at him. He could see the words *I'm fine* forming on her lips and he called to whatever power bound them together to stop her from saying them. He willed her to tell him the truth.

"No, I'm not," she said, and he nearly collapsed in relief.

"Come on," he said. "It's Friday and I have a bottle of wine in the fridge. We'll close up early."

He watched the tiny lines appear across her forehead and beside her lips. He spoke before she had a chance to say no.

"It's sunny and almost warm enough to sit on the beach for an hour. If we wait, the sun'll be down or it'll rain or the wind will be too cold. In the spring you have to take advantage of these moments. Here."

He thrust a blanket from the back room into Josie's arms—he kept it there for the babies. Parents sometimes left them for him to watch over when they couldn't find a sitter and had an appointment they couldn't miss. He grabbed the wine and two glasses from the cupboard beside the sink. It held dozens of cheap wineglasses, enough to last out his lifetime. The previous owner loved to throw parties.

"I bought two hundred glasses," he'd told Gray when he first showed the huge cupboard sparkling and full. "What if everyone I invited came? Wouldn't want to run out, now would I?"

And Gray had nodded and put the glasses down to eccentricity. He took a few home but this was the first time he wasn't just laughing at John when he thought of them. "Thanks, John," he whispered. "You were right."

"I've got another blanket in the car. We can wrap them around our shoulders if it's too cold on the beach."

He thought she might bolt when he stopped to lock the office door, or on the walk across the street to the car, but she stuck with him, the blanket clasped against her chest.

Gray felt a ping in his abdomen, the ping he associated with his soul and he panicked. His heart raced, his face and throat and neck flushed. His breathing stopped and not just for a moment. Or at least it felt that way. It had never happened this way before, never happened without the writing. But there it was. A tiny piece of what was left of his soul detached and left him for Josie.

She flinched and he knew, without question or hesitation, that she now held a piece of him. And she'd felt it happen. He thought of the boxes in his living room and the unnecessary and excessive care he'd taken with them lest he finally lose his soul completely.

Gray smiled at Josie as he started the car. "It regenerated, you know. I'm not sure you can lose it, not anymore. I think it just keeps growing."

He turned his head to her, just for a moment, though he didn't need to do that to see the bewilderment on her face.

"Don't worry, I'm not crazy. Just figured something out that's been bothering me for a while."

He chatted about work and Julie and the Shelter Ball and

the sergeant the rest of the short drive to the beach. He avoided mention of Fred or Marlene—it was obvious what was worrying her and he wanted to give the subject his full attention once they sat down.

A glass of wine wouldn't hurt, either. He sat Josie down on a log with a blanket around her shoulders and one of the glasses in her hand. He poured the wine then moved to the far end of the log. He watched her relax as he moved away from her.

"Tell me," he said, speaking not only to Josie but also to the part of him now residing inside her. "Tell me what's up."

"I have to see Marlene tomorrow. And I don't want to. I don't know… You won't believe this, it sounds stupid, but she scares me. She has two, not just personalities, but two bodies. And I don't know which one I'll find when I get there."

"Do they both scare you?"

"Yes. No. I don't know. What scares me is I don't know what to expect. She doesn't want to see me and she'll be angry when I show up. Not just because of that, but she's sure to know…" Her voice faded away.

Gray took a sip of his wine. Should he let on that he knew? Sure. Why not? He had nothing to lose. She didn't respond to his overtures, so what did it matter if she got mad at him? And she needed to talk about it, that was obvious.

"What? That Fred might have gone back to Florence when you promised to keep him away?"

Josie's head whipped around to glare at him.

"This is the second time he's disappeared, but at least this time he's not with Joseph. So he must be with Florence. I checked Joseph's first thing."

"You didn't call Florence, did you?" he asked.

"No. I'm hoping…"

Gray laughed. "You're hoping what? That Florence had enough sense to send Fred away if he showed up at her door? Or that your father had enough sense to stay hidden if he went back up to Sechelt?

"Josie, you know neither of them is capable of doing the sensible thing. They're too much in love."

Josie glared at him again.

"Whoa." He grinned. "Everyone knows about Fred and Florence and the deal, not just me. Rose told me the other night."

"But only Marlene and Florence and I…"

"Nope. You told Fred that you guys had made a deal. And Fred told Mercedes and Mercedes told Rose, and now everyone knows." He laughed, then continued. "This is Gibsons, remember? Not Toronto. Everyone knows everyone else and gossip about love travels faster than news of a lottery win. I'd be surprised if Marlene didn't hear it almost as soon as Fred did."

"God. And I tried so hard to keep my part of the deal. Keep Fred here even if I couldn't keep the deal a secret. I might as well not have bothered."

"No, I think you were right to keep your end of the bargain. That way, the consequences can't be laid at your door. You'll have a clear conscience."

"I'll have a clear conscience and Marlene's going to tear Fred and Florence apart. She's going to make Fred come home so she can spend the rest of her life punishing him, making him as miserable as it is possible to be. And she'll figure out a way to ruin Florence's life, too. I tried to hold her back until I thought of a solution that would please everybody but I guess that was wishful thinking."

The wind picked up, blowing the scent of salt and seaweed and damp sand in their faces. Josie held out her glass and wrapped the blanket tighter around her shoulders.

"Too cold? Do you want to go home?"

"No, I love the smell. I'm from Ontario and it smells nothing like this. I don't think I ever noticed that water had a smell except when it was overflowing with sewage after a storm. And that wasn't water, was it?"

He knew she didn't expect an answer but he gave her one anyway. "I know what you mean. I grew up in the Kootenays—about as far away as you can get from the ocean in B.C.—but every once in a while, when the wind blew hard from the west, I could smell something in the air. I thought it meant escape or adventure or the call of the wild." He laughed. "When I moved to the coast I found out it was the ocean. So I guess it was all of those things. I wouldn't live anywhere else, not now."

Josie looked at Gray, the faded Hudson Bay blanket draped over his shoulders. He looked like a derelict, one of the street people in Toronto. His hair and beard fared badly in the wind, as if someone had tugged each hair away from his head and then just left them there in a tangled mess. He had spots of color high on his cheeks and his eyes were half-shut against the blowing sand.

She should find him disgusting, Josie thought, instead his

dishevelment made her comfortable. And besides, she probably looked just as bad. She felt her hair flying around her head, the grains of sand scouring her face and her scalp, and amended that. She looked worse; and she didn't care.

"When I came out here, I came to convince Fred and Marlene to get back together. I thought they'd had a fight and Marlene had got on her high horse and all it would take to put things right was for me to appear. Josie their very best friend. Josie the savior."

She stayed silent for a moment, then shrugged. "It all seemed so simple when I was driving across the country. But as soon as I saw Fred and Florence together I knew."

Gray poured the last of wine into the glasses while he mulled over his response.

"Anyone who saw the two of them together would know that. When it first happened, people would come into the paper with this look on their faces, as if they'd just seen a puppy or a kitten or a perfect sunset and I'd ask them what had made them so happy. I just ran into Fred Harris, they'd say. Or I saw Florence at the grocery store. Everyone would say the same thing, just that and nothing more. You can't tamper with that kind of love."

Josie drank her wine and watched as the sun disappeared beneath the island and the last colors of the day began to fade from the water. She'd felt that happiness too, the one time she'd seen them together, but she'd forgotten or misplaced it in her worry over what Marlene was going to do.

The deal wouldn't work because there was no way on earth that, having found each other, they would be able to stay apart.

"When I saw Marlene, when I knew her for who she truly was, not the person I'd all my life imagined her to be, I got scared. Because I'd never seen her out of control. I didn't know she could be. And her real self was a stranger, a mad old woman who might be capable of anything and wouldn't care at all about the consequences.

"She's going to do something, probably is already doing it. And I have to go up there and try and stop her. It won't work. She's never listened to me and she won't now, but I have to try. Because I don't know what else to do."

"Do you want me to come with you? Maybe an outsider…"

"No. Thanks, but no. I have to do this on my own." She stood up and felt the wine flow into her knees and her head. "I should go home now. I want to get an early start."

Josie raced home, tired and happy and worried at the same time. Julie was waiting for her on the front porch, clutching a bottle of champagne.

She actually squealed when Josie pulled up, a high-pitched squeal of pure joy. Josie couldn't help herself. She squealed right back, a teenage ritual she'd never before indulged in. It felt good.

Julie Jones grabbed her hands and spun her around the porch, laughing and crying at the same time.

"He loves me. He loves me. I can't believe it. He loves me. He has forever."

Josie sat Julie back down on the steps and poured the champagne into the waiting glasses.

"Tell me," she said.

Julie smiled her perfect smile. "You'll never believe it," she said.

* * *

It had been a truly miserable day. The lab she'd found on the beach the night before had died in her arms and the shelter rent was due in a week. She'd make it, she always did, but it never seemed to get any easier.

Julie Jones tidied up, shed a few more tears and then did the one thing she usually avoided like the plague; she drove to the Way-Inn, sat herself down in the dark back booth and ordered herself a bottle of wine.

"Nothing to eat," she said, lying to Rose. "I had a big lunch."

She felt Rose watching her as she sipped the wine. Rose was waiting. Josie knew she was waiting to see if Julie was okay. Julie watched her back, wondering if Rose would phone her mother, but Mercedes didn't show up. Ron did.

He sat down across the table from her, his gorgeous body covered in jeans and a T-shirt.

"Not on duty tonight?" She fought to keep her voice steady.

"Nope," he said, pouring himself a glass of *her* wine.

"Hey, I paid for that and I'm going to drink every drop of it."

"We'll order another bottle." He waved at Rose.

Julie nodded. It was all she could manage.

"Julie." He reached across the table and took her hand. "Are you okay? Rose called me."

Julie laughed, a peel of bliss. "And I was worried about her calling my mother."

"You'd rather have her?"

She grabbed at his hand. This was her chance and she wasn't going to waste it.

"There's no one I'd rather have than you."

She waited for the fear to show up in his eyes, holding her breath until she felt light-headed.

"Is that true?"

The grin on his face said it all, far more than those three simple words, and Julie responded to it, rather than the question.

"Of course it's true. You haven't noticed me mooning over you since the first day you arrived?"

"No, mostly I've noticed you avoiding me."

Julie didn't see how it happened, but suddenly he was beside her in the booth, holding her tight against him.

"Julie Jones, don't you dare tell me that I've wasted all this time fretting about my unrequited love for you."

She turned to him, their faces only inches apart, her beautiful eyes warm with laughter.

"Yes, you have."

Julie looked at Josie and said, "I haven't even told my mother yet."

Josie couldn't help herself. She broke into gales of laughter. It took a few moments but pretty soon Julie joined her, the two of them doubling over with the giggles.

"I don't have to tell her, do I?" Julie giggled.

"I'd bet not, especially if one of you didn't make it home last night."

Julie blushed and Josie felt a jolt of envy. Maybe one day she'd feel like that. And for the first time in her life she knew it to be possible.

CHAPTER 19

The drive up to Sechelt wasn't long enough. Josie wanted to keep driving, to keep going north until she hit tundra and moose and polar bears. She'd rather face any number of angry polar bears and hungry blackflies and huge mosquitoes than face Marlene. And that was saying a lot because the blackflies took bites out of your skin and then the mosquitoes added itching to the pain.

Josie had spent a single summer in the north and still occasionally woke in a sweat, dreaming of being chased by blackflies.

The weather had changed in the short time since she arrived on the Sunshine Coast. The damp foggy days were shortened into damp foggy mornings and by ten o'clock the sun burnt off the dampness and the mist disappeared. The Sunshine Coast was beginning to live up to its name. Even Josie, in her blind rush to solve the problem of Marlene, saw that.

She heard the songbirds each time she stopped at a light or a stop sign, a ceaseless accompaniment of cheerful trills and chirps and whistles. She smiled at the sun and the birds but the smiles lasted only a few seconds. What awaited her at her destination tugged at her.

Marlene, her mother, the woman who'd given birth to

her, had somehow in the past days turned into the wicked witch of the fairy tales. Josie expected warts and a tall pointy black hat.

When she thought about it logically, which she was almost incapable of doing in relation to Marlene, she knew how the transformation had happened in her mind—it was obvious. The two Marlenes. Just like Snow White's stepmother— beautiful on the outside, a wicked old crone on the inside. And deadly, too. Josie would have to remember not to eat any apples.

But it wasn't just that. It was the way she'd blinded Josie to her real self. Marlene convinced Josie that she was the best mother in the world, that Josie was an integral part of the perfect family, and nothing could ever happen to change that.

Josie believed these things right up until she arrived in Sechelt last week. That was the worst part of it and that new belief, more than anything else, was the reason she didn't want to go to Sechelt.

She didn't want to face Marlene with this knowledge inside of her. Because Josie had a terrible feeling she might explode and that would not do her father or Florence the slightest bit of good.

So she drove the now-familiar highway and tried not to think of how she'd been lied to, mistreated, snookered, how her whole life had been based on a lie, how her once-best-friend was a liar and a cheat and a complete and utter bitch and had been since day one. But of course it didn't work.

Josie got angrier and angrier the closer she got to Sechelt. Her pulse sped up, her face reddened, her breath grew shallow and fast. Her fists clenched on the steering wheel until her knuckles turned white. Her eyes teared up—tears of rage, not of sorrow—and her mouth dried. She readied herself for battle. The dragon lady waited and Josie would be prepared, finally, to meet her.

The years of subservience, of complete and blind obedience were over. The blinkers fell from Josie's eyes and they broke into a million pieces. They couldn't be repaired; Josie couldn't go back.

The world as she knew it was gone, as if a filter had been removed, changing the photograph from color to black-and-white, or a layer of wallpaper had peeled away, leaving a whole new wall. Familiar on the surface—same houses, same friends, same conversations—new and frightening underneath. Because everything she thought she knew, including herself, was changed.

The parking lot by the beach was empty. Josie drove through it and around the back of Marlene's building to check for her car. It was missing. A reprieve.

"She must be out shopping or getting her nails done. I'll just wait here." Talking aloud to herself in the car was a habit she'd acquired on the drive across the country. "But maybe the car's in for servicing or she lent it to someone. I'll have to go in and see."

Josie couldn't avoid this task even though the walk across the parking lot seemed to go on forever. She wanted to turn back, but Josie didn't grow up stubborn for nothing.

She held her head high and her shoulders back, just as Marlene taught her, and took deep slow breaths to calm herself. Josie laughed out loud at that thought. Wasted effort.

"Damn. Damn. Damn. I have to go in. But she's not home. So why am I worried? But she might be home, might be, probably is, and how do I know which Marlene will answer the door? Doesn't matter. Just push the button."

She stood in the elevator and pushed the button for Marlene's floor. "Less than a minute, Josie, just hold on. The worst will be over in a minute. You'll know."

The elevator door opened and she peered out. Nothing. No one. Marlene's door was at the end of the brightly lit hall—closed, thank God.

The piece of paper—carefully printed in perfectly shaped letters and equally carefully taped perfectly straight in the exact middle of the door—contained perhaps the most shocking thing Josie had seen since her arrival.

We have left for our honeymoon.
We will be gone indefinitely.
Marlene

Josie gulped back the panic and thought about the Fred she'd talked to on the beach, who'd told her to go easy on Marlene. The man whose love for Florence was as clear as a full moon on a cold winter's night. Could Marlene have convinced that man to return to her? No. Could Marlene have a new man? Not much of a stretch.

Josie read the note again, then a third time before she realized what it meant. Marlene saving face, of course. It meant she'd given up on Fred but even more than that—because she wouldn't give up without something better in hand—she'd found a new man. It must be Bert and he would be rich. That went without saying. It would also be good-looking and not too bright. All the men over the years had been all three.

Marlene, as always, had fallen on her feet. It also meant that Fred, wonder of wonders, hadn't been seen with Florence or Marlene wouldn't have left.

She pulled the note from the door. She'd take it to Florence and Fred and free them to go on with their lives.

That note could only have been taped to the door recently or Josie—certainly Gray—would have heard of it. In fact, it could only have been up since this morning.

Josie stood, pulling the tape from the note and putting it in her pocket. She checked the door. Locked. She put her ear to it and heard only the dead silence of an empty room.

Her footsteps back across the parking lot were faster than when she'd arrived. She would tell Fred and Florence the good news, they'd jump up and down and kiss the messenger and then they'd all go off to dinner somewhere in town to flaunt their freedom. And when she got home, Josie would set the gossip queens searching for Marlene and Bert.

She stopped midstep. Odd, she thought, that she'd heard so little about Marlene's new man. Josie shrugged. Marlene was an expert at keeping secrets—look how she'd kept them from Josie. But the gossip queens were experts too, give them a lead and they'd bring home the goods.

The geraniums on Florence's front porch drooped from their stems and petals and dirt littered the ground. The curtains veiled the windows. A general air of unease enveloped the little cottage. Josie grinned and then grimaced. They were either more discreet than either she or Gray had imagined possible or they were completely engrossed in each other. She couldn't blame them. She'd bet it wouldn't take long for things to get back to normal once they heard her news.

Josie knocked on the door and waited. And waited some more. She put her ear to this door. Someone was definitely home.

She knocked again. "It's Josie. You don't have to worry anymore. Marlene's gone away. Florence? Are you there? Fred? Let me in."

Josie heard a pair of feet pattering toward the door and fumbling hands unlocking it. The cheerfulness she'd felt since she'd read the note on Marlene's door—she clutched it in her hand as evidence—faded as she waited, and disappeared completely when the door opened.

Josie only recognized Florence by her height, the color of her hair and the pink sweatsuit. The beautiful face was gone, replaced by a mask of suffering. Red swollen eyes, gray skin and pain delineating every line and crevice. Florence looked her age and then some. Her sweatsuit was dirty and her hair stood out from her head in clumps.

Florence blinked at her. "Josie? What are you doing here?" She peered around her. "Did you bring Fred?"

"He isn't with you?"

"No, of course not. We promised, remember?" The anger in Florence's voice seemed to revive her a little and she straightened up. "He's sick, isn't he? That's why he hasn't phoned." She stepped out onto the porch and closed the door behind her with a snap. "Let's go. I need to see him."

"He's not sick. At least, I don't think he is. Maybe he is. But the sergeant would have phoned the paper and told me if he was in the hospital. No, no. He's not sick."

"Why are you here then? And why hasn't he phoned me? There's no way Marlene could know we've been talking on the phone." Her eyes turned inward for a minute and then she looked back at Josie. Florence's fear was palpable. "She couldn't know, could she?"

"I have no idea," Josie said. "But with Marlene anything is possible." Thinking of the note in her pocket, thinking of Fred back in Marlene's clutches but dreaming of Florence and happiness. Fred wasn't strong, but would he really go back?

"Come on, let's go inside."

Josie opened the door and followed Florence in. She sat Florence down on the couch, flung aside the curtains and raised the windows.

"Where is he?" Florence asked again. "I know he's not with Joseph. He wouldn't dare do that again. He promised after the last time that he wouldn't. And I was mad enough that I'm sure he got my point." She smiled a bitter smile. "But if he's not with Joseph anymore, then where is he?"

"He's not with Joseph," Josie said. "I checked."

"Mercedes?"

"No, I talked to her this morning."

Josie was avoiding mentioning the one place she was really worried about. She hated to admit it, but there was a possibility that Fred had gone with Marlene. But she also knew that Florence would be devastated by that idea, so she schooled her face into anxiety and away from the fear she was feeling.

Josie realized that while she'd learned a great deal about herself and about Marlene over the past weeks, she hadn't considered exactly what that knowledge might mean if she applied it to Fred. Why had he stayed with Marlene after Josie left for university? He'd stayed up until then for her, that was obvious, but once she was gone?

She didn't want to see Fred as a weak man but she didn't want to blame herself, either. She blurted out the question before she could stop herself.

"Why *did* he stay with Marlene all those years? He's so happy with you."

Florence sat up a little straighter, as if those few words had steadied her.

"He was scared, I think, although he never came out and said so. I know he wasn't sure he deserved any better." And she blinked away a tear. "And I understood that."

Josie looked away to hide *her* tears. She had no right to be feeling sorry for herself—she should have seen Fred's unhappiness. She should have talked to him about it.

Florence seemed to read her mind.

"There was nothing any of us could have done for him until he was ready to do it for himself."

"But you…"

"I think meeting me helped him because I understood. I'd been there myself. But even more, I think moving here helped him, taught him that he could have friends, that people liked him, were interested in him. They wanted to spend time with him. So, really," Florence smiled and this time it wasn't bitter, "Marlene helped him to his freedom."

Josie's confusion had to be obvious because Florence didn't stop there.

"Once Marlene and Fred moved here, Marlene loosened the handcuffs. Maybe she thought he was too old, too tame, too conditioned to make a break for it. So she got busy creating a new life for herself and Fred, once a necessary accessory, lost his cachet in Marlene's new world. He had a chance to make friends of his own—and he took it. I think that companionship—Joseph and Mercedes, the crib players at the club—gave him the courage to love me. So it was Marlene's doing."

Josie's tears fell now without restraint. Florence reached out her hand and touched Josie's knee.

"Don't cry, girl, we need to find your father."

And with those final brave words, Florence lost her composure. The couch wrapped itself around her, trying to support her tired body, as if it understood the depth of her pain.

Josie sensed the anguish and tried to imagine her own anxiety magnified a thousand times. Because Florence truly understood what it would mean to Fred if he returned to Marlene. Josie was worried and unhappy but Florence was scared to death. Josie did the only thing she could think of.

"I'll make a pot of tea," she said.

Even in her pain, Florence kept a spotless kitchen. As she waited for the kettle to boil, Josie imagined Florence scrubbing the counter, washing the floor, doing the dishes, while tears rolled down her cheeks. Telling her about the note would be the hardest thing Josie had ever done, but not telling her would be cruel. Josie braced herself and took the tray with tea and homemade cookies back out to Florence.

"I'll pour, okay?" Josie tried to buy herself a little time but Florence would have none of it.

Her body had abandoned the comfort the couch offered and now sat straight, shoulders squared to meet whatever Josie was going to throw at her. Her face set, color returned, she was ready. But Josie wasn't.

"Milk?" she asked, holding out the pitcher. "Sugar?"

Florence nodded to both, her impatience barely contained. She took the teacup from Josie and placed it on the table.

"Josie. Tell me. Now."

"Were you a teacher?" The voice threw Josie back to Grade Five and Miss Howick, and the first time Josie realized there was a teacher's voice, the first time she served detention for throwing paint at Joey Carmichael after he put red and green handprints on her chair and ruined her new dress.

"Yes. Now tell me."

Josie handed her the note. "I found it on Marlene's door." She waited for Florence's face to crumple to match the paper.

But it didn't. She stared at the note for far longer than it deserved. Josie had memorized it in a shorter time. Florence's face didn't change but Josie felt a buzz enter the room.

She tried to ignore it but it was like ignoring a swarm of African killer bees. Florence didn't say anything, simply sat straight up on the couch, her feet not quite touching the floor. The buzzing came from her. Josie checked again but she hadn't moved, not even a single line on her face had flickered. The note in her hand was perfectly still, as if she wasn't even breathing. God, maybe she wasn't.

Josie sprang from her chair and went to Florence. Or tried

to. She couldn't get past the buzz. It stopped her right where she stood, next to her chair with her arms outstretched.

"Florence? Are you okay?"

The buzzing stopped so suddenly Josie fell back into the chair.

"Florence?"

The room filled again but only for a moment. Josie almost caught the buzzing as it appeared and disappeared, turning her head to one side and squinting out of the corner of her eyes. It came from Florence, extending out around her like an aura, a thick black ugly one, and then reversing itself and vanishing back inside that tiny pink body. Florence looked incapable of containing something so big. But even gone, Josie felt it, waiting to be released.

"She kidnapped him."

Florence's voice changed. Gone were the sweet bell-like tones, what remained was raw emotion. Anger, mostly, with a deeply buried pain and a smidgen of despair. But the rage overwhelmed everything else.

"Maybe they've gone away together." Josie pointed at the note in Florence's hand. "Maybe she convinced Fred to come back. Maybe she threatened him. Or you. Or me. And Fred knows her, better than anyone. He knows what she's capable of."

Josie thought that explanation wasn't bad and might even be true. The ache in her ears from the buzzing hadn't returned, so she went on.

"He went with her to keep us safe."

"Bullshit."

Josie almost fainted. Her Miss Howick would never have used that language.

"Florence?"

"Bullshit. He didn't go with her to save us. He didn't trust her enough to believe anything she said. So even if she promised to leave me alone, he would have known she lied."

"Give me that note," Florence demanded, ripping it from Josie's hand. "It says *we*. Marlene means her and Fred. There is no other *we* for her."

"There might be. Florence. You've got to have faith." Josie laughed inside using that phrase, a woman who'd just rediscovered it. "Fred wouldn't leave you."

Florence simply looked disgusted.

"He's with her." Her face crumpled as she spoke and Josie's faith in Fred wavered. She didn't understand what Florence was telling her.

"Maybe. Well, maybe he just… You know, maybe he decided it was easier to go back with Marlene. They've been married forever and he's used to it, isn't he?"

Florence's smile wasn't a pretty thing.

"Josie Harris."

She used the teacher voice. Josie sat up straight and placed her knees together and held her hands lightly clasped in her lap. She waited for the pronouncement.

"Are you insane? Have you been paying the slightest bit of attention to what has been going on around you this week? Did you even see your father?"

Josie swallowed nervously and opened her mouth to defend herself.

"No, of course you didn't. Because you have never seen who he is, how unhappy he's been. You just lived your charmed life while he got eaten alive, year after year, for your sake. And now you think he might have gone back to that on purpose?"

Florence sounded mad enough to spit toads. Josie couldn't look up, didn't dare look up. Because her face would betray her. Every word Florence said hit Josie like a rock shot from the wheels of a passing car, hit hard enough to shatter glass, shatter Josie. Her body shook.

"Stop it. Right now."

Josie felt rather than saw the admonitory finger but she stopped anyway.

"Feeling sorry for yourself is not going to help. We are going to find and rescue Fred and then you can fall apart. But not yet. Pull yourself together. We've got work to do."

Josie regressed to fifth grade and spent the next few hours answering questions and feeling stupid because her answers were mostly, "I don't know," or "I never noticed." Florence's eyebrows rose higher on her forehead with each useless answer until her face resembled an amazed cartoon character, eyebrows poking out of the top of her head like miniature wings. Josie filled page after page with notes, forcing her aching fingers to keep writing. Her throat was dry—Florence didn't offer even a glass of water—and her toe had started throbbing to match her headache about halfway through the interrogation.

And the worst of it? Josie knew they weren't getting anywhere. Everything she knew was years out of date and suspect even then and Florence knew even less because her scruples had made her ask Fred not to say anything at all about Marlene. He couldn't speak of her without being mean, and Florence wouldn't have that.

Somewhere long past the nonexistent lunch hour, Josie snapped.

Florence responded by losing her grade school teacher persona. She replaced it with the quavering, sad woman who had met Josie at the door that morning.

Josie wondered if everyone was, at one and the same time, two quite different people. Or more. She thought of Marlene and Fred. Perfect couple on the outside, huge mass of anger and hurt on the inside. Of Mercedes—mild-mannered motel keeper and goddess of justice. Of Florence. And, finally, of herself. Happy, lucky woman hiding a lonely frightened child inside. But not any longer. She was damn well going to take charge.

"Enough, Florence. We're not getting anywhere. We need help."

"We can't call the police. Fred would hate that. And Marlene would…"

"What? Kill him if she heard sirens? Don't be ridiculous."

"She'll hurt him. Maybe not physically, but she'd hurt him. Badly. She may be your mother but she's capable of evil, I've seen it. What she did to Fred was cruel."

"That's why we need help. Go have a shower and pack your bag. We're going down to Gibsons."

"What if he gets away? This is the first place he'll go."

"We'll leave a note so he can phone if he gets home."

Josie didn't allow Florence to see her despair. If Fred wasn't with Marlene—and she almost hoped he was—where was he? She didn't hold out any hope that Fred would manage to escape from Marlene. It had taken him decades the first time. A few days wasn't going to get him anywhere except deeper into despair.

She knew what that was like. The trouble with despair—which was where she'd mostly been the past two years—was it gave you nothing to hold on to. Anger was different, you could use anger, make it take you somewhere, scream and yell and throw things until you were worn out and then you could let it go.

Despair made you feel as if you were in a pit so deep you could see no light, the walls slick and sheer, and you knew there was no way out. Despair went on forever. Because it perpetuated itself. Josie knew that now. She could see exactly where she'd been for the past two years—deep in the pit of despair.

They had to get Fred out before he lost his will, before he decided, like she had, that nothing could be done to change his life so he might as well accept it.

They needed to get into Marlene's apartment as well. Josie didn't think they'd find anything but they couldn't go back to Gibsons without checking it out.

"We need to stop at Marlene's."

Florence grabbed her bag. She looked like she was ready to hunt rhinos on the Serengeti. Oh, she wore another pink track suit with matching pink runners and her white hair puffed out around her head in sweet little curls, but she might as well have been carrying an Uzi. She looked seven feet tall and as tough as any movie commando. She'd abandoned all sweetness and replaced it with discipline. She turned warrior, and Josie shuddered to think how many other Florences there might be hiding under that sweet pink exterior.

"I think I can convince the manager to let me in so I can see if everything is okay. I'll say they phoned or something."

"No need," Florence said, strapping on her tiny pink purse like a .45. "I know the manager. I had him for Grade Four and Five. And his mother and father. No need for lies." She picked up her suitcase and headed for the door. "Let's put this in the car and go over. Marlene won't have left any clues, but we should check."

Florence was right. Nothing in the apartment said where she'd gone or even when she'd left. They checked the closets but Marlene had so many clothes she could have packed for an around the world cruise and they wouldn't have noticed. Fred's clothes all looked the same. Khakis, golf shirts, tweed jackets.

There were some of each in his closet, but neither Josie nor Florence could tell if any were missing. His closet smelled like him, the one place in the apartment that did, and the two women lingered there, breathing him in.

"I'm sorry, Dad," Josie whispered. "I shouldn't have interfered. I just made it worse. And I'm sorry I didn't understand your life. Or hers. Maybe I could have helped."

Florence reached up and put a hand on Josie's shoulder. "It's okay, honey. She was too smart for all of us. Let's go get some help."

CHAPTER 20

The drive back down the highway to Gibsons began and ended in silence. Florence didn't dare open her mouth. Once before in her life she'd felt this combination of fear and rage. She'd pulled the carving knife from its sheath, laid its already razor-sharp edge against the whetstone—once, twice, a third time—then held the knife in her hand.

She was far past weighing her actions. The knife felt good, and her accompanying smile was something only the most recalcitrant of fifth graders would have recognized.

Her husband—fat, sloppy, mean-spirited—sat, as always, in his chair in front of the TV. The screen flickered with images of young women in tight red swimsuits. Dan didn't watch sports; he watched *Baywatch*, cheerleading and fitness competitions, and he lived for the Miss Universe pageant. He sat in that chair every single hour of the day and he bawled.

He bawled for coffee and bacon and eggs in the morning. He bawled for Coke and fried chicken at lunch. He bawled for roast beef and mashed potatoes and gravy at dinner and he bawled for beer the rest of the time.

Florence tried to ignore his voice, tried to remember him as he'd been when they first met, tried meditation, Al-Anon,

Dr. Phil, and *Chicken Soup for the Abused Woman's Soul.* Nothing worked. Dan's voice cut through whatever layers of peace or stillness Florence managed to construct for herself.

The knife felt solid and balanced and real. It cut through the despair and touched her fear, turning it, just slightly, until it met the deeply buried anger and the two emotions combined to form something else. If it had been a color, Florence thought, it would be green, a deep, dark, flat green, speckled with drops of blood-red. It had no name, or at least none she knew, but she clasped it to her bosom, worshipped it, warmed it when it started to cool.

Because it cleansed her, changed everything until it all made sense. For the first time in years, Florence felt in control. She smiled again.

The sergeant convinced Dan not to press charges, telling him it would be embarrassing to admit that a woman less than half his size had chased him down the street with a carving knife. The sergeant also found a room for Dan in Pender Harbour, forty-five minutes away.

Florence paid the rent, paid for the beer and the food and the cable until Dan died, and considered herself lucky. Lucky to live without him and even luckier not to have killed him. Because she knew she would have done it—stabbed him a thousand times, stabbed him until the blood ran down her body, stabbed him until her arms ached and her fingers could no longer hold the knife—but the sergeant had stopped his car when he saw her.

Florence felt the exact same unreasoning combination of fear and rage right now.

In one part of her mind, she hoped someone would stop her again.

But in the other she wanted, more desperately than anything since she pulled that knife from its sheath, to find Fred, to punish Marlene for treating him so badly, to punish Fred for convincing her he loved her, and then allowing Marlene to kidnap him. Because no matter what Josie thought, Florence was pretty sure they'd gone off together.

But maybe Florence's desire for vengeance was also for Josie's sake. A child who'd been abandoned by her mother. A child who would have been better off if she *had* been abandoned by her mother.

Florence, even through the haze of fear and pain buzzing around in her head, could see how badly Josie had been damaged. And she saw the struggle Josie had undertaken to understand and change the way she saw the world. Although it was obvious Josie had taken control of her life, Florence could see the struggle it had been and what it had cost Josie to wage it.

So Fred and Marlene were both toast.

Josie drove in silence not because she didn't want to talk, but because her brain was working so hard she couldn't. A couple of times she tried to say something, to see if Florence was okay, to ask a question, to somehow break the silence that had taken on a life of its own within the car, but no sound came out.

The silence built itself up, forming a force shield so strong and solid it kept out all noise. Josie didn't hear the birds though the windows were open; she didn't hear the sound of the tires on the pavement or the roar of the huge eighteen-wheelers rushing by.

The silence felt as thick as a castle wall, the heavy stones hauled from miles away, then piled one on top of another and the spaces between them filled in with smaller stones and plaster. It was cold and still and impossible to break, even with a battering ram. And Josie, even at her best, didn't have a battering ram in her arsenal.

She glanced at Florence. Women. First Marlene, then Mercedes, now Florence. She wondered if that personality split came with age or simply with anger. Josie knew she'd never been as angry as Florence was now, or as Marlene had been when Fred left her.

What would Josie's other face look like? Would she end up like Marlene, an old crone? A witch to scare young children? Or like Mercedes? She'd prefer that, dispensing justice without mercy. She'd like to be a goddess because she definitely didn't want to end up like Florence, all her life peeled away to leave only raw anger and determination.

Florence scared her in a totally different way than Mercedes. Mercedes became more herself, adding layers of meaning and power, while Florence stripped everything away, leaving only implacable rage and an insistent drive to solve her problem at any cost. Mercedes considered other people, then made the best decision possible under the circumstances; Florence didn't give a damn about anyone else except Fred.

But Josie knew she didn't have it in her to be a goddess or even a common garden variety heroine.

Her foolish try at saving the world had only made things worse. She should have stayed at home—Marlene would have got over it eventually, Fred and Florence would be happy in their little cottage and she'd never have known that her whole life was a lie.

Of course, she'd still be working at Jonco, and she'd still have the worst luck in the world, but Fred and Florence would be safe and happy.

But she'd never have come to the Sunshine Coast, either, never have met Gray or Mercedes or Rose or Florence. She'd never have met Julie Jones, the most beautiful woman in the world, and her friend.

Mercedes sat behind the counter, the green-tinged TV playing *Jeopardy* without sound.

Josie stepped up to the counter and waited. Florence was still in the car, her hands resting demurely on her lap.

"I'll wait here," she said. "Maybe it's better if you explain things without me." A pause and shrug of those tiny shoulders. "And I'm tired. I'll try and get a little sleep."

Josie looked up at that, wondering if Florence was joking. But her eyes were closed and her head leaned back against the seat as if it were too heavy for her to hold up any longer. So Josie had left her there. It felt wrong but surely Florence was old enough to make her own decisions. Besides, she was right, it *was* easier to explain things to Mercedes without a schoolteacher watching over her shoulder.

Josie remembered to watch Mercedes's face when she handed her the note. She wanted to see the transformation.

But nothing happened except that Mercedes said, "This is Marlene's handwriting? You're sure of that?"

"Oh, yeah. She practiced that for years. Got it out of some book somewhere."

"Did you check the condo?"

"Uh-huh. I couldn't tell if anything was missing. And it was spotless. But it always is. Was. Marlene said a good wife kept her house as if Her Majesty might show up for tea any minute."

Josie remembered what it felt like to live in a house made ready for the queen. One toy at a time, and only in her own room. And silence. The house was always quiet, waiting, she thought now, for something that would never happen.

"What are you going to do now?"

Josie sat in one of the green armchairs with a cup of tea in her hands. The tea didn't even put a dent in the cold she felt. She looked across at Mercedes.

"I'm going to find them. Together or not."

Mercedes smiled and even though it wasn't the goddess smiling, Josie felt reassured.

"Go get Florence," Mercedes said. "We'll start from there."

Josie's heart skipped a beat. Her car was gone. She looked down the row of units, down the road toward the Way-Inn, down the path to the beach. No car, no pink sweatsuit, nothing.

"Where's Florence?" Mercedes had come out of the motel behind her.

Josie waved her hand at the parking lot and shrugged her shoulders.

"Oh." Mercedes didn't waste time on "maybe she's at the beach" or "did you check the dock?" She pulled Josie into the office and offered her the phone.

"Gray, it's Josie. We've got a problem here and I need your help."

"What is it?"

"Fred's still missing and now so's Marlene. And Florence." She laughed bitterly. "If you don't get here soon, I might be gone, too."

"I'm on my way."

Gray kept hearing that laugh. It held a trace of panic and why wouldn't it? Gray felt a trace of it, too. Fred. Marlene. And Florence. It didn't make any sense. But Josie's laugh also held a hint of humor. The weeping woman was gone for good.

He picked up his cell phone and called the sergeant.

"Ron, it's Gray. We've got a problem. Can you come by the motel?

"It's complicated. And change out of that damn uniform, will you? I'll pick you up. We don't want the squad car in the lot."

While she and Mercedes waited, Josie went back over the day she'd spent with Florence. She'd missed something, that was clear. Because Florence wouldn't leave unless she had somewhere to go, some clue to follow.

"Florence must know something we don't," she said to Mercedes.

"Yeah, I thought that, too. The good news is that she let you drive her down here. So she must think they're this way, not north."

The sergeant and Gray came in while Josie was speaking. The sergeant grinned when he saw Josie and she knew that Julie Jones had talked about her. On their first night together. Josie's heart warmed with the idea of it.

Mercedes handed the note to Ron, who took it gingerly between his fingertips, and listened while Josie told the whole story as clearly and concisely as she could.

Josie focused on the individual words, each one dropping into the silence like a rock in a pond. She followed the ripples to shore, the stone to the muddy bottom, but found nothing except more rocks.

Gray glanced at Josie when he first came in, then headed directly for the arm of her chair. She leaned her head against his arm and finished the story.

"So now we're down three people and I have no idea where any of them are. Do I file three missing persons reports?"

The sergeant laughed. "I don't think it's that serious. Do you think Fred and Marlene are together?"

"No," she said.

Gray squeezed her shoulders and breathed into her ear. "Good for you, Josie."

She continued. "But in a way that makes it harder. Because we have to look in more than one place."

Mercedes piped up. "We do know they're not north, though. Or at least Florence—who'd be the one to know where Fred, and Marlene for that matter, might go—doesn't think so."

The sergeant nodded.

"Good. That narrows it down. The whole rest of the world is at the other end of the ferry."

Josie pulled two small blue books from her pockets, passports, and handed them over.

"Nope. Only the rest of Canada."

The sergeant smiled again and Josie realized what it was that attracted Julie Jones. He smiled with his whole body, his entire self. It was a smile that held nothing back, not a single molecule. It wasn't the fake, perfect smile of a movie star or politician, all teeth and signifying nothing.

The sergeant's smile was for Josie, full of pride in her foresight, joy in her intelligence, and included warmth and good nature and a whole world full of friendship. Josie couldn't even imagine what that smile would be like if the sergeant loved you. It was already irresistible.

"Great."

And then the sergeant, with an occasional interjection from Gray or Mercedes, went over the whole story again.

Josie told them things she didn't know she knew. They started from the moment she woke up and moved, excruciatingly slowly, through the drive, the note, her hours with Florence, the drive back down to Gibsons.

They were good, all three of them experts in interrogation. At the end of it, Josie felt like a damp towel after a long, hot day at a cheap motel pool. But none of them looked too happy until Gray sat up with a start.

"Florence is waiting for the ferry. It's the only place she can be. And I have an idea where Fred and Marlene are, too."

"Where?" Josie, Mercedes and the sergeant asked in unison.

"Give me a minute. I need to think about this."

Gray went into muse-mode. Josie had seen him do it before, when he was writing, or maybe when he was thinking about what to write. His eyes glazed over as if they were looking in at something in his brain, his nostrils flared and his forehead smoothed out. He looked both younger and more mature, if that were possible.

Josie sat next to him, barely breathing. She didn't want him distracted.

She just hoped it wouldn't take long; the tension was getting to her. Even though she didn't believe Marlene would hurt Fred, Florence's scorn at Josie's naivete had marked her. She murmured another one of Fred's platitudes—*better safe than sorry*—and waited.

CHAPTER 21

Gray knew he'd heard something, a clue, from Josie. A little arrow struck his brain when she said it. He'd felt the strike but he buried the sensation beneath the much bigger shock and joy and pure physical rush of Josie leaning against him. So now, though he knew he'd heard it, Gray had to dig.

It was a little like digging up potatoes or carrots too early in the season but even as a boy Gray never could wait. Almost all of them were useless—too small to cook or even for a single bite out in the garden—but once in a long while he'd find a perfect miniature bite-size carrot, sweeter than any other carrot.

So he kept digging, turning over everything Josie had said. He had an idea it was something seemingly unrelated to a destination but he ignored it. He knew better. He'd spent way too much time looking for a book with a blue cover on the top shelf of the left hand bookshelf and, finally, after wasting hours, when he found the book it was orange and on the bottom shelf of a completely different bookshelf. Those kinds of impressions—blue book, top corner—were often wrong. So he examined everything without judging it ahead of time.

There, there it was. He pictured it hiding behind a mass

of what seemed to be more important information, a slight shine the only thing making it visible. He snuck up on it, coming at it from behind so it wouldn't disappear on him again. Gray had plenty of practice at this; he was always losing bits and pieces of his stories and having to find them again. Pretending to ignore the bits until you were close enough to grab them was the only way to find them again.

"Aha. Got you, you little sucker." He held out his hand to Josie. "Here. This'll help."

She solemnly took his hand and waited for him to speak.

"Let's assume Fred's with Marlene, okay? I think Josie's right. He's not with Joseph anymore." He leaned down and kissed her forehead. "And he's not with Florence."

Josie chimed in. "I've checked the hospitals. He's not in any hospital within forty miles."

Josie couldn't say it out loud but she'd also checked the morgues. Ron looked over at her and nodded. "Good work," he mouthed silently.

"We'd have heard if he was staying with anyone around here, and I've already checked at Joseph's. Someone would have told Rose or Mrs. Suzuki..." Josie paused, shaking her head.

"They would have told me," Mercedes said, rapping her hand against her forehead. "And no one's said anything. They're not on the peninsula."

"Marlene's only been over to the mainland a few times since they moved here," Gray said. "To Mary Kay conferences and seminars, somewhere out in Burnaby, right?"

"Right. And Fred didn't go with her. I remember because

we always watched his favorite movie together—my phone bills were astronomical when she was away. *Bridge on the River Kwai* is a very long movie."

Josie sat in her big old ugly comfortable chair, the chair she loved, partly because it fit her body like it was made for her but mostly because Fred had picked it out.

When she walked into her first apartment—the one Florence found for her when she got home from university—the chair stood out like a stained glass window on a sunny day. Marlene's taste was everywhere else, her taste in furniture, in daintiness, in femininity. But Fred had somehow snuck the big brown suede chair in, probably after Marlene thought the room was finished.

He had to have known even then that Marlene would never visit Josie's apartment though it would take Josie years to figure it out.

The chair was big enough for Josie to curl up in and the suede was as soft as a kitten. It faced the television, dropped in amongst the white wicker and delicate peach and green floral like a linebacker at a bridal shower. Josie loved it. She never sat in any of the other chairs, only and always in Fred's chair.

She sat at home and watched the clock. She had a date with Fred at eight. The VCR was ready, the popcorn popped, the red licorice on the table next to her with the large bottle of orange crush. Movie food, bought specially for this night. Josie never ate it otherwise.

She picked up the phone and dialed as the clock clicked over to the hour. She switched off the lights and turned on the TV and the VCR.

"Hi," said Fred over the opening credits.

"Hello," Josie replied.

For the rest of the movie neither of them spoke more than to say, "Oh, I love this part," or "I forgot about this." Josie listened to Fred breathing and laughing and occasionally sniffling. She listened to him eating popcorn and slurping his pop. And she knew he did the same. He knew when she reached for a tissue and she felt his hand pat her shoulder. He knew when she smiled and his teeth shone in the darkness beside her. And always she heard the movie in the background, exactly aligned to her movie, not even a second off.

At the end—they always watched it right through until the white noise came on—they said goodnight and hung up. No conversation necessary or wanted.

Josie went right to bed, leaving the movie unwound, the popcorn bowl and licorice wrappers on the floor, the tissues piled up next to the empty bottle of orange crush. She'd clean up in the morning, but leaving the mess made it feel more like a movie theater. A theater with only two patrons. A theater playing the best war movie ever made every single night.

"Marlene and Fred have never been to Vancouver, to anywhere else in B.C. They moved right from Toronto to Sechelt without stopping," Gray said.

"Right. We never vacationed out here, either."

"And I'm assuming Marlene liked to go places where people know her? Where she's kind of a VIP?"

"She likes to be recognized."

"Bingo. They've gone to that hotel. It's the only place they can be."

"But isn't that kind of obvious?"

"Why? She thinks we all think they're on a second honeymoon. Why would we even bother to follow them? Where would she go on a second honeymoon?"

"Hawaii. Paris. Maybe Bali. Somewhere exotic. Romantic. Foreign."

"Right. Certainly not to Burnaby. So she thinks we think they're thousands of miles away but we know they're not." Gray pointed at the passports on the table. "We know they're not across any borders."

"But they could be anywhere in the country." Mercedes grimaced when she said it.

"No," Josie said. "I think Gray's right. I think she'd go somewhere she knew, somewhere she felt comfortable and safe. Because Fred wouldn't be happy and she'd want to know her environment."

"Yeah. If you've got one complication, you don't want any more." The sergeant stood up and reached for the phone. "I'll call the Burnaby detachment."

"Wait. Ron, don't phone yet. We need to think about this for a minute." Mercedes looked around at them. "First we need to stop Florence. Fred's safe until we can get to him but Florence is a loaded gun. Can we stop her?" She looked at the sergeant. "Without arresting her?"

"Without embarrassing her," Josie added. "No flashing lights or sirens."

"The next ferry doesn't leave until six. We've got forty-five minutes."

"Okay. We need to get down there, get her out of the lineup and back up here. Without fuss. That means you—" Ron pointed at Mercedes "—and you—" he pointed at Gray. "Walk the lineup until you find her, then get her to pull out.

"Mercedes can drive Josie's car back with Florence in it. Gray can follow. Take this." He handed them a cell phone. "Gray, you keep in touch, let us know what's happening. Now go."

Gray looked down at Josie and smiled. She still held his hand and he didn't want her to let go. He leaned down and kissed her lightly, whispered, "I love you," and felt her shock as he spoke the words. "We'll be right back. Order a pizza or something, will you? I'm starving."

Josie sat in Mercedes's living room and waited. She was careful not to move, not even a single inch. She remembered being six and Marlene on one of her health kicks— open windows no matter what the weather. A storm outside, wind and snow and bitter cold, and Josie in her bed, wrapped in all her blankets with snow piling up on the inside of the windowsills.

She knew, even then, if she moved the smallest muscle the cold would get colder and she'd start to shiver. She'd wake up in the morning, tears and snot frozen on her face, every muscle in her body locked solid from cold and tension. The weird thing was that Marlene had been right.

Josie didn't miss a single day of school that winter. The next winter the windows stayed closed. She remembered that as the winter of vitamin C—Dr. Salk and orange juice and plenty of exercise. That year, Josie had a cold almost all of the time.

Getting Florence out of the lineup was easy. Mercedes walked up to the car, opened the driver's side door, said, "Slide over," and Florence, after a glare vicious enough to skin a cat, did so. She reached for the door handle once but Gray and Mercedes had discussed that possibility on the way down and Mercedes simply grabbed Florence's arm and said, "No." Florence stayed.

Gray never knew what they talked about although he could see Florence's head shaking. But Mercedes could be amazingly persuasive and he wasn't surprised when whatever Mercedes said kept Florence in the car while the rest of the ferry traffic drove around them.

Gray hurried back up to the Sand Dollar Motel, alternating between joy and despair. Josie hadn't rejected him. He worried that he'd made a complete fool of himself. Gray had been tempted to drive right onto the ferry to avoid the consequences of his actions but he didn't. Because, more than anything, he wanted to see the look on Josie's face when she saw him again. He'd know then if he had even the slightest chance with her.

He wasn't sure she'd moved at all while they'd been gone. She sat in the same chair, her feet curled up under her. Josie looked at him and smiled. His whole future was in that smile. He sat down on the arm of her chair and touched her shoulder, just once.

Gray sat there, his body inches from hers, while the most peculiar and unexpected thing happened.

They hit him with the smallest of pings, like miniature mosquitoes, or maybe even smaller than that. But they had discernible weight, as if a kitten, four or five weeks old, placed a single paw on his skin. He saw nothing. Or, wait, a flash. He focused on it, but it was gone. He could only see them when he wasn't looking, those flashes of light hitting his arms and his legs, his torso, even his eyes.

He sat perfectly still because even if he couldn't see them, could barely feel them, he knew what they were. The pieces of his soul had escaped from the boxes where he'd kept them, out of the letters he wrote to his ex-wife and had raced the length of Gibsons to find him. He waited while they burrowed in under his skin and rode his veins and arteries to his exact center.

He knew when they coalesced into a single entity and felt the solid weight of it settle somewhere below his heart, in front of his spine, above his belly. And he knew a small piece was still missing and knew, too, that he'd never get that one back. Josie had it and its transfer was permanent.

Josie sat in her chair and waited for Mercedes and Florence. She wanted to tell everyone at the same time what was going to happen. She sat still in the chair—the feel of Gray's body still humming against her skin, the echo of his words a great roar in her ears. And she thought about those words and what they meant, thought about the consequences of them spiraling out through every piece of her world, like a rock dropped in a still pool of water.

Her life, if she wanted it to, would change completely as a result of those words. Josie could see her future as clearly as she saw the sergeant pacing the room in front of her.

She'd be here, in Gibsons, part of the community, working at the *Sunshine Coast News*, knowing everybody and their business. When one of the gossip queens retired, she'd take her place. Like them, she'd pass on the things everybody wanted to know about their neighbors—births, deaths, illnesses.

But Josie would specialize in love. She'd be able to see its earliest beginnings, the first tender spark that might, by someone less skillful, be mistaken for something else, like friendship or simply warm companionship.

Would-be lovers would consult her.

"Is it possible?" they'd ask. "Can he be interested?"

And Josie would tell them the truth. If it were possible, she'd fan the flame, if not she'd tell them straight out.

"No, it's not going to happen." And she'd watch as the tiny spark went out, leaving only the faintest of scars behind. Because she'd have seen the pain of all kinds of love: unrequited love; obsessive love; angry, jealous, hateful love, and she'd know it was better to stop those kinds of love before they got started.

She'd spend every afternoon at the Way-Inn with the other gossip queens, sitting in regal state at the center table while petitioners and informants dropped by. She'd laugh so much her face would wrinkle up like a year-old apple and then she'd laugh some more. She'd cry and dance and swim in the ocean. She'd run on the beach. She'd wear bright colors and hats and long, flowing scarves. She'd dye her hair red and keep it that way even when she was ninety.

She'd spend time with Marlene and her new man, if she had one and whoever he might be, with Fred and Florence and enjoy every minute of it. She'd learn to sail, to paint, to weave, to make pottery, and she'd always have something ready for the craft ladies.

She'd bake cookies for the Scouts, make lemon poppy-seed cake for wedding showers and chewy rice bars for baby showers. She'd knit a blanket for each and every new baby and she'd say, "I love that name," even when she cringed at the thought of it.

She'd go to every amateur theater night and maybe even take up acting. She'd help run the white elephant sale and the animal shelter fund-raiser. She'd help out at the library.

She'd go to Vancouver every couple of months and visit the art gallery and Chinatown and the movies. She'd stand on the top deck of the ferry and watch the mountains and the eagles and the sailboats.

And her life would be charmed not only because Gray would be beside her, but because she'd know the truth of it, the piece she'd been missing for the last two years. She'd know who she was—flaws and problems and all—and where she belonged. She'd know where she came from and who her friends were. She'd take off the rose-colored glasses she'd worn for most of her life, the smudged and scratched glasses, which gave her headaches, and replace them with the clear, cool light of truth.

Josie knew it wouldn't be easy. She was skilled in self-deception; she'd spent a whole lifetime at it. But she thought there was a door opening for her, a door that might let her luck back in.

She sat in the chair and watched the sun on the window. The past few weeks had changed her life. She had spent her time fighting that change, trying desperately to ignore it, because she remembered what had happened with the last change. She'd lost everything. Or at least she'd thought she had.

The thing was, Josie thought, she'd learned to live with that change and though it took some time, she did manage to grow a new life. She watched the crows, and TV, she went to work and watched her coworkers and her boss. She watched the world go by. She avoided involvement because she believed she couldn't afford to lose one more thing.

But now she had a chance to get back in the world. It was risky, and Josie wasn't sure she was ready for it.

She laughed out loud. Things weren't so clear, not in real life. Movies and books were the only places where the crossroads bore signposts. This way to a happy ending…this way to ruin. In real life, things just happened.

Oh, you tried to pinpoint them, those life-changing moments, but really what you did was make them up. Like Josie's haircut. Or Gray's words. They weren't the moments of change, they were only a representation of it, the physical manifestation of something so ephemeral, so slippery, no one could touch it.

We made things up because we needed a sign, a symbol, a way for it to make sense. Josie laughed again. Samson and Delilah. She'd spent two years blaming her misfortune—her missed fortune—on a haircut. But she wasn't watching the world go by anymore.

She wanted to watch the sergeant and Julie Jones get married and have babies. She wanted to meet Mrs. Suzuki and get to know her daughter and her granddaughter. She wanted to know if Rowena Dale would ever stay engaged long enough to get married. She wanted to meet the hermit and learn his story. She wanted to know what brought him here to live on the beach and why he never left.

She wanted to be there when the whole Fred and Florence and Marlene thing got solved. She knew, somehow, that it wasn't up to her. The situation was so far out of her control it might as well be taking place in Katmandu and she watching it on CNN. Not her problem to solve, she thought again, and felt a rock or two roll off her shoulders.

All she'd wanted to do was to put things back the way they were and that was impossible. She knew too much. She had learned too much about herself and her life to ever go back. And she didn't want to.

She wanted to go ahead, to find out whether she could live a different life, one where instead of ignoring everything outside of her, she embraced it. Mercedes and Rose and Sam. Mrs. Suzuki and her family. Julie Jones and probably one of her damned stray animals. The sergeant and the hermit. Fred and Florence. Hell, even Marlene. The whole Sunshine Coast. And Gray MacInnis. She didn't know what would happen but she'd see. She'd just have to wait and see.

CHAPTER 22

Josie heard the cars pulling up outside the motel, then footsteps racing down the gravel footpath to the beach.

"You told Florence where he was, didn't you?" Turning to Mercedes standing in the doorway.

"It was the only way to get her out of the lineup," Mercedes replied, a few fine lines creasing her face. "He damn well better be there. Florence is so pissed that I don't want to see her again until she's vented most of that anger right where it belongs. On Fred."

"No, wait," Josie said. "Florence wasn't angry. She was hurt. And scared. But she'll be okay now. Anger's good."

Gray sat on the arm of Josie's chair as if he belonged there. He did. Josie put her hand on his leg and heard his voice in her head saying again, "I love you," and wondered if she'd dreamed it, wondered if he'd ever say it again, wondered, mostly, if he'd feel that way tomorrow. She had no answers, though she thought if she gave him a chance, he would.

And once Josie was through wondering about that, she wondered how she felt. She watched Gray, his thin body comfortable in the space he carved through the air.

Maybe that was her answer. She wanted to be touched by

Gray MacInnis. She wanted to talk to him. She wanted to spend days with him walking on the beach and evenings at the Way-Inn. She wanted to have breakfast with him, and lunch and dinner. How much clearer could it be?

Florence came into the room and sat down, the light fading from the window beside her. Mercedes had explained everything and Florence understood. It didn't make her less angry or panic-stricken but her good manners, the presence of the sergeant—even in plain clothes his police-ness was obvious—and of Josie kept her in the room and not running back down the highway to the ferry terminal to catch the next sailing.

They didn't understand. Well, they wouldn't, would they? She was the one person who did understand, who knew what it was like to be under the spell of someone you despised, someone so hateful and appalling that your skin crawled whenever you were in the same room.

But Florence knew that if the sergeant had told her to put down the knife, get back in the house and stay, she would have done it. Because she had that one, single moment of escape in her and if she hadn't made it then, she'd never have tried again. And Fred was in the same position. If he got left for too long with Marlene—and maybe it was already too late—he'd be stuck there forever.

But no one else understood her urgency. They were sitting in the room, drinking beer and waiting for the pizza delivery guy, while Fred's life was turning back into hell.

"I know you don't understand," she said. "You don't know

what it's like. All of you—the sergeant because he's seen his share of domestic violence, Gray because of his ex-wife, Mercedes because she's a goddess in disguise—" everyone looked up at that "—Josie because she grew up with Marlene—all of you think you get it. But you don't.

"Fred's in danger. And the longer you leave him there, the smaller our chances are of saving him."

The sergeant turned to the phone. "I'll get the Burnaby..."

"No. Wait." Mercedes stopped him again. "That won't help, will it?"

"No. He has to want to get away. He has to do it himself. We have to help him in a way that'll give him the power. We may already be too late."

Josie watched Florence rub her eyes and saw the tears glittering on her cheeks. She said, "She won't hurt him."

Florence's smile wasn't pretty. "No, she won't hurt him. She won't need to. She broke him so long ago there aren't even scars anymore. But it won't take her long to peel off the fragile layers of peace Fred's managed to grow in the last few months.

"She'll rip away the happiness, uproot the self-esteem, and he'll be right back where he started. And I'm not sure he'll have the energy to start over again." Florence glanced at the sergeant. "There's only one chance to get away."

Josie watched Florence sitting on the stool at the front counter, the lights from passing cars flashing on her pale face. She radiated Do Not Disturb with every breath.

Josie had gone over to her once with a cup of tea. "Here, Florence, it's hot. I put in milk and sugar. You need the energy." She put the cup down in front of Florence. The steam immediately stopped and the milk curdled. When Josie picked up the cup again the cold stung her fingertips.

Florence turned, just enough for Josie to see her face. Still and blank, Florence might have sat for a portrait titled *Grief*. The bones of her face were dragged down so the skin looked loose and waxy and out of place, as if someone had sliced it away then carelessly put it back, slightly askew. Josie wanted to touch her but that face brooked no interference. She took the cold cup and backed away.

Josie straightened her shoulders, picked up the phone and dialed the hotel.

"Yes, Mrs. Harris is registered."

Josie thought about it for a minute and then shrugged. "Put me through to her room, please."

She waved off Florence, then Gray, mouthing to them with her hand over the mouthpiece, "Trust me. I know what I'm doing."

"Marlene," she said, when her mother had answered the phone. "Where's Dad?"

Marlene ignored her question. "How did you find me?"

"It wasn't that hard. This is a small town," Josie said. "Everyone knows everything about everybody."

Marlene sniffed. "I'm disappointed in you, Josie Harris, listening to gossip."

"Where's Dad?" Josie asked again.

"Just a minute."

Josie heard Marlene put the phone down and a man's voice in the background, quickly stilled by a snapped order from Marlene.

"Marlene, let me talk to Dad."

"He's not here."

"I just heard him."

"That's not Fred, it's Bert. Bert Hickman."

Josie's confusion must have showed in her face because she heard a chorus of "whats" from around the room. She held up a hand to silence them.

"Bert?"

"Yes, Bert," Marlene said. "My fiancé."

"Where's Fred, then? Is he with you, too?"

"Not now."

"But he was?"

"Of course he was. He came down with me to sign the divorce papers."

"The divorce papers?"

Josie felt like an idiot repeating every word of Marlene's but she was flabbergasted. Of everything she had imagined might happen when she phoned Marlene, this was the very last. In fact, she was pretty sure she couldn't have, in her wildest of wild dreams, imagined this scenario.

"Marlene?"

"Yes?"

"Where is Fred?"

"I imagine he's on a bus on his way back to that little floozy."

Josie ignored the slight to Florence and asked again.

"When did he leave?"

"A couple of hours ago. He thought he might catch the last ferry back. I have to go now, Josie. We have an appointment at the jewelers." And she hung up without a goodbye.

Josie slowly put down the phone.

Once the whole story was related and exclaimed over and kisses and hugs were exchanged all around, Florence grabbed Josie's keys and disappeared. This time they knew where she was. At the ferry terminal waiting for Fred.

Pizza, Julie and Ron's mutt Aska appeared just as Florence pulled out of the parking lot.

Josie took Julie aside to tell her the story, Julie murmuring reassurances and rubbing her arm the whole time.

"She's not a good person, my mother. Not a good person at all. Why couldn't she be like your mother? She's wonderful."

Julie smiled and gave Josie a hug.

"My mother has faults, too. Look. I'm thirty years old and she watches over me like a mother hen. She has her face in my business all the time and she uses her friends, her gossip network, to spy on me. No mother's perfect, Josie. You won't be, I won't be. It's impossible."

Josie hugged her back. "I guess all we can do is our best, huh? And try not to make the same mistakes as them."

Josie watched as Julie honed in on Ron like a bee to a flower in the middle of summer.

She reached for Gray's hand and kissed his palm before tucking it against her cheek. She felt his heart beat faster, his arm tighten around her shoulder, and closed her eyes. This, then would be all right.

CHAPTER 23

Gray's nerves were bouncing around like jumping beans—
up, down, sideways. He felt slightly queasy, as if he were waiting to go on stage to make a speech, a scary feeling but not
altogether bad.

His palm still tingled from Josie's kiss. He understood that
teenage compulsion now—he didn't want to wash his hand,
not ever. Because that kiss had a physical presence. He
checked to see if it had left a mark. He felt the exact shape
of her lips, the slight dampness they left behind, the weight
of them on his palm.

Josie watched Gray and smiled to herself. She knew exactly how he felt. She was pretty sure she couldn't walk across
the room, let alone engage in a comprehensible conversation.
Overwhelmed didn't come close to how she felt.

She didn't worry any longer about whether Gray loved her.
She knew he did. She didn't worry about the future or the lo-
gistics of making a life with him. She knew they'd work it out.

Josie had always thought that love, true love, the kind
she'd believed Marlene and Fred had, meant hard work.
Compromise. Negotiation. Now she knew differently. Any

relationship—with friends, at work, with family—took time and effort, it was only natural. But she could see already that negotiating with Gray was going to be fun because she already knew they'd work it out, whatever it was.

And maybe that was the difference. Fred and Marlene had never begun any discussion with that kind of inherent goodwill and confidence.

And Josie wasn't at all sure whose fault that was. She'd started blaming Fred, then shifted to Marlene, but she was pretty sure now that neither of them was wholly to blame. Relationships were about compromise and no one person could bear all the fault.

The door slammed open again and Florence dragged in a very bedraggled Fred.

"Sit your bony butt down." She pushed him into the chair next to Josie's. "You owe all of us an explanation. And an apology."

She hammered on his shoulder. "You scared the shit out of me, Fred Harris. Don't you ever do that again."

Fred tried to smile but the glacial temperature in the room didn't shift a bit.

"I didn't know what to do," he started. "She asked me to go to the lawyers with her and I thought if I hesitated, she'd change her mind." He shot a quick glance at Florence and then looked back down at his hands.

"I don't know what I thought. Too much was happening, too much I couldn't control."

When Josie looked over at Florence, she saw nothing but

her anger and worry, overlaid with… What was it? Part of it was love. That was clear in her softened lips.

But there was something else, something stronger than Florence's love for Fred. Josie shivered. It was desire. Once she figured out what it was, it become perfectly clear. The skin pulled taut on her cheekbones, the white space around her pupils and the flaring of her nostrils. Passion, pure sexual passion.

Josie wondered if she looked at Gray like that. And she understood that now she knew what it looked like, she'd recognize it anywhere, even in her own mirror. It was frightening, and also exciting. She only hoped that Fred was too scared to have that particular look on *his* face.

She was glad she didn't see desire on Fred's face. His breathing had quickened, his eyes were wide open, whites showing, and his muscles were tight. Fred was scared.

"Falling in love at my age, at any age, is frightening." His voice quivered but he carried on. "I wasn't sure I could do it, change my whole life. Maybe I'd lose my daughter." He reached toward Josie. "I didn't know what to do. But I wanted a chance, Florence," he said. "I'm divorced."

Florence walked across the room and pulled Fred from his chair.

"I'm here," she said, wrapping her arms around him and rocking.

"We're here," Josie added, running her hand down his arm. "We're all here."

Josie knew all about fear. Fred and Florence were going to have to learn to live with it. You never forgot fear, never forgave yourself, either. It was insidious and self-perpetuating.

When Roosevelt said *you have nothing to fear but fear itself*, she knew exactly what he was talking about.

The trouble was that fear didn't give you much room for self-analysis or allow much space for critical thinking. The worst thing about it was its insistence on taking over your life, of being in your thoughts and your guts every single minute. You never got a break from it. And even when, if you were very, very lucky you got over it, it still snuck back.

When you were tired, or having a bad day, or after a fight with your partner or an encounter with a snippy waiter or salesclerk, it came back. It never really gave up. Once you let it in, it was like the worse of all houseguests, the one who stayed and stayed and stayed.

Fear was forever.

Josie knew all about that. She'd spent the last two years scared to death. And she knew she'd never get over it, either. Even though she knew her life was changing, knew she'd be happy and loved—and lucky—she'd still wake up dripping wet, full of fear. And it wouldn't matter that Gray was lying there next to her.

All you could do, she thought, was try to avoid the whirlpool. Do your best to cling with all your strength to the wooden struts of the lifeboat—your friends and family, love and desire and laughter. And don't give in to the temptation to let go, and allow yourself to be sucked down into despair.

Once you'd got to the whirlpool, once fear entered your life, it wouldn't leave. You just had to work on making your boat stronger and more seaworthy. And yourself stronger and smarter, better able to steer it clear of the whirlpool.

Gray headed straight for her. The look on his face made her move away from Fred and Florence and open her arms. He settled into them as if he'd always been there, as if he were coming home. He was, Josie thought, just as I am.

Josie turned in Gray's arms and put her head on his chest, comforted by the steady thump of his heart, the rise and fall of his breath. She'd fight for him, for what they had together. She'd fought for Fred and Florence, their right to make a life together. And despite everything, she felt better because of it. She'd gained a life, Josie thought, a real family and love and a future. She didn't need to watch the crows anymore.

And it came to pass just as Gray said it would. Fred and Florence and Marlene never became friends but they managed to say hello when they passed each other on the beach and all of them spent Christmases and birthdays and anniversaries and christenings at Josie and Gray's house. Florence and Fred lived happily together, never marrying. "It isn't necessary," they said, and Josie, watching them over the years, knew they couldn't possibly be happier.

Marlene married Bert Hickman and they spent the years traveling, buying gifts from exotic places for her daughter and her grandchildren.

And Gray and Josie? They did get married, although Florence and Fred convinced that all marriages were ill-fated, tried to talk them out of it. Josie understood their fears, even shared them, but she chose to ignore them and married Gray on the beach, the sea their only music.

When she told this story to her children and grandchildren, she always began with the exact same words.

"I always lived a charmed life."

Detective Maggie Skerritt is on the case again!

Maggie Skerritt is investigating a string
of murders while trying to establish her
new business with fiancé Bill Malcolm.
Can she manage to solve the case
while moving on with her life?

Spring*Break*

by *USA TODAY* bestselling author
CHARLOTTE DOUGLAS

A forty-something blushing bride?

Neely Mason never expected to walk down the aisle, but it's happening, and now her whole Southern family is in on the event. Can they all get through this wedding without killing each other? Because one thing's for sure, when it comes to sisters, *crazy* is a relative term.

The
GOOD KIND
OF CRAZY

TANYA MICHAELS

HN35

Available March 2006
TheNextNovel.com

REQUEST YOUR FREE BOOKS!

2 FREE NOVELS TO INTRODUCE YOU TO OUR BRAND-NEW LINE!

Ne^{xt} ™

There's the life you planned. And there's what comes next.

Where can a woman who has
spent her life obliging others truly
take time to rediscover herself?
In the Coconut Zone...

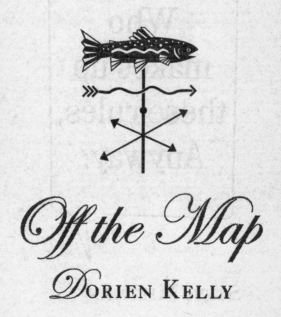

Off the Map

DORIEN KELLY

HARLEQUIN
Next™

HN31 Available February 2006
TheNextNovel.com

Sometimes the craziness of living
the perfect suburban life is enough
to make a woman wonder...

Who
makes up
these rules,
Anyway?

BY
STEVI MITTMAN

Available February 2006
TheNextNovel.com

HN30

What happens when new friends get together and dig into the past?

Ex's and Oh's
Sandra Steffen

A story about secrets, surprises and relationships.

If her husband turned up alive—she'd kill him!

The day Fiona Rowland lifted her head above the churning chaos of kids, carpools and errands, annoyance turned to fury and then to worry when she realized Stanley was missing. Can life spiraling out of control end up turning your world upside right?

where's Stanley?

Donna Fasano